FROSTED
Christmas

Alane Middleton

Dedication

To my mother who always encourages me every time I have a crazy idea. I couldn't do this without you!

contents

Chapter One

COMING HOME

Home is where the heart finds comfort, and hope is renewed.

L emon Frost was home. As her black SUV hugged the last bend on the road to the town's edge, she didn't know if she wanted to laugh or cry.

Harper, Colorado, hadn't been home since leaving the day after graduation. Six years ago, she said goodbye to everything she knew to pursue her culinary dreams, and for a few years, she had succeeded.

She graduated at the top of her class and earned a coveted internship at Opal's. Under the tutelage of the head chef, Lemon discovered her full potential until she made the stupidest decision possibly in her entire life. She fell in love with her mentor.

Her face burned with embarrassment whenever she thought back on how naïve she had been. She wished she could hide her shame, to tuck it away in a secret place where it could be forgotten. Unfortunately, memories had a way of crawling out from under the rocks that buried them.

In the beginning, Jeff had been any girl's dream. Handsome, charming, attentive, he made her feel special. For a while, she had been, but then the new class of students came through, and one in particular caught his attention. Overnight, Jeff changed. It had been foolish of her to ignore the signs, but faced with a truth she didn't want, she immersed herself in denial, clinging to a familiar sense of normalcy. Perhaps it had taken her too long to notice, but when the kitchen staff began exchanging sympathetic glances, she reached her breaking point. As the festive melody of "Santa Claus is Coming to Town" filled the car, her last words with Jeff echoed in her mind.

"Jeff, we need to talk," Lemon had said after the dinner shift ended. He stood at the employee lockers, shrugging into his supple leather coat.

"What about?" He asked, not bothering to look at her.

It was funny how quickly a man could lose interest when a blue-eyed bimbo with a way too generous amount of cleavage was in the vicinity.

"I was thinking of spending Christmas in Harper this year."

"Where?"

"Harper, my hometown." She'd reminded him, though his vacant stare didn't help bolster her courage.

"Right." He muttered absently as he gathered his things to leave.

"Well, you haven't met my family yet, and I thought this might be a good time."

Jeff smiled at her with a mixture of pity and superiority, as if he considered her to be foolishly innocent. "I don't think that would be wise."

"Why not?" Her heart sank with a nauseating anticipation as she asked.

He put his hand on her shoulder, patting her like one would a child. His voice became tolerant, as if he had been about to explain a complex concept. "I think we both know this relationship has come as far as it can go. I can't carry you any longer. It's time for you to fly on your own."

"What are you saying?" Lemon had asked stupidly.

"You're fired."

Lemon's brows furrowed as she looked through the windshield, the sinking sun casting long shadows in her rearview mirror. Well, that's what she got from dating her boss. Fired on November twenty-seventh, just three days after Thanksgiving. With no job and no way to pay her bills, she'd fled; she'd folded up camp. Granted, embarrassment likely triggered her abrupt departure, even though she would never admit it.

Harper had a single lengthy road that ran through town, while all subsequent streets meandered in a labyrinth of convolutions, ultimately culminating in a succession of dead ends. Lemon often wondered who had been the brains behind the town's design.

Due to the unfortunate lack of a grid, Main Street held the only valuable real estate, with all businesses lining up along its stretch. The first of countless childhood memories loomed on the horizon. Harper High School stood imposing, its dark silhouette stark in the distance. Standing tall and proud, the red brick buildings were a testament to their nearly century-old construction. However, it was the field in the background that drew her gaze. Her eyes fixed on the football field as memories flooded her mind. Walking the hallway in her green and black cheerleader uniform. Flying in the air with a broad smile on her face. Riding in the back of the old convertible during the homecoming game as part of the royalty court.

For many, the four years spent in high school were a mere stepping stone toward more promising endeavors. Lemon, however, couldn't shake off the nagging fear that she had already peaked in high school. All she had in front of her was an endless stretch of road leading nowhere. When Jeff dumped her, Lemon found herself adrift, floating in the middle of an uncharted sea without a life raft.

Tears stung her eyes when the familiar sight of Frosted came into view. The bakery had been in her family for years. The idea for Frosted took shape after a kindergarten bake sale, where her mother's cookies had sold faster than all the others. One year later, her parents opened Frosted. The business, her parent's pride and joy, was the driving force behind Lemon's decision to attend culinary school. Even though she studied savory, Lemon's love would always be in sweets.

Lemon brushed a tear from her cheek and concentrated on the road ahead. The life she'd thought she wanted was in the past. Now, she needed to focus on the future.

"Mama, are you home?" Lemon called into her childhood home, letting the screen door slam behind her. The enticing aroma of cinnamon and pumpkin spice lured her towards the back of the house, where the heart of her memories lingered.

Evelyn Frost stood at the stove, old country music twanged from the speaker on the counter. She wore a pink ruffled apron tied tightly at her waist, covered with flamingos. Her hips swayed as she cracked an egg over a metal mixing bowl.

"What are you making?" Lemon asked from the doorway.

Evelyn shrieked, the shell crumbling in her hands. "Oh no," she groaned. Routing out the white pieces from the bowl. "You're here sooner than I expected you?" Wiping her hands on her apron, she held out her arms.

Lemon ran into her embrace, tears threatening to fall again. Her mother's arms were as warm as freshly baked bread. Her mother brushed the hair from Lemon's face, looking into her eyes with concern. "You hungry? I was just about to start dinner."

"A little," Lemon shrugged. "What are you making? Can I help?"

"Lasagna. Why don't you go get yourself set up? The boys should be home soon."

"Where are Dad and Berry? I expected to see them."

"Berry had to turn in his uniform, and you know how much your dad loves walking the halls of Harper High."

Lemon laughed. "How did the season end?"

"We made it to the playoffs; Berry scored the winning field goal until the refs threw a flag. With the penalty, the boys weren't able to make it back to the goal line."

"That's too bad. How is Berry handling his small-town royalty status?"

"Oh, he loves it. Imagine both of my babies crowned their senior years."

"Really, Mama." Lemon groaned.

"What? Do you think I'm the only mother who wanted her babies to be crowned royalty? I know for a fact that Karen Whitting wanted nothing more than to have her pride and joy steal the crown from you."

"Oh, Mama, don't you think it's about time you let that go? After all, it's been six years."

Evelyn gasped. "Never. Not after that little tart tried to ruin your beautiful dress."

Lemon rolled her eyes. The whole incident had bothered her mother more than it had her. Nicole had lived in Lemon's shadow, always coming in second. For Nicole, homecoming queen had meant everything, but for Lemon, it had been another day to have fun.

The real upset had come when she found Brian, her boyfriend since their Junior year, kissing Nicole outside the girls' bathroom. Her mother didn't know about it, nor would she ever.

It was a bitter irony how life had a way of circling back around. First Brian and now Jeff. What was it about her that left men looking elsewhere? Pain shadowed her face. "There are worse things," Lemon admitted.

"What's wrong, honey?"

"Nothing, I just got a headache. If you're sure you don't need me, I'll go get my things from the car."

"Yes, go, go. Dinner won't be ready for another hour, at least."

Lemon gave her mom a quick hug. "It's good to be home."

The yellow and green striped wallpaper still covered the walls of her old bedroom. Lemon sat on her childhood bed, her knees pulled to her chest as she watched the luminescent clock minutes change.

The evening unfolded in a customary fashion, as if time had not lapsed and she was still in high school. Family dinner. Teasing at the table. Her mother's warm smile. Nothing changed; well, that wasn't exactly true. One thing had dramatically changed: she was older and shouldn't be living with her parents, even temporarily.

Just for the holidays, she'd promised herself as she had pulled into the driveway six hours earlier. The same litany Lemon recited to herself as she carried box after box of her possessions into the garage. She could do this. After all, who wouldn't want to spend time at home for the holidays?

Coming home: there was a phrase that held a new meaning now. Before, it was filled with anticipation of a few days spent with loved ones, time allocated to rejuvenate before facing life and the real world again. Now it was time she would spend licking her wounds. Maybe by New Year's Eve, she might have a resolution worth working towards.

Lemon smiled at the framed family photo resting on her antique white nightstand. Her dad had been pleased to see her, giving her a hug before situating himself on the couch with the recaps of last week's football game highlights. Berry had been less enthused. Not because they fought. Being seven years apart in age didn't lend too much of an overlap in life. Lemon supposed it was because he was almost eighteen and was already counting down the days until he could make his own splash in the world. She could only hope his experience would go smoother and last longer than hers.

After a brief head nod, he grabbed a slice of the freshly baked French bread as he left the house. Her mother sighed, rolling her eyes and giving Lemon a wry smile. "Boys." She'd muttered, but Lemon wondered if there hadn't been more going on than her mother let on.

Lemon shook her head. No, now wasn't the time to get involved in whatever Berry had gotten himself into. She wasn't here to fix the world. The reminder didn't help her feel any better, but maybe if she recited it to herself enough, it might just start to sink in. She'd had enough drama in her life. What she needed now was calm. If she had any hope of salvaging her future, she had to focus. Excitement wasn't something she wanted or needed anymore.

Predictable. That's what life was in Harper, Colorado. That's what had her fleeing six years earlier. It didn't matter how much she loved her family or the bakery. She wanted excitement and adventure. Well, she'd found it. Little did she know that the excitement she desperately wanted would lead her back home again. It was a lamentable truth now that she longed for the same predictability of her old life. Lemon never imagined she would have too much excitement or that adventure could be overrated.

Her eyes felt hollowed out, as if she had cried every drop of moisture from her body. Lemon stared sightlessly into an unknown future. All of her hopes and dreams were no longer plausible. Stupidly, she had wrapped them up in a happily-ever-after scenario with a man who had no intention of staying with her. Hindsight was a malicious bitch, and it kept biting her in the ass.

Lemon reached behind her head, clutching one of the many lace-covered pillows her mother insisted on using. With little effort, she hurled the pillow across the room, knocking over her row of cheerleading trophies in its wake.

Her door flew open, and the silhouette of her mother stood stark against the yellow glow of the hallway light. "What on earth was that?"

"Nothing," Lemon mumbled. "I tossed a pillow, and it knocked over a trophy, is all."

Evelyn walked further into the room. The soft light accented her features. Despite her fifty years, Evelyn was an exquisite woman. Her hair continued to possess the same golden hue, and her eyes remained the purest blue. Mother and daughter shared many of the same characteristics but for the eyes. The eyes were the one thing she had gotten from her father.

"Looks like more than a trophy was knocked over." Evelyn bent to pick up one of her cheerleading awards, setting it back on the shelf before turning to face Lemon. "You want to talk about?"

Lemon shrugged. "There's nothing to talk about."

"We'll see." Walking towards the door, her mother gave her a knowing look. "If you change your mind." Then, she closed the door softly behind her.

The way her mother seemed to be cognizant of her moods always caught her off guard. Lemon often wondered if this was a talent all mothers had or if only her mother had the frightening skill.

Lemon's brow furrowed as she contemplated her closed bedroom door. Eventually, she would have to explain what happened with Jeff. Though her mother never came right out and asked, she could see the curiosity in her eyes. The mere fact that her mother wanted to know and still allowed her privacy had made her coming home all the sweeter. Lemon wasn't disillusioned. She knew she had it pretty lucky. Her parents were like shooting stars, rare and spectacular.

Before going to bed, her mother had reminded her that tomorrow was December first, and certain traditions needed to be upheld. The first was unloading all the Christmas decorations from the attic. Every Christmas season, her mother stuck to the same traditions, saying *traditions help us remember who we are and keep us focused on where we want to go.*

Christmas had always been Lemon's favorite holiday. When the first snow fell, blanketing the earth in white, it was like a welcoming salvo into the season. Normally, she couldn't wait for the festivities, and this year, she wouldn't have to miss a single one. But instead of feeling excited, Lemon worried. She pulled her bottom lip through her teeth and tapped her fingers against the eyelet comforter. Lemon couldn't afford to allow Christmas to distract her. She needed to remain focused if she had any hope of saving her future. This year, Christmas would have to wait.

As far as this holiday season was concerned, she couldn't afford to screw around. Her life had taken a sharp turn that left her spinning in circles. It was as if fate dumped a gross pile of muck on the table and said, "Eat up." All the while expecting her to say, "Yum, that's good." Well, she was done being forced to do things she didn't want to do. The first step had been getting rid of Jeff, even if he had been the one to end things. The fact remained. She was free. Free to choose what she did with her life from here on out.

The clock numbers changed, signaling the new day. This was her time.

A new day.

A fresh start.

Today was the first day of her new life. Come what may, she was going to get the future she wanted. December was going to be her month. Lemon drifted off to sleep with a firm resolve in her mind.

Chapter Two

MONDAY, DECEMBER 1ST

For some, mornings symbolize a rejuvenating beginning, while for others, they represent a taunting letdown.

Lemon stumbled blurry-eyed through Frosted's back door.

She breathed in the familiar scent of sweet bread. Her eyes closed at the onset of emotions. Maybe it was the early hour, but suddenly, she found herself on the verge of tears and let out a shaky breath.

Today was the first of her 4 a.m. shifts. Early mornings were something she hadn't missed for those six years she spent away from home. Indeed, the shift in hours had been a determining factor when she had deliberated on which culinary path to pursue. Little did Lemon know she would be right back where she had started, with no other option available even though she had graduated at the top of her class. The culinary community was small when you wanted to work in an elite kitchen. She had no doubt Jeff had begun to spread his vile rumors, destroying her reputation in the process.

It didn't matter, she reminded herself for the hundredth time. She couldn't change him any more than she could change the snow-capped mountains surrounding Harper. What she needed to do now was take some time to rediscover herself and, more importantly, what she wanted in life.

"Good morning, sunshine," Evelyn said with a brilliant smile. "Did you sleep well?"

Lemon wouldn't categorize three hours of sleep as a good night's rest, but she wasn't about to mention that to her mother. If Evelyn knew her only daughter wasn't sleeping well, she would insist on providing every known kind of sleeping aid as a way to help her sleep. Every morning would turn into twenty questions as her mother drilled her about what worked and what didn't. Just thinking about it made her shudder. "I slept fine." The corners of her mouth curled, unveiling her cheerleading grin. It was the smile she mustered when she needed to feign happiness despite her inner turmoil.

"Good, come over here and dive into this dough. I'm going to start working on the cookies."

"Why do I feel like I'm getting the raw end of the deal?" Lemon asked while drying her hands.

Evelyn's wounded expression was impossible to ignore as she turned to face her. "You honestly think I would do something like that?"

Lemon tilted her head, eyes narrowing with suspicion. "I suppose not."

"That's right. Now, if you'll excuse me, I'm going to get started on the cookies."

"Yes, Mama," Lemon muttered as she approached the metal bowl holding the dough for cinnamon rolls. It was the largest in the kitchen. Almost one and a half feet tall and two feet wide. Once the dough was rolled out and prepared, she would have fifty warm, gooey cinnamon rolls laid out in the display case by the time the first customers came into the bakery.

Lemon hummed to the jolly Christmas tune playing over the speaker as she split the dough into manageable sections. She drove her fingers into the malleable texture. Her mind wandered when her mother came back in with a stack of sealed containers. Lemon watched with a dawning awareness as her mother pulled out several large cookie sheets, lining them with parchment.

Evelyn began swaying to a holiday classic as she peeled a lid off the first container. Lemon's eyes widened when her mother broke off a row of dough, dropping the pre-sectioned squares in a row on one of the baking sheets.

"Mama," Lemon gasped. "You lied to me."

"I did not."

"Yes, you did!" Lemon pointed to the damning evidence. "You said you were starting on the cookies. Those are not only stared, they're already made."

"Nonsense. I still have to bake them."

Wagging her finger, Lemon claimed, "You are terrible. You know how much I hate making cinnamon rolls."

"No, that's not true. You just don't enjoy waking up early."

Lemon laughed, surprised to find how good it felt. The sound was rough, proving it had been too long. "When did you start freezing cookie cubes?"

"A couple of months ago. I had a harder time getting everything ready in time to open, and after a few mishaps," Evelyn waved her explanation away. "It's been easier."

The initial surge of guilt came out of nowhere. Lemon pushed the feeling aside. "What mishaps?" she asked, thinking to steer the conversation into a less uncomfortable topic. When her mother didn't immediately respond, Lemon turned around, the wood rolling pin in her hand. She stared in stunned silence as a red hue spread across her mother's cheeks. She couldn't recall a single instance in her memory where her mother was visibly embarrassed. Evelyn Frost had a knack for staying positive, even in the face of adversity.

"It was nothing. It doesn't matter."

Torn between curiosity and empathy, Lemon debated whether to ask her mother for clarification or let the matter go. Even though her mother tried to pretend whatever had happened didn't matter, the truth was obvious. She was as red as Rudolph's nose.

"After we close today, we need to talk about the town's Christmas festival. I have some ideas I've been wanting to try but couldn't when I didn't have an extra set of hands to help me."

Guilt made Lemon's cheeks pink. "Okay, Mama."

The bakery opened right on time. Its doors unlocked by seven on the dot. Lemon filtered back and forth between the kitchen and storefront, stocking the display case and the storage area below. The spicy aroma of cinnamon and the sweet scent of frosting permeated the air.

Lemon had almost forgotten how wonderful it was to pull a sheet of cookies from the oven or to hold a bag of icing in her hands. The years spent away from Harper had been good, aiding her in discovering her path in life. Yet now she wondered if the place she belonged hadn't been here all along.

The last of the cinnamon rolls lined the metal countertop, cooling before she added the icing. The secret family cream cheese frosting sat next to the pans. Lemon swept a finger around the metal bowl, popping the icing into her mouth. Her eyes closed in bliss as the delicious flavors exploded on her tongue.

A soft chime came from the front, signaling the arrival of a customer. Absently, Lemon listened to the cheery greeting given by her mother and a deep, rumbled response.

She loaded a tray with pecan buns. Her mother's sticky buns were almost as popular as her cinnamon rolls. Because of their charming look, they occupied a central position on top of the display counter in a decorative crystal cake holder. It had belonged to great grandma Mimi, as did the recipe. It only seemed fitting that the buns be shown at their best.

Lemon turned her back to the swivel door as she passed through the opening, juggling the sticky buns and a pitcher of lemonade to fill the dispenser.

"It's so nice of you to help your mother. I'm sure she is so grateful to have your help," Evelyn said.

The sound of her mother chatting with a customer wasn't anything new. So she didn't spare the man behind the counter more than a fleeting glance. "Oh. Lemon. Come, say hello to Nancy's boy." Her mother said, holding out an arm for her to step forward. Lemon hesitated, her pulse leaping in her throat. The turn she made was slow as if every second stretched out into eternity. As Lemon looked up, her eyes met a pair of dark, gleaming eyes behind a set of black, wide-framed glasses. "Hi, Jace. How are you?"

Jace stood taller, taller even than she remembered from high school. Back then, when he'd graduated the year before her, he was only a few inches taller. But now he had to be at least a head taller than her. His once reed-thin frame had filled out. His notable muscles bunched under the fabric of his long-sleeved sweater.

"Well enough." His gruff voice rubbed along her nerves with a delicious stroke.

"Are you here visiting family?" She asked, her eyes soaking up the sight of him, noting not only the differences but the similarities to the boy he once had been.

"Uh, no. I'm going to be sticking around for a while."

"He's going to run the bookstore for his mother," Evelyn explained. "You remember. I told you how Nancy had been battling breast cancer this past year."

The End was the business next to the bakery. When her mother decided to open Frosted, she approached Jace's parents about leasing the adjacent space. After years of good business and an amicable working relationship, Nancy and Evelyn had decided to connect their businesses by opening the wall separating them. The entrance was six feet in width, and on the bakery side, there were tables and chairs. While on the bookstore side, Nancy created a few cozy reading spaces with plush armchairs and coffee tables.

Both areas were designed to allow customers to shop and eat at their leisure.

However, since Nancy's diagnosis, The End hours had become sporadic, and French doors were added so that the bookstore could remain closed on those days when Nancy was too ill to come in. With Jace back in town, it seemed the doors would remain open again, which was good, especially with the fast-approaching holiday season.

The reminder of Nancy's illness deepened Lemon's color, leaving her unable to meet his eyes. With everything going on in her own life, she had forgotten. Of course, he would be here helping his mother. "Right, sorry. How is your mother feeling?"

"Depends on the day."

"Does she need anything? Can I help in some way?"

His lips twitched, a smile teasing the corner of his mouth. His eyes warmed as his gaze locked onto her mouth.

"No. She's doing okay for now. I'll let you know if something changes."

Heat spread across her cheeks as her gaze dropped to the countertop.

"I hope you do." Her mother broke the awkward silence that stretched between them.

Jace nodded, his eyes flicking to Evelyn before returning to Lemon.

"Such a nice boy," Evelyn gushed after the door closed behind Jace. "And just think, him giving up his big career in San Francisco so that Nancy wouldn't have to sell her store."

"Big career?"

"Oh yes, Nancy bragged about it all the time. He worked for a big graphic design company. Nancy said he was on track for a management position if circumstances hadn't forced him to leave."

"Can't he go back? I mean, when Nancy's better."

"That's the problem. There is no set time frame for Nancy's recovery. It could take weeks or months. Right now, the whole family is taking it a day at a time."

"So he gave up his career to help his mother?" Lemon asked, unable to fathom the selflessness of what Jace had done. Her heart tightened. To be loved by a man like that. Before Jeff, she had thought there were men out in the world like that: caring, considerate, and selfless. Then Jeff had taught her that her fantasy expectation didn't apply in real life. Men were only interested in what helped them in life. Now, she couldn't wrap her head around the idea of a man willingly making such a drastic change in his life.

"Yes," Evelyn gushed, her hands clasped together.

Lemon poured the lemonade into the dispenser. Then she lifted the sticky buns from the counter and walked over to the cake display. Already, half the buns were missing.

She frowned down at the empty spots. "Mama, did you sell any sticky buns this morning?"

"Jace bought his usual two."

"Any others?"

"No, why?"

"Well, there are four gone, and I just stocked them before we opened."

Evelyn came to stand beside her, resting a hand on her shoulder. "That is odd." She murmured, lifting her eyes to meet Lemon's, when her brow creased as she frowned. "How long have you had icing on your face?"

"Mama," Lemon said warily, "What are you talking about?"

"Icing. You have a glob of icing on the side of your mouth and across your chin."

"I do not!" Spinning around, Lemon ran to the bathroom. The light flicked on once she crossed the threshold. She stood in front of the sink, her hands braced on either side, and groaned. She looked like a child after eating a frosted treat. The goop of white icing at the corner of her mouth was the size of a dime. How on earth did she miss that? How could she have walked around without realizing her face was covered with frosting?

"Mama," Lemon wailed, "Why didn't you tell me?"

"I just did, honey."

"No, I mean earlier when I was talking with Jace." The image of Jace's face smirking at her expense flooded her vision. "I am so embarrassed. I can't believe I stood there talking to him with my face looking like a toddler learning how to use a fork." Her voice hitched at the end of her tirade, reminding her she was dangerously close to having a tearful breakdown.

"It doesn't matter. I'm sure Jace didn't even notice."

"Want to bet?"

"Don't be so hard on yourself. After all, it's Christmas time. People are always more forgiving when it's Christmas."

"Oh, Mama. This is Jace. He's not forgiving. Believe me."

"Why would you say that? He's a sweet boy. Just look at what he is doing for his mother." Evelyn reminded her.

Lemon rubbed the back of her hand against her chin, wiping what remained of the frosting off her face. She fixed her gaze on the far wall that connected the bookstore to their bakery. She could picture Jace sitting behind the desk used to ring up customers, his nose buried in one of his graphic novels. Despite what her mother said, Lemon knew just how mean Jace Torte could be.

Chapter Three

TUESDAY, DECEMBER 2ND

The attic is the gateway to a family's historical narrative.

L emon sorted through plastic tubs, setting aside those with green and red lids.

Every year since she turned twelve, it had been her job to climb the old attic stairs and bring down the holiday decorations. When Lemon was younger, the task was exciting. To her, the attic held mysteries and the promise of hidden treasures. As she grew older, her imagination waned some, but she still loved the adventure of pulling down the decorations. In her eyes, the dust-covered containers held years of holiday traditions and memories.

The wood-covered floor creaked under her weight as she sank to her knees, opening a tub, excited to rediscover what lay inside. Lemon wrinkled her nose in distaste as she caught a whiff of the musty air seeping out of the closed container. Glancing at the rows of red boxes, her heart lifted with anticipation, knowing each contained a piece of her mother's cherished Christmas village.

Over the years, the collection grew steadily, boasting over fifty painstakingly selected additions. Every year, her mother would buy a new item and place it at the forefront of her display. Last year, she had found a darling white lighthouse with a miniature green wreath adorning the door.

"You done?" Berry asked, poking his head through the attic opening.

"Not yet. Probably would go faster if I had some help." Lemon gave him a meaningful look.

Berry smiled in his easy way. "Why do you think I'm here?"

"Because Mom finally nagged you enough," Lemon said sweetly.

With his head tipped back, Berry let out a roaring laugh as he squeezed his broad shoulders through the opening. Like all members of the Frost family, Berry carried the same physical characteristics that distinguished them from everyone else in Harper. His honey-blonde hair and green eyes were the same shade as hers and their father. The attractive genes ran in the Frost family, as many found the children to be just as appealing as their father.

Lemon observed her brother with a critical eye, taking in his chiseled good looks and impressive physique, quickly reaching exemplary standards. "Are you dating anyone?" She asked. The question had become a game between them.

"No one worth talking about." He said, just as she knew he would.

"Be careful, Berry. You never know when someone might turn into someone worth talking about."

Berry frowned. "What's that supposed to mean?"

"What it means," Lemon said, enunciating each word, "if you keep treating the girls you date as interchangeable, you might miss out on one special one."

Berry stalked across the floor, stopping only when he was an inch or two away. "Why don't you mind your own business?" He growled.

Lemon's eyebrows rose, her eyes twinkling with humor as she watched Berry stomp across the floorboards, jerking one of the tubs off the stack. "What's wrong, Berry? Did you already mess up a chance with someone you liked?"

"No." He snapped.

Taking in his dark expression and barely contained anger, Lemon figured Berry was suffering from a bruised ego. And what kind of sister would she be if she didn't tease him just a bit.? "What's her name?" Berry flashed her a warning glare that she promptly ignored. "Come on, you can tell me. Do I know her?"

"What bins should I take down first?" Berry asked, stubbornly refusing to acknowledge any of her questions.

Lemon threw a stuffed snowman at him. "You are no fun, you know that?"

Berry snatched the white ball of fluff from the air, tossing it back at her. "I'm loads of fun," he grossed, his lips curving into a sneer. "Ask anyone. I'm the guy you call when looking for a good time." He lifted a container, turned on his heel, and went to the ladder.

Well, that was odd. Lemon leaned back against the wood beam in stunned silence. Her eyes followed Berry's stoney expression as he maneuvered down the attic opening. She had only been teasing, but evidently, she had managed to hit a nerve. If there was a girl who wasn't interested in Berry, which she had a hard time believing, why did he care?

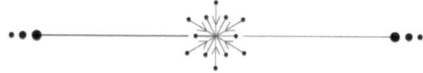

Like every holiday season, Evelyn transformed their home into a magical winter wonderland in a few hours. The Christmas tubs now held all the everyday knick-knacks that Lemon and Berry would haul back up the stairs and into the attic until January 1st. Every surface donned signs of the season in festive colors of red, green, and gold.

In the four hours since Berry had helped her bring down the Christmas decorations, the house had changed into a picturesque holiday scene. Holiday cheer was in every corner, with fake snow-covered furniture pieces decorated throughout the house. Garland, strung with twinkling lights, adorned the banister and dangled over the mantle. At least half a dozen wreaths ranging in size and decorations hung over the doors and windows of their home. Every time Lemon passed by, it looked a little more like Christmas.

Once the Christmas village, set on display in the front window, was completed, the holiday festivities would finally begin. The warm amber glow in the window would draw in the neighbors, and her mother would bask in the attention.

"I want these three tubs to go to Frosted," Evelyn said, stacking the identical containers next to the front door.

"All right, Mama," Lemon said, placing the last of the stocking holders over the fireplace. The stockings, which were the same plaid pattern with fury white tops, wouldn't be hung until the night before Christmas. It was a tradition that her mother insisted on carrying through, even though Santa's secrets had long since been revealed. She turned away from the fireplace, eyeing the three large bins by the door with a wary dread. "What do you want me to do with them once they get there?"

"After you close Frosted for the day, I want you to hang the lights around the bakery. Make sure you use the white lights around the trim and the colored ones around the windows and door. There is also a mistletoe that hangs over the doorway leading to The End. Oh, and I also have a smaller version of the Christmas village you can set out in the store window. Just use the shelf that we have the vintage baking tools on."

Lemon frowned at the ever-growing list of tasks. "Since when did you start putting a village up at the bakery?"

"Oh, a couple of years ago. You know how much everyone loves my display. I thought it would be a great pull to get people into the bakery, and boy, was I right. I think this is just the thing to help get our sales back up."

"What is that supposed to mean? Has the bakery been losing money?"

Evelyn grimaced, color rising to her cheeks. "No, nothing so dramatic. Just a minor dip. Nothing we won't be able to come back from."

"But why a drop at all?" Lemon asked, worry creasing her brow.

"Don't worry about it. I shouldn't have said anything. Remember, the town festival is on Saturday. We'll need the next few days to prepare; the decorations must be done by tomorrow night."

Lemon wanted to groan. If she weren't an adult, she'd stomp her foot, maybe even throw a fit. "But Mama, I can't hang the lights by myself. Why can't Berry do it?"

Evelyn sighed, moving another emptied Christmas container aside. "Because your brother has another obligation after school."

"He does?" Lemon lifted a pale eyebrow. "What is it?"

"Nothing that concerns you," Evelyn stated as she retreated to the kitchen.

Lemon hesitated for about half a second before following her mother. "Mama, what is going on? You and Berry are both acting strange."

Evelyn paused in arranging her collection of holiday salt and pepper shakers to glare at Lemon before turning back to her task. The longer her mother refused to comment, the more worried Lemon became. "Come on, Mama. Just tell me. Is Berry okay?"

"Of course, he is. Why wouldn't he be?"

"Then why is he acting so cranky, and why do you keep avoiding my questions?"

"Don't be silly. I'm not avoiding anything." Evelyn said after closing the lid of the last Christmas tub. She brushed her hands off as she took a step back. A look of pure satisfaction spread across her face.

Lemon stood next to her mother, setting her hands on her shoulders. "You've outdone yourself this year. Everything looks great, Mama."

"It does, doesn't."

"I think you are forgetting something." Lemon turned to the sound of her father's voice.

"What's that dear?" Evelyn asked.

William Frost was a quiet, unimposing man. His pale features, the same as his children, sat comfortably on him. In his heyday, Lemon knew he'd been the catch of the town. Now, well into his forties, he could still turn women's heads.

From his nimble fingers dangled a green plant with white flowers tied together by a red ribbon. "Mistletoe." He said, as his handsome features spread into a smile. He held the mistletoe over Evelyn's head, wrapping an arm around her waist. Then he dipped her back and kissed her.

"Oh, Dad," Lemon groaned as her face brightened with pleasure. Even though her love life was in shambles, watching her parents together gave her hope for her future.

Lemon left her parents to themselves and went looking for Berry. Perhaps, with the right inquiry, she could finally understand the reason behind his strange behavior.

She found Berry perched precariously on an aluminum ladder, a strand of Christmas lights dangling over his shoulder. "Do you need any help?" She asked, resting her arm on a metal rung.

Berry grunted as he attached another section of lights to the house. "Did it without your help last year. Don't know why you think I need your help this year."

"There's no need to be snippy."

"I'm not snippy; that's a chick thing," Berry grumbled, descending the ladder faster than she was comfortable with.

"Be careful," Lemon cautioned. "Is it necessary for you to rush down the ladder like that?"

"Since when did you become such a stick in the mud?"

Truly offended, Lemon narrowed her eyes at her brother's back. She suddenly itched to kick him soundly in his backside. Before she thought better of it, Lemon dipped down, scooping up a handful of snow that lightly dusted the front lawn. Working the white flakes into an oddly shaped ball, she wound up and let it fly, smiling smugly when it landed squarely in the back of Berry's smartly styled hair.

His hand shot up, rubbing the spot. Berry turned his head, giving her a frosty look. "What in the hell was that for?"

Dusting the snow from her cold fingers, Lemon smiled. "*That* was for calling me boring."

Before she knew what he was about, Berry's long arms swept up a handful of snow that had gathered on the window ledge, hurling a ball of ice at her chest. Lemon squealed, ducking as the ball flew by, striking the tall oak tree behind her. "How dare you?" She shrieked, her heart racing, as she sprinted for cover upon realizing that Berry's assault was far from over. "I'm your sister. You're supposed to protect me?" Lemon reminded him.

Berry laughed, his head thrown back in confidence. Taking advantage of his distracted state, Lemon pelted him with handfuls of snow she didn't bother shaping into balls. Unfortunately, the loosely packed snow crumbled in midair, dusting the ground before reaching him. Not to be outdone, Berry gave up trying to scoop the limited snow from the ground and instead took off after her. He chased her around the cars and twice around the oak tree before catching her around the waist. With her tucked under his arm, Berry carried her to the garden hose. Lemon's eyes widened in alarm. "You wouldn't dare?"

"Want to bet?" Berry said, laughter clear in his deep voice.

"I'm sorry!" Lemon cried, but to no avail. With an evil cackle, he dropped her unceremoniously onto the dead grass, turning on the spigot before she could run away. Lemon sputtered in outrage when he hit her full in the face with a cold spray of tap water. It was over almost as quickly as it had begun.

Berry flicked the water off, grabbed the Christmas light strand once more, and worked his way back to the top of the ladder. Lemon sat cold and shivering as she watched her brother, wondering when he had grown so much bigger than her.

"Jerk." She muttered. "I'm going to get you for that."

"Yeah, we'll see," Berry called out, not bothering to look down at her.

A smile tugged at the corner of her lips as she opened the front door. It was good to be home.

Chapter Four

WEDNESDAY, DECEMBER 3RD

Time seems to fly by only when dreaded tasks lie ahead.

The day had passed at an unusually fast rate. It seemed as if every time Lemon looked at the clock, closing time had leaped closer than she wanted. She had taken to singing about a grumpy green creature more and more with every passing hour.

Aside from the dreaded end of her shift, Lemon had been pleased by the steady stream of customers. Even though most had been strangers, there had been a few familiar faces sprinkled throughout. Nothing brightened the holiday season quite like the friendly faces from Christmas past.

"You're a mean one," began to strum out of the speaker when the front doorbell rang. Lemon turned, a welcoming smile on her face when Jace crossed the threshold. Surprised, Lemon's eyes darted to the now-closed, joining French doors. "Are you closing early?" She asked when he approached the counter.

His lips twitched as if he was struggling not to laugh. Although she couldn't fathom what he found amusing about her question. "Did I say something funny?" Lemon asked. Her bottom lip, which was already prone to pout, stuck out even further.

Jace's eyes glimmered with a mysterious hint of wickedness. "Not at all. I closed the store a few hours ago. I guess you missed when I locked up."

"It's been busy today," Lemon explained, though she wasn't entirely sure why she felt the need to defend her inattentiveness to him.

"I noticed." He said, his eyes holding hers. Then his expression darkened as if a storm cloud rolled over him. "Don't worry. The idea of you acknowledging me in the slightest never crossed my mind."

Lemon straightened her shoulders. "Excuse me?" She gasped, certain she misunderstood him.

"I said, you don't have to worry about being embarrassed for not noticing when I come and go. After all, you're the last person I would expect to care one way or another what I was up to."

The more Jace spoke, the hotter her face became. She felt like a kettle about to boil over, her anger escalating with each passing moment. She couldn't decide what she wanted to do first. Her hand itched to hurl one of his favored sticky buns at his head. On the other hand, the ice-cold pitcher of lemonade on the counter behind her might just be the thing to cool him off. But before she could decide, his next words flatted her as a pancake.

"My mother had an appointment I didn't want to miss." He confessed the smooth timbre of his voice wavered with emotion.

Lemon's face tensed with concern, all thoughts of retribution fading from her mind. "Is she okay?"

"Yes, the cancer was all removed. Now she just has to finish her last round of radiation treatment."

"Oh, that's good. How is she feeling?"

"Better," Jace said, stepping closer to the counter. His arm rested across the smooth glass surface. "Not back to her usual self yet, but she's doing better every day."

"That's great news!" Lemon exclaimed, moving forward. She laid her hand over his forearm. "I bet—" she said, but her voice trailed off when the front door swung open, and her past walked through the opening.

"I don't believe it. Lemon drop. How are you?" Brian Reeds asked jovially as he strolled up to the counter. His bright blue eyes sparkled with pleasure.

Lemon felt a rush of heat to her cheeks. "Just fine." She said, her weak smile not quite reaching her eyes.

Brian had been her high school sweetheart. They had dated for part of their junior and all of their senior year of high school. Aside from the unfortunate incident during their homecoming dance, their time together had been fun. Which had been all that Lemon cared about at the time. After graduation, they had parted ways. Deep down, they knew it would be too challenging to make a relationship work while attending college in different states. Her education took her to Los Angeles, a place where she had discovered the magic of culinary arts. Meanwhile, Brian found himself, by way of a football scholarship, at a prominent Texas university.

When they stood together six years ago on the top step of her front porch, Brian had promised if neither of them married, they would reconnect at their ten-year high school reunion. Never had Lemon imagined she would be back in Harper long before that day.

"What have you been up to?" Lemon forced herself to ask, knowing the time for her explanation was coming. Unfortunately, amidst her slight embarrassment, she had forgotten Jace was standing by the counter. Her focus had so completely shifted to Brian.

"I sell real estate now," Brian replied, flashing his wide smile and showing off his bright white teeth. "How about you?"

Lemon's smile slipped. "I graduated in culinary arts and interned with a popular restaurant in L.A. for a stretch. But I'm home for the holidays, or at least until I decide what comes next."

Brian's smile grew. "So it looks like you and I will have some time to catch up."

"I suppose." Lemon allowed, her mouth tilting up in an impish grin.

"I hate to interrupt this endearing reunion." Jace cut in, his voice barely above a growl. "But if you don't mind, I'd like to finish my order."

"Finish? I hadn't realized you started one."

"Why the hell else do you think came in?"

Lemon's eyes widened at his agitated tone. "I'm sorry. I thought you were just saying hi."

"No, my mother wanted me to pick her up a cinnamon roll."

"Sure, of course." Lemon's eyes darted to Brian, and she mouthed a quick apology.

"No, don't need to," Brain assured her. "Unlike Jace here," he said, clapping a hand on his back. "I did come in here only to say hi. So I'll get out of your way."

"You don't have to leave yet?" Lemon assured him.

"Don't worry, I'll see you soon," Brian assured her as he pushed open the glass door, stepping into the sun's golden rays.

Lemon's narrowed eyes turned to Jace. "You didn't have to be so rude."

"I was rude?" Jace challenged. "Since when is asking a vendor to do their job rude?"

She fumbled with a white paper bag clenched in her hand, trying not to drop the large cinnamon roll. She slammed the paper sack against his chest, momentarily distracted by the solid wall of muscle her hand collided with. In all the years she'd known Jace. She would have never pegged him as someone who spent time lifting weights.

She vaguely remembered him in high school as a short boy with a slender build and black, square-framed glasses. Most of his time was spent in the computer lab, and she distinctly remembered him sitting behind a computer, quietly typing away.

Lemon jerked her attention back when Jace snapped a finger in her face. The action made her want to reach out and bite the insulting fingers. Instead, she suggested he leave.

"How much do I owe you?"

"Nothing, it's on the house."

"I can't accept that." He said, reaching for his back pocket.

"It's not for you."

"Oh."

The slight inflection in his voice made Lemon wince. "I mean, I wanted to do something nice for your mother. Not that I wouldn't mind doing something nice to you." Lemon's eyes widened. "For you. I meant for you."

A flash of hurt faded from his eyes. A cocky smile softened his full lips. "What did you have in mind?"

"Oh, will you get out of here already?" She groaned, though the urge to laugh took her by surprise.

"These blasted lights!" Lemon growled loud enough to cause a couple across the street to look up in surprise. She didn't care if the entire town lined the street to watch her. At that moment, she was a minute at most, a mere sixty seconds from losing her top. She was fairly certain steam was coming out of her ears, but that didn't matter either because nothing changed the facts. And the facts were simple: whoever put the Christmas lights away after last year failed to roll them correctly. Now, the rows of tiny white lights were tangled in a web of knots Lemon knew was bound to send her to crazy town. It didn't matter how she tugged, pulled, or threaded, the damn line refused to let loose.

She tossed the end she'd been struggling onto the ground with a huff. Her boot stopped on the ice-covered sidewalk. Which wasn't smart because the momentum set off her balance, and her foot slipped out from under her. She let out a high-pitched squeal of alarm, her arms flailing windmills in a desperate attempt to regain her balance. Amid gravity's imminent triumph, Lemon felt herself being snatched from the air. A pair of firm hands were locked around her waist, steadying her wobbling feet beneath her.

Lemon turned her head, a thank you perched on her lips. The sound faded away as a pair of brooding brown eyes peered at her. When Jace's hand fell from her waist, she experienced a discerning tug of disappointment she shook off with a scowl. "What are you doing out here?" She asked in a tone that was not very friendly. She couldn't explain why, but thanking Jace for catching her was out of the question.

Jace eyes narrowed, his black-framed glasses adding to the hard line of his brow. "Saving you. Or didn't you notice?"

"Last I checked, I had everything under control."

"Oh, really?" Jace insisted, his face darkening with a thunderous expression. "So, the next time I look out the window and see you struggling, I should just ignore it?"

"Struggling? I wasn't struggling; my foot slipped on the ice. That's all."

"I'm talking about the lights. I could hear you throwing a hissy fit even before I looked out the window."

Lemon's eyes widened. "I was not throwing a hissy fit! I can't believe you were spying on me."

"Please." Jace huffed. "Why don't you get over yourself, Princess? I've got better things to do than listen to you yell at me." As he stormed back to the door of The End Bookstore, she could hear him grumbling, "See if this isn't the last time I offer to help." He cast a narrowed-eye look over his shoulder as he pulled the door open.

It took her a second after the shop door closed to feel dreadful. He was right. All he'd done was offer to help, and she had nipped at his heels like some ankle-biting dog. She caught her bottom lip between her teeth as she hovered with indecision. She swung the glass door open before she could talk herself out of it. The End Bookstore was a lovely shop. Every wall was covered with floor-to-ceiling shelves in an aged-barrel colored wood. Rows of books lining the bookcases, the decorative covers full of colorful images and fun fonts. Wagon-style chandeliers with vintage-looking bulbs hung from the ceiling, casting a warm, inviting glow. Overstuffed chairs were scattered throughout the store, creating cozy reading nooks for customers. Nancy had an eye for style, and she did a wonderful job of keeping her shop up with the times.

Lemon wound her way through displays and furniture. When she didn't see Jace manning the front desk, she began to search for him. Though, the further she went, the more she wondered where he had disappeared to. As she approached the back of the store, there were only two options: the back door or the set of stairs to her left. A glance at the lock confirmed that Jace hadn't gone outside. Lemon looked up the dark staircase, where a single light illuminated the top. She knew there was an apartment up there. Its floor plan spanned the entire building. Nancy had rented the space out a few years ago to a newlywed couple who were saving to buy a house. But Lemon didn't remember if anyone since had moved in.

She stood at the base, undecided of what to do. After a quick look over her shoulder, she latched onto the railing and walked up the stairs. The stairway was a narrow, straight shot to the top. Once she reached the landing, only one door was to the left. The door sat slightly ajar. Lemon experienced a momentary pang of guilt. However, curiosity got the better of her.

She pushed the door the rest of the way and crossed the threshold. The studio apartment resembled the one she had left behind in Los Angeles. It was a wide-open space divided into separate living areas. Before her was the living room with a loveseat, a square coffee table, and a floor lamp, all facing a large screen television mounted on the wall. In the corner was a fireplace that still held remnants of a fire.

A muffled shuffling sound brought her attention to the opposite side of the apartment. She walked toward the king-size bed. It appeared tousled and unkempt, as if someone had just woken up. Her eyes widened as realization dawned into horrifying clarity. Suddenly, the shirt on the floor by the bed and the pair of pants tossed over the back of the sofa held new meaning.

Jace was living here.

She had walked, unannounced, into his home. Her pulse jumped in her throat as she spun on her heel. Lemon darted to the door, her movements resembling a skittish rabbit, frantic to escape unseen. She had almost made it when her step halted at the sound of an all too familiar voice. "Should we add trespassing to your growing list of transgressions?"

Lemon tensed, her body bunching with the need to flee. Her only hope to save face was to play the part of the wounded party. When she turned to face him, her head was up, and she looked him in the eye. With her chin lifted high, she arched her eyebrow, attempting to exude confidence. "List? What list?"

It dawned on her with a jolt that she had unknowingly interrupted him since he was preparing to shower. He stood barefoot, leaning against the bathroom door frame. His shirt dangling between his fingers.

The sight of Jace, bare-chested, had never been something that caused her to stop and look. She had a vague memory of him running the track field after school. But he had changed sometime over the six years since she had seen him. His chest was spattered with rich chocolate hair that tapered and extended below his navel, vanishing behind his worn blue denim. Jace had always been thin, leaning toward willowy, but now his chest was hard with muscle that rippled beneath taunt sun-tanned skin.

When she finally managed to tear her gaze away from his naked chest, her eyes met his. His mouth curled into a knowing smile, his eyes gleaming. The gloating look on his face made her blush. "The list is something I've been working on. I'll be happy to show it to you when it's finished. Although I should probably be honest and admit, I don't know if it will ever be complete."

"You know, you can be a real jerk."

"I'm the jerk? Shall we have a recap on what happened?"

Lemon narrowed her eyes as she strode forward, momentarily forgetting she wanted to leave. When she was only a few inches from him, she poked him in the chest. Her red and white candy-striped nail dug into his muscle. "I'll have you know I was trying to find you to apologize. You are the one who is ruining it."

When her finger jabbed him again, Jace folded his hand around the nail. His calloused palm rubbing against her sensitive skin set off a ripple of sensations she didn't want to consider. "Apologize, huh? Don't think I would mind hearing that."

"Well, it's not happening now." Lemon snorted.

"Why not?"

"Because I'm mad at you."

"Oh, I get it. You only apologize when you are in the mood, too?"

"No." She snapped. "I only apologize when the person deserves one."

"And I don't anymore?"

"That's right."

"That's too bad."

When she realized he was still holding her hand hostage, she tugged but felt his grip tightening in response. "What's too bad?" She asked while tugging on her hand.

"I always reward a sincere apology." He explained. Letting go of her hand, he turned his back on her, returning to the bathroom. Just before he managed to close the door behind him, she asked, "What does that mean?"

"I guess you'll never know."

Lemon stared at the closed door. Despite herself, she felt a spark of joy deep inside herself.

Chapter Five

THURSDAY, DECEMBER 4TH

Memories are only as good as the people in them.

J ace sat behind the counter, his laptop humming as
he typed. The backlight cast a neon glow against his
pensive expression. He remained only partially attentive to
the sporadic influx of customers as they wandered through
the store. As the holidays drew near, he anticipated days
like today would become increasingly scarce. That was
the reason he diligently typed away at his keyboard, fully
focused on seizing any available opportunity to work on
his other job. His actual job. The one he hoped would
be waiting for him. Because even though his life was the

bookstore for now, he would eventually need to return to his previous existence.

His mom needed him right now, and he was happy to do what he could for her. When his father had called to let him know about his mother's diagnosis, he'd been devastated. The news had come as a swift right hook, sending him reeling. Luckily, he'd been home when his dad dealt the heavy blow. He'd dropped onto his sofa and sat in a dazed silence, the world around him fading into a blur.

He and Brynlee rallied together, offering what support they could. During the first few months, Brynlee bore the brunt of the burden because she was closer. Denver was a far more reasonable distance to travel than San Francisco. However, after the need for surgery became apparent, Jace wasted no time making arrangements to be by his mother's side.

Whether by chance or fate, his boss happened to be a breast cancer survivor and was very sympathetic to his plight. When he'd asked to take a sabbatical, she had offered him the option to work remotely. At that particular moment, he hadn't even entertained the thought as a possibility.

Jace loved his job. Working as a website designer was a rewarding and lucrative field. And although he hadn't worked remotely for a few years, taking the opportunity to do so again was heaven-sent. When his father asked if he could keep the bookstore going for his mom, he hadn't hesitated. How could he? Especially knowing how much his mother treasured it.

Even though he'd been willing enough, the thought of sitting behind the counter—something he hadn't done since high school—day after day turned his stomach. He kept his sanity by working in his free time on his current project.

A shriek of laughter coming from the opening between the bakery and the bookstore made him smile. He supposed it wasn't only his option of working remotely that made his days enjoyable. Lemon Frost was back. He still couldn't believe the timing of it all. He had thought her gone for good, especially after landing that job at an upscale restaurant in Los Angeles. However, destiny had different plans. Lemon was the type of girl that could drive a man to madness. He remembered all too well his last year in high school when Lemon would walk the hallways, her slender body adorned in the black and green cheerleading uniform. The skirt skimmed the top of her shapely thighs. He shuddered at the memory.

Now, she was all grown up and still could make a man forget his name. Her silky hair and soft green eyes, the delicate sprinkle of freckles across the bridge of her nose, all of the things that made her irresistible, were no more than twenty feet away from him. Sadly, he couldn't have a sample of her without entering into a committed relationship. Even though he wanted her, he didn't particularly like her. From what he could see, she had things handed to her far too easily. It made her ungrateful, and she expected people, particularly men, to bend over backward for her.

Well, he wasn't that kind of man. If he were looking for a woman to have a relationship with, it would be someone who would give as much as she took. It was too bad Lemon didn't know how to give. No, a princess like her only knew how to take.

The laughter erupted again, breaking through his concentration, though admittedly, it wasn't hard to do. Since Monday, he couldn't focus on anything worth a damn, not when Lemon was around. His eyes lifted to the adjoining door, and he wrestled with the urge to see what the ruckus was about.

After Lemon had walked into his apartment yesterday unannounced, he'd made a point to avoid her today. While the encounter had a touch of awkwardness, there was an undeniable energy that captivated him. His thoughts couldn't help but wander to the nearby bed, envisioning how effortlessly he could gently place her on its plush mattress. When he'd wrapped his hand around her finger, he couldn't think of anything but the jolt of desire coursing through his body. His blood heated to a feverish pitch. Damn, if he didn't want to sample that pouty mouth of hers. It had been a struggle, but he found the strength to stand his ground and let her walk out of his door. The truth was, she'd left him rattled, and that wasn't good. It was best to let things cool down before they crossed paths again.

But not catching even a glimpse of her today had been eating a hole in his resolve, leaving him with almost nothing left. With a grunt of impatience, he shoved away from the counter and strode to the open doorway. His eyes took in one wide sweep of the complete chaos of Frosted's storefront.

Open boxes of Christmas village pieces lay in disarray on one table and scattered across the floor. Styrofoam dusted Lemon's hair, looking like a blizzard had swept through. Positioned under a shelf spanning the front window was an A-frame ladder. The usual clutter of kitchen decorations that adorned the shelf was stacked precariously around the ladder's base.

Lemon, as usual, was the star of the show. She sat straddling the top rung. Her slender legs perched on either side as she pelted out the many ridiculous things a woman, especially like Lemon, wanted for Christmas.

"A yacht," her honey voice crooned, "and really, that's not a lot." Although he doubted how much of an angel she had been. He was skeptical she could manage the masquerade for a day, let alone a year.

Jace leaned against the wall inside the bakery, his arms folded casually across his chest. He couldn't help but smile when another rambunctious giggle broke through her lips again. It seemed the cause of her insatiable laughter lay on the other side of the store window.

He had to rise onto his toes from where he stood to see what caught her attention. A litter of kittens, their long fur making them resemble balls of fur more than a cat, were scurrying frantically on the sidewalk. The wind had picked up while he'd been working and was blowing a plastic bag in a cyclone around the heads of the kittens. In their frantic efforts to snatch the bag, they climbed on each other. Only the ones on the bottom couldn't handle the weight of their siblings. Consequently, the tower of kittens would collapse, causing them to roll apart.

Even though he wasn't much of an animal person, he had to agree the kitten's antics were vastly entertaining, but for him, Lemon was more so. The delight on her face as she sang and decorated the shelf while watching the kittens had an odd effect on him. For a moment, he worried he was having a flare-up of indigestion.

He said to cover up his reaction, "They're pretty cute." Fortunately, he was keeping a close eye on her and noticed the exact moment his comment caused her to lose her balance on the ladder. With a startled yelp, the ladder began to sway backward, her arms shooting out to grab the shelf just as he held the ladder still beneath her.

Lemon shot him a deadly look, her cat-like eyes narrowing dangerously. "Why did you have to scare me like that?"

"Sorry, I didn't mean to."

"Right." She huffed. "What are you doing in here, anyway? Frosted is closed."

He hitched his chin toward the opening he passed through. "You didn't shut the French doors, remember?"

"Oh, right? I guess I forgot."

For some reason, a faint blush began to spread across Lemon's face as if she were embarrassed, though he couldn't begin to guess why. "What's with all the decorations?" He asked, not yet ready to return to his work.

Lemon sighed, placing a small cottage coated with fake snow next to a tiny Christmas tree. "I was supposed to do this yesterday, but it took me so long to hang the lights outside. I had to finish decorating the interior today. My mom is coming in to help me prepare for the Holiday Festival, and if this isn't up by the time she gets here, I'll never hear the end of it."

"Want some help?" He offered before he could think better of it. The surprise on her face, he was sure, reflected on his own, but he wouldn't take the words back even if he could. It was a startling feeling, this desire to help. Never in his life would he have ever thought he would extend such an offer to Lemon Frost.

He could see the hesitation on her face. Her teeth caught her bottom lip as she worried over his offer. When he found himself wondering what she would do if he nibbled on her lip for her, he frowned. He was about to rescind his offer and go back to his computer where he belonged when she broke the silence.

"Sure. You know, I think that would be great."

Good and stuck now, Jace looked up at her, perched like a bird in a tree. Her lips had spread into a wide grin, flashing her bright white teeth. "What do you need?" He grumbled, wishing he would have stayed away like he meant to.

"The other village pieces. Thank you."

Jace stood to the side, handing her piece by piece until the shelf was filled with a white-covered town decorated for the holidays. "There should be a white extension cord around here somewhere. Do you see it?"

No, he didn't. How did she expect him to find anything in this mess? Jace nudged a few boxes out of the way with his shoe but didn't see anything resembling a cord. "Do you remember where you last saw it?" He asked, trying to ignore the sweet scent of sugar and spice that clung to the air around her. Even in the bakery, the unmistakable scent of Lemon lingered in the air. One that made his mouth water and gave him the strange desire to nibble his way along her butter-soft skin.

"No, not offhand. Oh, wait!" She exclaimed, pointing to the corner by the front door. "I think I see it."

Sure enough, the cord was folded up on the floor under a pile of styrofoam. After handing her the plug to connect the village, the remaining tail dangled down the side. He couldn't imagine how Lemon intended to get light to the village when the nearest outlet was five feet away and the cord was three feet short.

Jace looked up when she started humming again as if he wasn't there and couldn't hear. "Why don't you sing?" She asked while stretching her arm behind the village, covering the cord with store-bought snow fluff.

"What?"

"I asked, why don't you ever sing?"

"I sing." He said, probably too impatiently.

"I've never heard you."

"When exactly is it you think you would have been in a position to hear me sing?"

She shrugged negligently. "Any time you come in to buy your sticky bun," she said, winking, "You don't sing then."

"Why would I? It's too early."

"Oh, so you aren't a morning person?"

"Definitely not. I prefer absolute silence until at least ten o'clock."

"That's no fun. What if you had something you were busting to share? Wouldn't you want to share it?"

"Nope, I just wait until I feel awake."

Lemon scrunched her nose. "Okay, so you don't sing in the morning. What about at night?"

Jace shook his head. "I like my nights to be quiet, too. That way, I can unwind and relax from a long day at work."

Lemon stopped what she was doing and gave him her full attention. Her eyes reflected her incredulous expression. "Hmmm. That is a quiet life you live, Jace." Lemon delicately tapped a finger to her lip as if engaged in profound contemplation. "Let me see if I've got this right. You don't sing in the morning because you prefer it to be quiet. You also don't sing at night because you need it quiet to unwind. I assume you don't sing during the day because you are working, so would you care to tell me again when exactly you are supposedly singing?"

"In the shower."

"Excuse me?"

"I sing in the shower."

"The shower."

"Yep. When I am in the mood to sing. I do it in the shower."

"Huh. So yesterday, after I left..." Lemon let her voice trail off.

She wouldn't meet his gaze, and he found a perverse sense of pleasure in that knowledge. "That's right. I sang."

"Oh, too bad I missed it."

"No one said you had to leave."

"Yes, I did. You were occupied."

"Was I?"

"Yes, hand me that bit of snow I accidentally pushed over."

Jace scooped up the pile of artificial snowflakes. As he lifted his hand, a trail of fairy dust floated back to the floor. Lemon leaned over, her hands cupped. He rested his hands against her palms, allowing himself a moment to indulge in what it might be like. To touch Lemon, stroke her without reservation. He lifted his gaze, meeting hers, when she let out a startled gasp. Her eyes held an emotion he couldn't fully interpret.

"How do you want to plug these in?" He asked, his voice a little rougher than it had been a moment ago.

"I have another cord in the kitchen. I'll get it later."

"Do you need me to help with anything else?"

"Just one thing."

"What's that?"

"The mistletoe. My mom wants it to hang in the doorway." Lemon explained, her skin glowing.

"Where is it?"

"On the counter."

Jace spotted the green shrub tied with a length of red velvet ribbon. He walked over to the doorway and reached up, his fingers slipping the loop of ribbon over the hook. As he let his arm drop to his side, Lemon had come up beside him. He couldn't help but notice one more step, and they would be standing under the mistletoe together. His heart did a funny flutter that he promptly ignored.

"What song?" Lemon asked.

He swung his head around, his focus centered on her once more. "Huh?"

"What song? You know, in the shower yesterday. What song did you sing?"

"All I Want for Christmas is You."

Chapter Six

Friday, December 5th

Is a coincidence an omen or a promise?

"**M**ama," Lemon called out as she walked into the kitchen. In her hands, she flipped through a printout of the sales numbers for the past week. Only raising her head at the sound of her mother's voice.

Evelyn stood at the sink, an apron knotted at her waist. She was the picturesque of a 1950s housewife. Even while cleaning, not a single silver strand of hair was out of place. "What's the trouble, honey?"

The lines in Lemon's brow deepened as she approached her mother. "I was going over Frosted sales and noticed your chocolate chip cookies only sell about half of what they used to. I remember when we'd sell fifty on a slow day. Yesterday, I sold eleven. Eleven! Is that normal? Did something change?"

With every question she asked, it was as if her mother's back got straighter. Her stance grew a little more tense. When Evelyn spoke, her voice was like the best peanut brittle, capable of breaking under the smallest amount of pressure. "Things change; customers have new favorites."

"But Mama, everyone loves your cookies."

Shutting the water off, Evelyn dried her hands on the red towel draped over her shoulder. When she turned to face Lemon, her eyes were shadowed with embarrassment and hurt, which made little sense. Lemon laid a comforting hand on her mother's shoulder. "What's wrong, Mama?"

"Nothing." With a forced smile, her mother turned away. "Everything is just fine. Why wouldn't it be? I have both my children home for Christmas this year. There is nothing like spending the holidays with the family. Don't you think?"

Lemon studied her mother's tense features, suddenly seeing a startling similarity between them. How many times during this past year had she used that same bright, cheery tone when talking to Jeff? How often had she smiled at him, knowing her heart wasn't in it? Too often, she allowed others to influence her actions. In her constant quest for approval, she had lost sight of herself somewhere along the way.

"Sure, Mama," Lemon said, her throat tightening under the strain of controlling her emotions. As she did every night, she asked if her mother needed help with dinner. And as she did every night, her mother politely refused. However, her mother didn't seem as eager to carry out the task this time.

Berry and her father sat in the two recliners, the television on low as they watched the latest football game recaps. Lemon hesitated in the doorway for a moment. She knew her father would be clocked out when the game was on, even if it was just the highlights. But she needed to talk to him. And with her early hours, she only had a limited time before bed at night. She may regret it, but she walked to the television, flipping the power switch as she stood in front of the screen.

"What the hell, Lemon?" Berry yelled, pushing his reclined feet to the ground.

"Don't bother getting up," Lemon said sweetly, facing her father's dark scowl. "What's wrong with Mom?"

Her father's scowl deepened, "What do you mean? Nothing's wrong with your mother."

Lemon braced her hands on her hips, tapping her foot in impatience. "Come on, Dad. I know something is going on with her. She keeps getting upset over the strangest things, and when I ask her about it, she tells me I am just imagining things."

The screen flipped on behind her. Berry smiled wickedly. "There. You see, nothing is wrong with Mom, and now you can get out of the way."

"Dad," Lemon whined.

"Sweetie, I don't know what to tell you. To my knowledge, your mother is fine."

She looked at the only two men in her life right then and wondered why she bothered dating. Men were blind and selfish, and she had the disheartening thought that they might even be a little indifferent. Lemon didn't know why, but she felt indifference towards the woman one supposedly loved would be the ultimate betrayal. Lemon stalked to the coach with a slight huff, flinging herself onto the cushion. Neither her brother nor her father spared her another glance. "Men." She growled.

Today was the final day Lemon had to prepare for the town's holiday festival. This year's theme was Harper's Winter Wonderland. The town council had given the task to a select number of committee members to organize, decorate, and run the event. As the event of the year, the town of Harper invested heavily in its success, meaning every vendor was screened and auditioned for the coveted spaces. Frosted held a place of honor every year right next to the Santa photo booth. This meant that cookies were hot ticket items. Every year, they sold more cookies than they had in the previous.

However, her mother wanted to step up the game this year. First, she wanted Lemon to make five hundred sugar cookies cut to look like snowflakes. Then Evelyn insisted on giant cinnamon rolls, large enough to feed four. Her thought had been to give an inexpensive option for parents to feed their children something that also had a little substance to it. Evelyn had also insisted on serving their famous sticky buns. She was convinced that sticky buns would be a hit.

The final and probably most technically challenging addition to her mother's grand plans was the addition of hot chocolate. The hot beverage was to be served with a pile of whipped cream and sprinkled with cocoa. Even though Lemon knew her mother was right. Everyone would go wild over the hot cocoa. It still would be a challenge to keep it made and heated to a temperature worth selling.

After baking for hours and then spending the rest of her afternoon icing snowflakes, Evelyn had shooed her out the door. Her mother had explained the hot beverage machine she had ordered online was lost in transit, and if they didn't purchase something pronto, the whole thing would be lost.

When Lemon had calmly suggested they place the hot chocolate idea on hold until next year, her mother had looked as if she'd slapped her. At this point, Lemon had no recourse but to do as her mother asked.

It had taken her over an hour to drive to Denver and another half an hour to get to the first store on her mother's list. After that, the drive time hadn't been terrible, but she was on to the fifth store on her list, and so far, no one had the machine her mother had set her heart on.

At first, the task had started as a major inconvenience, but now it was more than that. Lemon had sunk too much time and energy into this to even entertain the thought of giving up now. She would tear the city apart before even considering coming home empty-handed. The more she hunted, the more driven she felt. She needed this win. If nothing else, she needed to be able to say. "Yeah, that rights, I did that." Although, the more she thought about her drive to win, the more she realized how out of her mind she was.

The aisles were no longer crowded with other shoppers, making the walk to the appliances much easier. Lemon scanned over the boxes, losing hope as her eyes struggled to locate the box she needed. Then, on the top shelf a few feet away, it sat like a halo of light. Tears smarted in her eyes for some unknown reason. Maybe it was because she was tired of feeling like a failure. Perhaps it was because she had a one-hour drive ahead of her, and her bedtime was in just thirty minutes. Tears or not, Lemon was thrilled to hold the end of her quest in her hands finally.

At least until her phone rang.

Lemon wrestled her phone free, dangling her purse from her curved arm. "Hi, Mama. You won't believe what I finally got my hands on."

"Wonderful, dear," Evelyn said.

The less-than-enthused response from her mom was surprising. Especially since her mom was the reason she was still out shopping at this hour. Lemon frowned, debating whether or not to question the reason behind the lackluster response.

"Listen, honey. You haven't left Denver yet, have you?"

"No, why?"

"Oh, good." Her mother sighed. "I need you to pick up Jace from the airport."

"What? Why?" Lemon groaned. Then, her mother's words sank in. "Wait a minute. Did you say airport?"

"Yes, his flight lands in about half an hour."

"I don't understand. I thought he was helping his mother with the bookstore."

"He is. Evidently, there was a meeting that he had to attend today. He said he shouldn't have to travel for the rest of the month."

Lemon scowled at the oversized box in her shopping cart. "Why doesn't his father pick him up?"

"Because Nancy isn't feeling well today, and Robert doesn't want to leave her alone."

"Where's Brynley? I thought she lived in Denver."

"She does, but it isn't feasible for her to drive Jace to Harper and then back again. Especially since you're already there."

"Fine." Lemon caved. "But you owe me, Mama. Just remember, someday soon, I am going to call in my order."

"Thank you, dear. I'll send you his flight information. Oh, and don't be late. Okay, honey?"

Lemon tried not to feel offended that her mother would think she would run late.

The pick-up from the airport had been uneventful. Luckily, the holiday travel hadn't started yet, so it was just the usual chaos. It had only taken two loops around the airport to spot him.

Jace stood out in the crowd. His dark hair was uncovered despite the dipping temperatures. When Lemon pulled up next to him, he had opened the back door, setting his small carry-on in the backseat before sliding into the passenger seat.

Lemon's SUV was small and purchased for economic purposes. It fit her size comfortably. However, with Jace occupying the chair next to hers, she felt an overwhelming sense of crowding. Every time she moved her hand from the steering wheel, she invariably bumped into some part of his body. The connection would send a spark of warmth through her body.

That wasn't even the worst of it. Halfway into the hour drive, he had barely spoken two words together. She had tried to ease into a conversation about the holidays, only to have it fall flat. When she brought up the bookstore, his expression had turned stoney, and she let it go. Then, grappling for something they shared in common, she brought up high school, which turned out to be the worst mistake. Not only did he give her a scathing look, he also said the most unkind thing. Her feelings were still smarting from the sting.

What was his deal? She gave him a sidelong look. People talked about high school with her all the time. It seemed anyone who came into the bakery brought up something about high school. None of them had ever told her to keep her shallow musings to herself. Her brows drew into a tight knot. If he disliked her conversational attempts, why didn't he initiate one himself?

When she couldn't stand the silence a moment longer. When he brushed his arm against hers for what seemed like the hundredth time, Lemon blurted out, "What's your problem?"

Jace turned to face her, his expression obscured by the car's dim interior. "What did you say?"

Lemon tightened her grip on the steering wheel, silently cursing her wayward tongue. "I asked what your problem is. I mean, you have done nothing but brood since I picked you up. Then you were mean when I asked you about high school. Did I offend you or something?"

"I have not been brooding." He challenged, though she wished she could see his face. There was something in his tone that made her suspect he was laughing at her.

"Dark looks, sour mood. What would you call it?"

"Frustration."

Lemon stole a quick look at him. There was a word laden with meaning. Part of her wanted to leave the word where it lay. However, another part of her, the reckless gambler, wanted to turn the word over and see what it revealed. "What are you frustrated about?"

"Several things."

The husky grumble of his voice had an odd effect on her. Instead of pausing to examine it, she threw caution aside and pushed forward. She'd always felt the best things in life only came when a person went after them. "Name one." She challenged.

He looked at her again. This time, a car passed by in the oncoming lane, illuminating his heated gaze before casting him back into the shadows. Lemon swallowed roughly, her blood pulsating through her veins in an uneven staccato. The silence stretched between them, and with a pang of regret, she worried he was quitting. That whatever this moment between them had been, he was going to let it pass by.

She jumped when he spoke, his voice shattering the silence. "Not being home."

Lemon spared him another glance before returning her attention to the road. "You miss home that much?"

"Don't you?"

Lemon shook her head. "No, not as much as I thought I would. I guess L.A. wasn't home for me. What about you? What do you miss the most about San Francisco?"

Jace relaxed against the seat, his head leaning into the headrest. "Everything."

"Well, that's specific," Lemon said, laughing. The mood in the car had shifted so unexpectedly, leaving her unbalanced. Yet now she worried the wrong word might send him back to his previous mood.

"Yeah, well, it's the truth. I miss my apartment and the neighborhood. There's a street I enjoy jogging along that has all these old houses. It's like walking back in time." Then he sighed, his voice softening. "San Francisco is a different lifestyle. There's art and history. You can't go anywhere without feeling wrapped up in it."

"Harper has culture," Lemon argued. She hadn't thought so before, but since coming home, she had begun to see the place with different eyes. "I think our town has a lot of character."

Even though she couldn't see Jace's expression, she could imagine it. "Don't confuse nostalgia with character."

"Let's agree to disagree," Lemon conceded. "What else are you frustrated about?"

She could see he had let his eyes close as another car drove by. His dark lashes blanketed his cheeks in a thick curtain. He had the kind of lashes all the girls wished they had and often paid good money to imitate.

"My father."

That surprised Lemon. She expected him to say his mother. After all, how could he not feel frustrated with her diagnosis and the unknown path of recovery? But his father. She found herself holding her breath, hoping he would confide in her. The dark cocoon of the car made their conversation feel all the more private. As if this time was a secret shared only between themselves.

She waited for a beat when he didn't offer anymore; she asked him cautiously, "Are you two arguing about something?"

"No, nothing like that. He just likes having me home, is all."

"What's wrong with that?"

"Nothing, except he doesn't want me to go back to San Francisco."

"Oh."

"Yeah, oh."

Lemon brightened. "Okay, so you miss home, and your dad is bugging you about leaving. Is there anything else frustrating you?"

"Yeah, there's one other thing." He said in a tone that confused her.

Clearing her throat, Lemon asked, "Oh, care to share?"

Jace peered at her from under his partially closed lids. Even his half-opened stare couldn't conceal the intensity of his gaze. After a prolonged silence, he looked away, the weight of the moment still hanging in the air.

When Lemon abandoned hope of an answer, his gruff response surprised her. "No, I think I'll keep that frustration to myself."

Chapter Seven

saturday, December 6th

Magic happens when the tree is lit, and merriment is all around.

T he Winter Wonderland Festival was off to a great start. With over a thousand people milling around, the streets in the holiday-decorated five-block area were alive with the sounds of laughter and Christmas cheer. Multi-colored strands of light twinkled from above, casting a magical glow on the tables of wares.

At the center stood the handmade Santa's workshop, meticulously crafted year after year by Ronny, the local carpenter. The wooden walls were painted to look like a charming brick house, complete with a snow-covered roof and a stout chimney made of Styrofoam. Inside the workshop, a labyrinth of walls guided families to the back room where a large wooden armchair, donated by Furniture and More, held the jolly man himself. Anticipation filled the air as children eagerly awaited their turn to sit on Santa's knee. The line to see Santa ran beyond the built structure, zigzagging through the street. The tail end lined up perfectly with Frosted's table, where Lemon and Evelyn stood ready to sell the tired parents and children hot chocolate and cookies.

Even though the festival had been running for less than an hour, it was still early. The big sales always came later, when hunger and patience ran thin. In the meantime, Lemon happily watched the crowd.

With the weather taking a sudden turn, the temperature had dropped dramatically in the last couple of hours. Despite wearing mittens, she could still feel the chill nipping at her fingertips. Lemon's ice-blue knitted cap and gloves matched her mother's. They had been one of her mother's many purchases in preparation for the evening's event.

If she didn't know better, she would have thought her mother was trying to prove herself. She hadn't seen her mother this competitive since the homecoming queen debacle when Nicole's mother and Evelyn had gone toe to toe over the crown. But she couldn't begin to guess why her mother would feel the need to prove herself as a baker. No one in Harper baked as well as her mother. Her sticky buns were well known not only in Harper but also in Wilson and Caplin.

"Now, here are two of the prettiest girls in town," William said, wrapping his arms around Evelyn's waist.

"Hi, Dad." Lemon smiled as she sprinkled cocoa on top of whipped cream. After handing the cup off with two snowflake sugar cookies, she dusted off her hands and turned to her parents. Their faces glowing with pleasure. She loved seeing her parents together. They had the kind of love story that Lemon dreamed of. "What are you up to tonight?"

"I hoped I could steal your mother away for a little stroll. The Christmas tree ceremony is going to start in fifteen minutes."

"Oh, I don't know William. What if Lemon gets busy and needs help?"

"I'll be fine, Mama. Go have a good time." Lemon untied the Frosted apron from her mother's waist, giving her a little shove forward. "Go, I've got this."

Lemon watched her parents blend into the crowd, her dad's arm wrapped around her waist. A smile played across Lemon's face at the endearing sight. She jumped when a deep voice sounded behind her.

"What's this amazing hot chocolate I have been hearing all about?" Brian stood tall, his mouth widening into a broad smile. Her face broke into a welcoming grin. He'd been to the bakery every day to say hi since she'd been back. Unfortunately, they hadn't had much chance to talk because he would inevitably show up when she had several customers in line.

"You heard about that?" She asked in mock surprise, her eyes twinkling like the lights hanging overhead.

"I sure did. There doesn't seem to be an empty hand on the street. I was beginning to feel left out."

"Oh, no. We can't have that. Let me get you a cup. Then you can tell me if it's worth all the hype." Lemon blushed with pleasure. It had been so long since she had been at ease with a man. It was just like her high school days when she walked with confidence. When she and Brian roamed the hallways together as royalty. She was flying so high that she handed him a chocolate chip cookie and winked. "Here, have a cookie on the house."

Brian held up his hands and took a step back. "Woe, what did I do to deserve this?"

Lemon looked at Brian in surprise. Their light banter had changed so dramatically she could guess why he'd gotten so upset. Since when was a free cookie construed as an insult? "What's the matter? Don't you like chocolate chip cookies?"

"Sure, normally."

"Why not now?" Lemon asked, her head tilting to the side.

Brian smiled in a way that made her realize there was some kind of inside joke she wasn't part of. She found her back straightening, her muscles tensing in anticipation of offense, even though she couldn't fathom the reason.

"I don't suppose it's something your mother eagerly runs around telling everyone."

"What are you talking about?" Lemon demanded after Brian didn't freely continue. She was seriously contemplating the benefits of climbing over the table and strangling the information from him when a large group of teenagers materialized from the crowd. Their exuberant voices tripped over each other as they called out their order to her. After filling ten cups with hot chocolate and providing four cinnamon rolls, Lemon looked for Brian, who had managed to disappear amidst the chaos.

"Well, damn," Lemon muttered. Her eyes scanned the sea of faces, unable to find the one she wanted.

"Not seeing who you're looking for?" Jace asked, walking up from behind.

"Where did you come from?"

"The alley leading from Maple Street." He explained as he snatched a chocolate chip cookie from the tray of cookies. After taking a sizable bite out of it, he grinned as if in triumph.

Instead of looking at Jace, Lemon studied the tray of chocolate chip cookies. The steady stream of customers had kept her mind occupied, and she had paid little attention to the dwindling number of cookies. Only when Brian made the odd comment about her chocolate chip cookies did she notice what remained on the table.

They had started the evening with ten dozen for each cookie. Now, with half the night over, there were only a third of the snickerdoodles and maybe a quarter of the sugar cookies left. However, when Lemon's eyes fell on the chocolate chip cookies, the tray was almost full, and she hadn't needed to restock once.

Her brow furrowed when she turned her attention to Jace. He had devoured the cookie and was reaching for a second when she asked, "Jace, did my cookie taste okay?"

"Is that a trick question?" With an arched brow, he asked around a mouth full of cookies.

"No, I'm serious. Does it taste okay?" Lemon asked again as she broke off a piece of the cookie he held in his hand, popping the soft morsel into her mouth. The sweet, butter flavor of the dough melded perfectly with the semi-dark chocolate chips into a flawless balance of gooey goodness. Her eyes closed in pure delight as the pleasure-filled flavors exploded on her tongue. When her eyes fluttered open, she found Jace watching her with a guarded expression.

She cleared her throat, letting her gaze drop to the top button of his flannel shirt. "I don't know what his problem is."

"Whose?"

Lemon lifted her eyes to meet his, the color surprisingly similar to the melted chocolate she'd just finished licking off her fingers. She found herself mesmerized by the molten intensity of his stare. Her tongue flicked out nervously, running along her bottom lip. "Brian," she squeaked, "I offered him a chocolate chip cookie, and he made it sound like it was some kind of punishment."

"Maybe he doesn't like chocolate." Jace offered with a negligent shrug.

A flood of more teenagers came through, each one asking for hot chocolate, which wasn't unexpected. However, as they started daring each other to buy a chocolate chip cookie, Lemon felt her temper slipping. Unlike Brian, Jace didn't slink away into the crowd. Instead, he played the role of cup-holder while she artfully adorned each cup with a dollop of whipped cream and a sprinkle of cocoa. When two of the boys started shoving each other toward the table, taunting, "Try it, try it." Jace took command, telling the boys to bother someone else, which brought Lemon nothing but relief.

It was another twenty minutes before the last of the rush of customers walked away, happily holding a cinnamon roll in their hand. When Lemon turned her attention back to Jace, she tried to smother the sudden overwhelming urge to laugh. He had another chocolate chip cookie in his hand and was busily polishing it off while reaching for another.

"I don't get it," Lemon muttered, perplexed.

"Don't get what?" His attention was clearly not on her.

"You heard those kids. They were practically goading each other to eat a cookie as if it was some form of torture."

As Lemon reached for another piece of Jace's cookie, he raised his hand above his head, out of reach. "Yeah, weird."

She laughed, pulling on his arm. His muscles flexed under her fingers as she tugged on his sleeve. "Why don't you want to share with me?"

He turned his back to her, saying over his shoulder. "You have hundreds. Get your own."

"There are not that many, and I don't want a whole cookie. I just wanted a bite."

With one arm stretched into the air, Jace reached behind her back. Grabbing a cookie, he spun her around, holding a fresh cookie under her nose. Lemon pinched her mouth shut, turning her head from side to side as Jace tried to feed her a bite.

"Come on, take a bite." Jace teased, holding the cookie against her mouth. His arm held her against his taunt body.

Lemon laughed, squealing when he pressed the cookie to her closed lips. "Jace," she gasped, almost choking when a piece of cookie made its way onto her tongue. "St...stop." Her laughter carried over the volume of the dwindling crowd.

"What's wrong? You don't want a cookie?" He whispered against her ear, sending a delicious shiver that had nothing to do with the cookie race down her spine.

At that moment, Lemon became painfully aware of two things. The first, Jace, was fun. She would have never believed that he could be like this. With his brooding stares and abrupt manners, she always thought of him as a big grouch. It was a delightful surprise to witness his playful nature, something she wouldn't have believed if she hadn't seen it with her own eyes. The second and more alarming thing was Jace made her heart race.

Somehow, in the last few days, Jace had become undeniably attractive to her. His charm and allure were so captivating that she couldn't help but be drawn to him. This was probably the most troubling reality. Jace wasn't someone she wanted to have a relationship with. After all, they had nothing in common, and she was pretty sure he didn't even like her. Not really, that is. But no matter what she tried, she could not get her heart to settle. The thundering beat drummed in her ears as she tried to push down the sudden flash of embarrassment.

"What on earth are you doing, Lemon?" Evelyn asked. Her prim voice broke them apart as if she had just touched a scolding hot pan.

"Hi, Mama," Lemon said brightly, her arms hanging at her sides. "Did you like watching the tree light?"

Evelyn's gaze swept from Jace to her and back again. "It was lovely. Thank you. How is the booth?"

"Good. I was just talking to Jace about your famous chocolate chip cookies. But it was weird. Some kids acted as if eating one of them was a punishment."

"Just ignore them," Evelyn said dismissively.

"But, Mama."

"No, Lemon." Evelyn cut her off. "I said to let it go."

More perplexed than ever, Lemon chanced to look at Jace. All the laughter was gone from his eyes. The sparkle of mischief dimmed. With a pang of regret, Lemon turned her attention back to her mother. "All right. If you insist.

Chapter Eight

SUNDAY, DECEMBER 7TH

A rigid adherence to traditions can be imprudent.

It was Lemon's first day off since coming home, and she couldn't wait to get started. First, she pulled on her oversized sweatpants, which she had to roll down three times until they hung loosely from her hips. Lemon turned on the television after sliding her blue toenails covered with tiny snowflakes into her fluffy candy-striped socks. She finally would have time to catch up with the new thriller series she'd heard a lot of hype about.

Lemon hummed happily as she stood at the microwave, waiting for the exuberant popping of kernels. She danced from leg to leg, her movements filled with restless energy. The same restlessness that had been plaguing her for days. Her body, unused to a day off, craved the usual routine.

How many hours, days, and weeks had she dedicated to work without a break? Even as an apprentice, the demands of working in a quality kitchen were high. Hunh. Lemon drummed her fingers along the smooth counter surface, contemplating the newfound emotion that had taken hold of her. Although the embarrassment and regret still lingered in the background, the intense yearning to run her own kitchen took her by surprise. It was the first time since her return home that she felt overwhelmed with this desire for the life she had abandoned.

Wasn't that just how life was? One minute, everything was fine, great even. Then, as if the notion of joy was a distant memory, life barged in, leaving one battered and bruised. "Oh, there you are," Evelyn said, sweeping into the kitchen. Her mother's voice effectively broke through Lemon's distracted mind.

"Hi, Mama," Lemon said over her shoulder. "Were you looking for me?"

"As a matter of fact, I was. I need to ask you a favor."

Lemon stiffened as her dreams of a lazy day on the couch with a warm bowl of popcorn slipped away. She turned around, a look of dread etched on her face. "Oh, no. No, Mama. You can't do this to me. This is my first day off since coming home. I made plans. Big plans." She explained with a broad sweep of her arms.

Evelyn lifted a brow. "I haven't even told you what I need."

"It doesn't matter because whatever it is means I won't be relaxing."

"Relaxing? I thought you said you had big plans."

"I do, and they involve relaxing."

"Well, once you do me this tiny favor, you can relax the rest of the day."

With a groan of defeat, Lemon whimpered at the microwave chime. Her scowl deepened, the mouthwatering smell of buttered kernels taunting her. "Fine. What do you need me to do?"

Evelyn's mouth twitched, her eyes gleaming with humor. "Really, Lemon. What is with all the dramatics? You act as if I just told you Santa Claus isn't real."

"What?" Lemon gasped, her hands pressed to her face in horror. "Santa isn't real?"

"Oh hush, you." Her mother swatted at her hands. "Enough of this messing around. He'll be here any minute, and judging by what you are wearing, you are going to want to change before then."

"Who's coming? And what's wrong with my clothes?"

Her mother's eyes swept over her outfit. "I think you mean to say, what's right with them?"

"Hey!" Lemon's arms instinctively crossed over her chest, a mix of indignation and embarrassment flooding her. "I'll have you know I am dressed for comfort. After all, this *is* my day off."

"Stop acting the part of a martyr. Go put your boots on and something you can walk a mile or so outside in."

"Why? What do you want me to do?"

"I need you to pick us up a Christmas tree."

The town set up a tree lot in the corner of the hardware store's parking lot, filling the side street with the intoxicating scent of fresh pine for weeks. Although not extensive, the selection had enough variety for early birds to find a tree that suited their needs.

"Come on, Mama. Why don't you have Berry go? He's almost a man. This is hardly a job for a girl." Lemon never minded playing the weaker female card whenever she didn't want to do something. To her way of thinking, monthly periods, cramps, and not to mention carrying another human inside oneself were enough to earn a pass now and again.

"Because Berry is busy. Besides, I need your eye. If I sent your father, he would wind up coming home with a three-foot cactus proclaiming, 'At least we won't have to water it.'"

The sad truth was that had happened. It was the only time her mother had asked her father to bring home a Christmas tree. Lemon privately wondered if it had been a deliberate ploy done by her dad so that Evelyn wouldn't ask him to do anything like that again. If that was the case, she had to give her dad props. Not only had her mother never asked him to pick up a Christmas tree, but to her knowledge, her mother never asked her dad to do anything involving the holidays. The man was smart. Lemon smiled. Her father certainly had learned early how to manage her mother. "Besides, it won't be as simple as driving over to Earl's lot." Evelyn held up a golden ticket printed with black ink. "I won a cut-down-your-own Christmas tree ticket at the grocery store, and I want you to go find us a beautiful one."

Lemon snatched the scrap of paper out of her mother's hand. Her eyes scanned over the information. "Mama, this says I have to drive out to Pike National Forest. That's at least an hour's drive one way. Besides, how am I supposed to cut a tree down? I don't have any tools for that."

"Your father has an axe and chainsaw you can take with you."

She looked at her mother with growing apprehension. Visions of bloody limbs lying amidst the dried leaves sent a chill of trepidation down her spine. "I am not going to use a chainsaw, Mama. Are you crazy?"

"Fine, like I said, you can use the axe just as well."

Lemon snorted, "No, I can't."

"Sure, you can," Evelyn assured her. Her expression changed into a smile when the doorbell chimed. "Oh, that must be your ride. Hurry and get dressed. You don't want to keep him waiting."

An altogether different kind of dread sent alarms off in her head. "Who, Mama?"

"Why, Jace, of course."

There was a light frosting of snow on the ground as Lemon walked silently next to Jace. The day had been spent in relative quiet, only punctuated by the occasional inquiry, which, once answered, caused the conversation to retreat into an unsettled stillness. She couldn't shake off the disbelief of walking through the forest with Jace. Her mother had claimed he, too, had been tasked with getting a tree for his parent's house, and it only made sense for them to have made the trip together.

The problem was that she didn't want to spend time with Jace. Any amount of time. She couldn't figure him out, not that she tried, but still. Men were fairly simple to understand. They had their primary needs and, provided those were fulfilled, were generally happy. In her limited time with Jace, he'd been anything but happy. One or more of his primary needs were not being adequately addressed. It was the only explanation she could think of. Since he'd picked her up, he kept giving her these hard looks beneath his darkly hooded eyes. If she didn't know better, she would swear he was upset with her about something. But she couldn't fathom what he had to be upset about or why he felt entitled to be upset with her, to begin with.

"What size tree are you looking for?" Lemon asked, his stiff back.

Instead of responding, his eyes kept sweeping from left to right again. Lemon found it hard to believe that he was searching for a tree, given how his eyes darted around so restlessly. His actions were far more suited for someone watching for a threat. The thought caused her awareness to intensify into a painfully acute realization. If anything were to happen to either of them, they would be too far away to receive help.

"Jace, is something wrong?" She worried, hurrying her steps to catch up to him.

His deep, pensive gaze met hers, electrifying her with a newfound awareness. "No, sorry." He let his stride shorten so she didn't have to run to keep up with him. "I was just thinking."

"About what?"

"What?" He asked sharply, his eyes dropping to hers.

"What were you thinking about?" She saw amusement flicker in his eyes and wondered what he found so funny.

He tilted his head as if trying to decide if he should share his thoughts with her. Lemon prickled at his scrutinizing stare. Then he said, "A job, the same one I was working on.

The client has asked for some alterations to the design, but I don't think they will work as well as he thinks it will."

"Did you share your concerns with him?"

"I did, but he wasn't in a very respective mood." He admitted, a wry grin forming on his lips.

"So, do what he asks, and when it fails, at least you will know that you warned him, even if he didn't want to listen to you."

"True. But my name is attached to the work. I don't know how much I like the idea of a bad design out in the world that bears testament to my craft."

Lemon lifted her gaze to his profile. The sudden, sharp stab of physical awareness surprised her. With her eyes off the ground, she missed the root protruding from the earth, catching her boot and causing her to pitch forward with a startled yelp. Jace moved fast. His hand locked onto her arm and pulled her back upright. "Are you okay?" He asked, his fingers tangling with hers.

"Yes." Lemon laughed. "Sorry, I should keep my eyes on the ground."

"If you do that, you might miss something great standing right in front of you." He replied, letting the words drop between them.

They stood facing each other. Her heart raced, its quick tempo matching the jumble of thoughts in her mind. Lemon looked into his eyes, frustrated not to be able to read anything in his expression. It was just like him. He had a way of saying something that held a deeper meaning, only never giving her enough information to decode his message. Why couldn't he say what he wanted to say in plain words, words that she could understand? Not these profound and deep phrases that made her heart race and her throat tighten with emotion.

She hoped he would say something more, something that would give her a clue to what he was thinking, but he didn't. Instead, Jace started walking, her hand still cradled in his. The realization sent a thrill of excitement through her, an explosion of emotions rippling off each other.

No matter what, she didn't want this sudden blossom of feelings to end. Her mind frantically searched for where they had left off their conversation. "Is it so bad having your name associated with a design you don't completely agree with?"

He flicked a quick look at her before turning his attention back to the path. "No, I suppose not. Though it hasn't happened to me yet."

"What does your boss say? I mean, I suppose you told them about what is happening."

"Yeah, I did. She told me the client is always right, and even if they come back and say they don't like the changes, we just have to fix it and move on."

"I'm sorry. That must be frustrating."

"It is." He laughed in a cold, humorless way. "The funny thing is, I didn't even want this project. They gave it to me because the client kept making the last project manager cry."

"Oh, my. That's terrible."

This time, when he smiled, a wicked gleam twinkled in his eye. "Not really. Cindy tends to cry a lot. And I mean a lot. She says it's how she gets her creative juices flowing."

Lemon laughed. Her heart lifted with the pleasure of the moment. "Wow. I need to remember that one. Maybe the next time my mother catches me crying, I can claim they are helping me to clear my senses."

"Or maybe, the next time you pick a man to date, you will choose one who doesn't see breaking your spirit as a way to build himself up." Jace ground out.

With startled eyes, Lemon met his gaze in amazement. "I don't know what you mean."

"I think you do."

"Even if I did, I don't see what concern it is of yours."

With an ironic bow of his head, Jace let his hand slip from hers. "True. There is no reason why I would be concerned with your happiness. I think I see a tree that will work over in this direction."

As he walked away, Lemon felt a keen loss. She looked at her hand, and a sudden emptiness washed over her as if something precious had been taken away.

Chapter Nine

MONDAY, DECEMBER 8TH

Even the best intentions can be overshadowed by the allure of tiny, shiny objects.

L emon bit back a groan when a group of middle-aged women strolled through the connected opening of The End Bookstore. Their bright smiles and chipper attitudes did nothing to quell her frazzled nerves. After helping her stock the display case for the day, her mother cheerfully told Lemon that she had an appointment with her father and wouldn't be in for the rest of the day. When Lemon had stammered her concern for being left alone to manage the bakery, her mother waved away her worries as if she were hysterical.

Now, four hours later, with a line ten people deep and a door that wouldn't stay closed, Lemon's hysteria was no longer hypothetical. With each demanding customer, she cursed her mother's name, and every time buns ran out, she grumbled as she stalked to the kitchen for a refill.

Later, when she finally had a moment to breathe and restock,she realized surprisingly few sticky buns were left. Every morning, she made five dozen. Sometimes, they sold out, and other days, there might be a dozen or so left. Lemon stood at the counter where the overstock of cinnamon rolls and sticky buns rested and stared at the empty pan in confusion.

She could have sworn the last time she came back to restock the glass display stand, there had been two buns left of the pan. Her brow furrowed as she struggled to remember. It had been the group of friends, Lemon recalled. Amidst their rowdy laughter and concurrent conversations, she had barely managed to comprehend their order. She had silently stood, observing with a pang of jealousy. It had been years since she had experienced such unrestrained laughter with friends like that.

When they each had wanted a sticky bun, she'd had to grab some from the back. The glass dome only holds two remaining. If the cake stand held seven, and they had purchased five, that meant she would have gotten ten from the back. The pan held an even dozen, but what she couldn't swear to was if the pan had been full or not. Usually, when she emptied a pan, it went into the sink. So why wouldn't she have done the same thing if the pan had been empty? Unless she'd felt rushed to return to the counter.

Reflectively, the day had been trying. She'd only managed to steal a few minutes of respite between each rush of customers. Maybe she had just been frazzled and forgotten. Not that it mattered, only it was strange.The last few end-of-shift inventory audits she'd run had seemed to come up with a miss count of one or two items. On the whole, that wasn't necessarily a bad thing, especially in the food industry. However, it may be time for her to pay more attention to exact product counts, just in case.

The bell chimed over the door. The once pleasant jingle now irritated her. Lemon glanced wistfully at the clock, what she wouldn't give for the time to read four o'clock. But it wasn't to be. With no help for it, she quickly washed her hands and swung through the door, a bright smile spread wide. "Welcome to Frosted. What can I help you with?" She said before her eyes found the crystal blue of Brian's. "Oh, hi." Her smile turned into a genuine grin.

Brian's dimple winked as he stepped up to the counter,resting an arm on top. With his button-down shirt rolled halfway up his forearms, his tan skin looked vibrant and healthy against the steel blue fabric. The barely perceptible golden arm hair dusted his arms, blending with the bronze hue. Unexpectedly, a vivid image of Jace's arms, adorned with deep brown hair accentuating his sinewy muscles, floated in her thoughts. Lemon pushed the image aside and the sudden desire to feel the soft texture beneath her fingertips.

"What brings you in today?" Lemon asked, trying to cool the abrupt surge of warmth to her cheeks.

"You," Brian replied in his usual easy way.

His smile suddenly sent her back to high school and all those old feelings she used to have for him. She raised her eyebrow, her smile widening. "Me? Sounds intriguing." She teased, her eyes twinkling with mirth. "Well, you've gotten my attention."

"Do I?"

"Of course. Do you see anyone else here?"

"Hmmm. I suppose that's true. But I wonder what would happen if someone else did happen to come in. Would I still hold your attention, then?"

Lemon laughed hesitantly, unsure of his mood. "What's with this line of questioning?"

Brian shook his head. "Never mind. Listen, maybe I could buy you dinner this Saturday."

"Dinner. Wow, it's been a hot minute since we've been on a date. Are you sure you want to go down that road again?"

The last meal they'd shared had been the night after graduation. It had been foolish, she realized now, but back then, she'd been full of dreams. She thought she'd go to school with a boyfriend and, after graduating, they would get married. When they had sat in that corner booth, she snuggled into his side. The scent of his cologne circled her. She never imagined he would whisper in her ear how much he loved her and then, on the very next breath, that he thought they should break up.

At the time, she'd laughed, thinking he'd made a joke. But when she'd pushed away to see his face, the seriousness of his expression left her cold. All the warmth and happiness she'd felt in his arms a moment before evaporating into the air.

His smile faltered as if he, too, was remembering their last meal together. Then his mouth widened, showing his white teeth. "Come on. That was years ago. When we were impulsive kids. We're adults now. We've both had our share of relationship experiences. What's the harm in going to dinner? We could catch up, maybe exchange some of our more interesting dates."

Lemon's eyes dropped to his hand resting across hers. She expected to feel something. Given their shared history, she assumed there would be some sort of spark. The lack of sensations was unsettling, causing her brow to furrow.

"Come on, Lemon." Brian cajoled, "Don't be like that. Give me another chance." Lifting her hand, he squeezed it between his own. She was surprised by how easy it felt to slip right back into the old patterns. Her mouth twitched when he bit the tip of her middle finger playfully. "Didn't we have fun together?" He prodded, and she felt her resistance slipping.

He was right. They had had fun together, and as long as she didn't dwell on the nightmare homecoming dance, things between them had been good. Yet, the slight twinge of doubt continued to haunt her.

"Okay," she finally said, just as the bell over the door chimed again.

Mrs. Butternick, the Harper High School principal for the last ten years, walked into the bakery. Her face brightened with recognition. "My, what a delight," she said. Her eyes fell to their joined hands. "It is so nice to see you together again. You two were a darling couple."

Lemon slipped her hand out of Brian's grasp. "Thank you, Mrs. Butternick. It's nice to see you again, too." Her gaze flicked to Brian's before returning to her old principal. "Can I get you anything?"

"Yes, please. I wanted to order a dozen Snickerdoodles. It's my monthly book club tonight, and I've gotten into the habit of picking up cookies for it. I used to get chocolate chip cookies. They're my favorite, or at least they used to be. But after that unfortunate batch, I just haven't had the courage to try them again." Mrs. Butternick explained with a grimace.

As her eyes swept from Brian to Mrs. Butternick, Lemon's mind flooded with a thousand questions. The two of them shared a conspiring grin. Of all the questions floating in her mind, one pressed forward. What happened to ruin the batch of chocolate chip cookies?

Instead of asking for details, Lemon filled the white box.Her mind puzzled over the strange turn in the conversation. When her attention was once again on Brian and Mrs. Butternick, she caught the tail end of an agreement that had her groaning inwardly.

Mrs. Butternick had her hands clasped tightly in front of her ample bosom as her voice took on a shrill pitch of excitement similar to a tea kettle setting off steam. "That is just fabulous. Just think, one of our schools favored royalty back for the winter formal."

Brian had the gall to wink at her horrified expression. "It will be fun to chaperone. I haven't been back to Harper High since I graduated.Have you Lemon?"

Lemon snapped out of her inner turmoil at the sound of her name. "What?"

"Have you been back to Harper High since we graduated?"

"Oh, ah, no. I haven't." She muttered, wondering how she had gotten herself into this mess. The last thing she wanted was to chaperone a high school dance, especially with her old boyfriend. As she looked into

Brian's laughing face, she had the sudden desire to throw the box of snickerdoodles at him.

"Well, it looks like we'll share the treat," he said, then almost as an afterthought, "After dinner, of course."

"Of course." She agreed. Now, as she looked at Brian, she wondered what had possessed her to accept his offer for a date. Sure, she could see remnants of the boy she'd once fancied herself in love with, but if life had taught her anything, it was to be careful of shiny packages. Rarely did they ever meet with expectations.

Whether Mrs. Butternick didn't notice the sudden tension in the air or simply refused to acknowledge it, Lemon marveled at her ability to chatter happily. "The dance starts at eight. We ask that the couples' chaperoning show up fifteen minutes early. The theme I think you are going to love, by the way, is Gumdrop Gala. The students have been working so hard creating the decorations. We got Al from the hardware store to donate a bunch of plastic containers. Then the student council spent all morning Saturday spray painting the outsides blue, red, orange, green... you know all the colors."Mrs. Butternick exclaimed, waving her hand like a flag. "The entire gymnasium is going to be covered in gingerbread cutouts. Snowflakes and strands of lights will dangle from the ceiling, with little gumdrops scattering the floor." With her hands clasped, she asked wistfully. "It's going to be a magically sweet wonderland, don't you think?"

"It sounds lovely." Lemon agreed, though she couldn't imagine why Mrs. Butternick thought gumdrops would be a good dance theme. The whole thing sounded ridiculous. Unlike her winter formal, which exuded elegance with an ice castle theme, this seemed to allude to a casual barnyard hoedown.She could hardly be expected to wear the champagne-colored evening dress she'd worn her senior year. Visions of tulle and rainbow colors danced through her mind. "I wonder what I should wear?" The question was out before she could stop it.

Mrs. Butternick's expression brightened. "I think you'll look lovely in anything you choose to wear. But if I may offer my humblest opinion, I think the long gowns look so much better than these short skirts girls are wearing today. It would be wonderful if someone the girls looked up to set the example and wore something elegant but tasteful. Maybe in a soft pink." She turned her attention to Brian, then said, "Don't you think Lemon would look angelic in pink?"

"I always thought she looked best in deep greens." Jace's deep timbre cut over Brian. Three pairs of startled eyes turned to the doorway where Jace stood propped up against the wall. His arms crossed over his chest.His expression was remote as his gaze locked on to hers.

"Well, if it isn't Jace Torte." Mrs. Butternick said with a warm smile. "How are you? What have you been up to since you left us? I know your mother told me, but

I can't recall what it is you do now. Have you enjoyed being close to your parents again? Your mother told me you were coming home to help, but I haven't been into your mother's shop in a few months, so I wasn't sure when you go back. Speaking of your mother, how is she feeling? It's just terrible. Breast cancer is such a nasty business."

Jace skipped over most of Mrs. Butternick's dialog, jumping to the last question. "My mother is improving daily."

"That's so good to hear. It's always nice when there is a happy ending." Turning back to Lemon, Mrs. Butternick asked, "Don't you?"

Lemon smiled, her eyes darting to Jace's. "Yes, it is always preferable to hear good news."

Mrs. Butternick glanced at the face of her watch and gasped."Oh, how time has flown? I have to run. My book club is due to start in fifteen minutes. How much do I owe you, Lemon?"

After a quick click of the screen, the total appeared, and Mrs. Butternick dug out her wallet, handing Lemon a few bills, a dime, and an odd-sized silver coin."

Lemon held the coin up. Looking first at the front, then the back. "What is this?"

"It's a fifty-cent piece. I got it as change in a store in Denver. I know they're rare, but I promised Hal I wouldn't keep anything else. Our house is busting at the seams as it stands now. So I thought the next time I paid with cash, I would make sure to pass it along."

"That's so nice of you." Lemon gushed, her fist closing over the coin protectively. Unlike Mrs. Butternick's husband, her dad loved to collect coins and would no doubt be thrilled with an awesome coin that fell into her lap.

As Mrs. Butternick turned to leave, Brian held open the door for her, wishing her a good day. Lemon followed her progress until she disappeared. Brian returned to the counter, his phone in hand. A frown deepening the ridges of his forehead. "It looks like I won't be available Saturday like I thought."

"What?" Lemon gasped, struggling to push down her panic. "You just told Mrs. Butternick we would chaperone for the dance."

"I know." He groaned, running a hand through his styled hair. "If it wasn't important, I wouldn't bail on you like this."

"What am I supposed to do now?"

Brian smiled, patting her hand. "Just go alone. I'm sure it won't matter whether I'm there or not."

Lemon could only stare. She knew her mouth was hanging open but was too stunned to close it. It wasn't until the chime of the door at Brian's exit that she managed to pull herself out of her mental fog. The mere thought of walking through the doors of her old high school gymnasium alone sent chills down her arms. She couldn't, wouldn't do it. Lemon slammed the cash register shut, remembering to keep the unusual coin out at the last minute.

She tapped her fingers on the counter, weighing her options,when Jace caught her eye. He still stood leaning against the wall as if he didn't have a care in the world. Lemon stepped out from behind the counter.With her slate blue apron tied snugly around her waist, she wore it like a shield. Her hands fisted at her sides. She took a deep, purposeful breath."Jace, what are you doing Saturday night?"

Maybe it was because she'd spent so much time with sweets,or perhaps it was the dim lights hanging overhead, but suddenly,Jace's hair wasn't simply a dark brown shade but a rich chocolate. Her mind became plagued with curiosity. She wanted to know if it would slip through her fingers like melted chocolate. Would it be as soft and malleable? She watched in fascination as his eyebrow lifted. "As of now, I don't have any plans."

It was funny how life kept throwing her into these unusual situations. She found herself contemplating something she never would have fathomed. Still, it wasn't so much that she was considering going on a date with Jace. No, Brian's actions put her in a tough spot, and Jace served as a sensible solution. Even as her mind continued down the forbidden track, she asked, "Will you go to the winter formal with me?"

Chapter Ten

TUESDAY, DECEMBER 9TH

It isn't until something is missed that the loss is realized.

B erry slammed the door, stomping to his room. The force of his bedroom door shutting rattled the ceiling. Lemon looked toward the stairs, her brow furrowing with concern. "I wonder what that was about." She said, shifting her gaze to her father, anticipating a reaction to her brother's intense display of emotion. She sighed with resignation. It shouldn't have been surprising to find her father's focus still centered on the vibrant screen in front of him.

Since closing Frosted for the day, she'd spent the remainder of the afternoon reading on the couch while her father watched some football recap. Lemon never understood the desire for her father and brother to rewatch plays they had already seen while watching the game. Nor could she grasp how they could be so engrossed that they ignored the actual happenings around them.

William sat reclined in his brown suede chair. His sock-clad feet crossed at the ankle. At his elbow sat a can of cola on the end table, condensation trickling down its smooth surface. The remote cradled in his hand, resting idly on the armrest.

After a few minutes, Lemon's expectation of a response from her dad dwindled. The lines of her golden eyebrows pulled down into a scowl. "Dad," she prodded. When he still didn't respond, Lemon sighed exasperated and grabbed one of the fluffy square pillows next to her. With a flick of her wrist, she sent the pillow flying. Lemon didn't throw it forcefully, but it landed where she wanted it to, directly on the back of her father's head.

With a grunt, he snapped his head around. "I'm pretty sure we had 'the talk' about throwing things when you were five."

Lemon laughed, her eyes sparkling with a wicked gleam. "You did, but throwing a pillow was the easiest way to get your attention."

"*Or* you could try saying my name."

"I did."

"When?"

"A minute ago."

"Huh."

"Maybe you would have heard me if you weren't zoning out."

William frowned. "Since when is it a crime for a man to relax in front of his own TV?"

"Only when you don't pay attention to your daughter," Lemon exclaimed. "Unless you don't want me to talk to you." Her eyes deliberately clouded up, and she turned her lips into a pout.

William's expression softened as he looked into his daughter's face. Like his wife, he couldn't be prouder of their daughter. From the day Lemon was born, she'd always been a shooting star, bright and dazzling, lighting up their lives.

He'd always known she would grow to be an amazing woman, and she hadn't disappointed him, not in the least. It was more than her pretty face that made her a success. Lemon had a fire inside of her. However, she had come home bruised with a fragility reminiscent of a wounded dove. But he knew once she found her footing again, she would take to the sky.

He only hoped she would accept the gift he and Evelyn wanted to give her. He doubted she would now, but maybe once Harper had worked its magic, she would remember her worth and embrace a new path in life that could be waiting for her.

"Daddy, are you even listening to me?" Lemon asked, standing at the side of his chair, her hands braced on her hips.

"Sorry, honey bee. What did you ask me?"

"I was wondering if you knew what was going on with Berry."

William's brow furrowed. "Berry? Why would anything be wrong with Berry?"

"Well, for starters, he slammed the front door and stormed off to his room a minute ago. Then the other day, he was grumpy..."

"Oh, that." William shrugged, his attention caught once again by the screen. "Some girl at school."

"Really? What girl?"

William spared her a half glance. "I don't know. Something about his grade in English slipping, and she's been tutoring."

"Oh."

"I guess your brother has taken a shine to her, but she says he is too conceited, and she doesn't trust him."

"Does that mean he asked a girl out, and she actually told him no?" Lemon asked, choking on her laughter.

"I don't know," William grumbled. "Look, Lemon, I am missing the recap of Saturday's game. Why don't you just go and ask your brother about it?"

Lemon's face broke into a wide grin, which meant she was fixing to cause mischief. William groaned, grasping one of her slender hands in his. "Just don't get him riled up. I beg of you."

"Who, me?" Lemon said, batting her lashes.

William's groan went unnoticed this time as he spared Lemon's retreating back with one last look. He hoped they didn't get Evelyn involved because it would inevitably lead to his involvement, causing him to miss his show.

There was a time not too long ago when she would have opened Berry's door and walked in without bothering to knock first. But somehow, in the time since she had moved out, the balance had shifted, and she found herself hesitating at the door.

Lemon shook off her hesitancy, raising her hand from the knob to knock on the door. Then, as a compromise for herself, she twisted the handle and pushed the door open without waiting for a reply. She found Berry lying across his bed, a double. Their parents had replaced his twin after his last growth spurt the summer of his freshmen year. He had a baseball out and was tossing it in the air. The only sound was the solid thump of the ball hitting the palm of his opposite hand.

Berry gave her a fleeting glance before resuming his game. "I didn't say you could come in."

Ignoring his snide remark, Lemon strolled around his room, walking past his wall of trophies and assorted recognitions. The glittering tower of triumphs represented years of athletic achievements. When she got to his dresser, she leaned against the smooth surface. "Why do you think I just walked in? A girl could grow old waiting for you to let her in."

The pain that flashed across his face came as a shock. Berry wasn't one who succumbed to hurt feelings. Even after getting hit with the harshest criticism, he always shrugged it away and went about his business. Though it rarely happened. No one bothered to correct someone like Berry. With his looks and charisma, he often escaped any disparagement.

Being placed on such a high pedestal couldn't be good for a person. After all, she should know, having been placed on a similar one for most of her life. A wry grin lifted the corners of her lips. Lemon fingered the miniature Christmas tree their mother had placed on Berry's otherwise immaculate dresser. The subtle reminder of the swiftly approaching holiday brought a smile to her face. "I'm surprised you let Mom put this tree in here."

Berry shrugged, the motion limited because his shoulders remained braced against the headboard. "Why wouldn't I? A little tree doesn't bother me, and it makes Mom happy."

Lemon stared at her brother, seeing him with new eyes. It wasn't fair to say that Berry had lived a charmed life because he was no more charmed than hers. However, having managed to breeze his way through life relatively unscathed had left him a bit emotionally stunted. It wasn't a matter of indifference; rather, his regard for others never reached a point where their opinions were relevant. The fact that he grasped the significance of their mother's Christmas decorations and remained silent about her decorating his room spoke volumes.

"What's that look for?" Berry asked, his expression hesitant.

"What look?"

"That one on your face."

"How about I tell you mine if you tell me yours?"

"What are you talking about?" He asked, the lines of his forehead deepening.

"Come on, Berry. Don't act like you don't know what I am talking about. You have been acting weird ever since I came home." She gave him a speaking glance. "I am assuming that this doesn't have anything to do with me, but I can't ignore it anymore. Especially when you are slamming doors and snarling at anyone who tries to talk to you."

"Leave it alone, Lemon."

"I wish I could." Lemon pushed away from the dresser, crossed the room, and sat on the edge of his bed. "I love you, Berry, and I would like to help you if I can."

Berry snorted, sitting up and swinging his feet to the floor. "This isn't something you can help with."

"Try me." The note of a challenge hung between them. She didn't push anymore. Instead, she waited for him to come to a decision. Either he would trust her with his problems, or he wouldn't. And though she tried not to let him see her earnest expression, she hoped he would confide in her. In the six years she had spent living away from her family, Berry had grown up, and soon, he, too, would be gone. If they didn't use this time to form an adult relationship now, they might never get another chance. The fear of them drifting apart pressed down on her. She had to remind herself to take a deep breath to relieve the crushing sensation in her chest.

"I have been struggling in English this year." Berry began, his eyes focused on the ball in his hands as he rolled it between his palms. "Coach said he could take care of the problem for me, but I turned him down. Football is great, but it isn't something I can do forever. I need to go to college, and it's going to be on me to get the work done when I get there." He explained, almost pleading for her to understand. She rushed to agree. "Of course. It was the right thing to do."

"Yeah, well. Mr. Porter suggested a tutor and recommended a student he had last year. He told me she was really smart and is taking college English right now."

"Okay." Lemon offered, though she wasn't sure what she was acknowledging or why.

"Anyway. Mr. Porter set up the first tutoring session between me and Mia. That's her name. Mia Spenser. She's amazing. Clever. Funny." He gushed, which surprised Lemon. She couldn't remember the last time her brother had ever spoken so highly of a girl that wasn't directly related to her physical appearance.

"Her family moved here from the south about a year ago, Georgia, I think. I had no idea she even went to my school. At least not until Mr. Porter introduced us. The whole time we were talking during that first meeting, her voice Lemon," he said earnestly. "I swear her voice sounded like sweet honey. But it wasn't just her voice. Her smile, her eyes. Pick a reason. There were so many of them I can't choose just one. I couldn't think of anything but her. Whenever I wasn't busy, my mind would go wild."

In a fluid motion, Berry surged to his feet, pacing in an agitated stride right in front of her. "So, she sounds like honey and is really smart. What's the big deal?" Lemon asked, though she had a feeling she already knew.

"I asked her out." He admitted, his cheeks growing red.

"And?"

"She said no."

She almost missed it and would have if she hadn't been watching him. It wasn't what she expected, the deep hurt that flashed in his eyes. She couldn't recall the last time any girl had affected Berry this way.

Even though he seemed to be genuinely upset by the rejection, they both knew he would move on to the next girl. "Berry," Lemon started out tentatively. She didn't want to upset her brother, but she had to know. "You have been out with dozens of girls. What makes this one so different?"

Berry spun around and faced her fully. His eyes glittered. "Haven't you been listening to a word I have said? I have never felt this way about a girl before, and she won't even give me a chance."

"Did she say why?"

"Yeah, she said that I was too focused on the superficial, and one day, I would look at her and really see her. She would be attached by then, and I would wind up breaking her heart. She told me she wasn't interested in facing those kinds of emotions."

"Wow." This Mia girl really had a good pulse on the situation. However, that information did nothing to help ease the pain her rejection had caused. "What did you ask her to do?"

"The first time I asked her to dinner. The second I asked her to go bowling with me. I was meeting some friends and hoped a group activity might give her a better chance of becoming comfortable."

"I take it that she didn't like either of those options?"

"Nope." Berry dropped his baseball, kicking it with his shoe until it rolled beneath his unmade bed. "I figured that maybe she might want a grand gesture." He explained.

Lemon wanted to cringe away. Already, she knew where this was going and could see the writing on the wall even if Berry hadn't. "What kind of grand jester are we talking about?"

"I thought she might enjoy going to the winter formal, so I wrote on the sidewalk leading to Mr. Porter's room."

"That's not so bad."

"Yeah, well, she didn't like it. She didn't even answer my question. Then the rest of the school found out I got jilted by her, and now I am the running joke."

"Okay, let's table that for a second. What about your tutoring? Are you still seeing her for it?"

"Yes. Mr. Porter won't let me switch, and now everything is awkward. Mia won't look me in the eye, and any time I accidentally touch her, she jumps like a frightened kitten."

Lemon started responding to his problem, yet the end of his explanation had her pausing. "She jumps when you touch her?"

"Yeah."

"How? Show me."

Berry laughed, "What? No, I'm not doing that."

"Come on, show me. I promise it will be worth it."

"Fine." He grumbled as he sat on the bed beside her. "Touch my hand."

Lemon brushed her fingers over the back of his hand, which he promptly snatched away. "Are you sure she moves like that?"

"Yes. Why?"

Lemon smiled, "Because, brother, you have her. You just need a little finesse to get her, is all."

"How so?"

"I would have thought it would be obvious to a lady's magnet like yourself. But if you can't figure it out, I guess I'll just have to explain it to you."

"Will you quit jerking me around and tell me what you are talking about?"

"It's quite simple. When a girl pulls away like that, she feels a connection but doesn't want to admit it."

Berry frowned. "How do you know this, anyway?"

The endless encounters with Jace flashed through her mind in rapid secession. "Trust me., I know."

"Okay, fine. Let's say you are right. Let's pretend that Mia is interested in me. What would you have me do? I've already asked several times and been shot down. I don't know if I can handle being rejected again."

"I thought you really liked her? Isn't she worth laying your heart on the line at least once more?"

Berry's shoulders drooped as he stared at his hands. "I thought so, but now I don't know."

Lemon glared at him. "Come on, Berry. How much do you want, Mia?"

"More than I want air to breathe."

Lemon smiled, her eye sparkling with mischief. "Excellent. You just leave it to me."

Berry gazed at her with a skeptical expression. "Why do I suddenly feel like I am turning my heart over to someone who only knows how to take things?"

"Hey!" Lemon gasped, slapping him in the chest with the back of her hand. "That is not true, and you know it."

He rubbed at his chest absently. "Okay, I'll let you handle it."

"Good, now stop pouting. I've got this." Lemon paused at the door. Before swinging it open, she asked him, "By the way. What exactly did you write on the sidewalk?"

With a smirk, Berry said, "I took it from your playbook. I told her I wasn't a fan of gumdrops and asked her if she would be my sweet date."

Lemon nodded before closing the door behind her. As she walked away, a new determination took hold of her. No matter what, she was going to get Mia to that dance.

Chapter Eleven

WEDNESDAY, DECEMBER 10TH

Once may be a fluke, but twice is a problem.

Lemon picked up the half-eaten sticky bun, examining it from one angle, then from another. She held the remains in her hand like an offering and pushed through the door leading to the bakery front. "Mama, is this your sticky bun?"

Evelyn turned, her crystalline blue eyes popping against the slate blue apron. "What, dear?"

After holding the bun up higher, Lemon pointed to the eaten side. "I found this on the tray in the kitchen. Is it yours?"

"No. I haven't eaten anything since coming into work this morning."

"Well, if you didn't eat it and I didn't eat it, then who did?"

"Maybe Jace." Evelyn offered as she turned back to the display case. She set another row of snickerdoodles on the white snowflake doilies they ordered for the holiday season.

"When would Jace have had the chance to eat half a sticky bun from the kitchen?"

"He came down this morning just before you got in. Which you were fifteen minutes late, by the way." Evelyn said. The reminder grating on Lemon's nerves. Her mother had always had a way of making her feel guilty for the slightest things she did wrong.

Lemon rolled her eyes. "Mama, I hardly think this is the time to get into something like that. Besides, you were here. What difference is it if I run a few minutes late?"

"I guess that all depends on how successful you want to be. Remember, I won't always be around to cover for you."

With her lips pursed, Lemon muttered. "I'm pretty sure I have managed a pretty successful career on my own, thank you very much."

"I suppose that's why you have found yourself back home again."

As far as jabs went, this one had staying power. Lemon bristled, fighting back the sudden rush of tears. If anyone else had said something like that to her, she would have told them to go to hell. But this was her mother, and no matter what, she could never speak to her that way.

"I think I will go ask Jace then." She mumbled, not bothering to wait for her mother's reply. She turned away, walking blindly toward the closed French door leading to The End.

Lemon fought to put on a brave face even though her mother's words continued to race around in her mind. When Jeff had broken her heart, she had come home, not considering any other alternatives. But maybe that choice had been wrong. She hadn't thought what it would look like to have left her job, even though she had technically been fired and returned home. While happy to have her home, her mother must have been embarrassed.

Despite all of this, one question continued to haunt her. Did coming home actually signify failure?

The End was closed; it wasn't even seven yet. The absolute quiet told Lemon Jace must still be upstairs. She didn't even think about calling out to make sure she could. She simply took to the stairs, the half-eaten sticky bun still resting in the center of her palm.

His apartment door stood half open, to which Lemon knocked as she pushed it open the rest of the way. With each step, her temper surged until she was boiling over.

It didn't matter that Jace probably hadn't done anything wrong. He was in her crosshairs, and she was primed and ready to fire.

She found him in his cramped kitchen. It held no more than five feet of cabinets, a cooktop, and a refrigerator. A small microwave sat on the bar-height table tucked to the side. He stood at the sink, the water running. She imagined he was probably washing dishes, though she didn't much care at the moment. Because he was about to catch hell, which was in the form of a green-eyed vixen.

Jace hummed under his breath, washing the last of his breakfast dishes. He'd already been up for two hours and felt the effects of a sleepless night. The sad truth was he hadn't been able to sleep for the past two nights, and it was all Lemon's fault.

This was supposed to be temporary. He would work the store for his mother until her health improved. Then, he would return to his life in San Francisco. That was the plan. And it had been, no, it still was. Nothing had changed. So what if Lemon came soaring back into his life like a comet, filling his life with wonder again? The point was simple. He may be crazy about her, but that didn't mean she felt or ever would feel anything for him. Besides, girls like Lemon never looked twice at guys like him. She wanted brawn, like Brian. Not brains.

Sure, after high school, he'd hit a growth spurt his freshman year. Then, he decided to join a gym and add some muscle to his lean frame. And he had to admit the difference was astounding. Not only had the college girls begun to take notice of him, but they appeared genuinely delighted by his ability to engage in conversations that surpassed the norm for men his age in college.

Life had been good. He had a great job. Dated all kinds of beautiful women. Even when his dad had called asking for help, it hadn't been that big of an inconvenience. No, everything had been going swimmingly until Lemon. Now, he couldn't get her out of his head. Whenever he thought he had a handle on this flood of emotions, she would do something to throw him off balance again.

The biggest was their upcoming date on Saturday night. Though he wasn't sure if she thought of it as a date. Call it fate, luck, or perhaps a case of bad timing, but he was taking Lemon to the high school winter formal. This was a dream come true. Every guy in his graduating class would have gladly given his left hand for the chance to date Lemon Frost, including him. Not that he would ever admit it. Especially not to her.

The problem remained. Was he supposed to take her to dinner first, make a night of it? Or maybe she saw it as him just filling in for the guy she wanted to go with. If this had been high school, he would have gone meekly along with whatever Lemon wanted. But this wasn't high school, and he hadn't cow-toed for anyone else in a long time.

Maybe it was a lack of sleep or his train of thought, but when he turned around and found himself face-to-face with his green-eyed goddess, something inside of him shifted.

"You know, if you continue to come into my home uninvited, I'm going to have to start locking my door."

"Why don't you? It's not like I'm the only one who could wander up here."

"During store hours, I do. But The End isn't open yet, and the only way up here is through Frosted, which isn't open yet, either. That leaves only you and your mother. Your mother has never barged in on me before." Jace watched with perverse pleasure as red spread across Lemon's face. His eyes followed the rising heat of her embarrassment, and an unmistakable desire to push her further overwhelmed him, shoving aside all sense of caution. He leaned against the sink, his feet crossed and his hands braced on the counter behind him. "Seeing as it's too late to lock the door, why don't you tell me what had you charging up here carrying half of a sticky bun? What? Were you hoping we could split it? Maybe set up a cute scene where you bring me breakfast, and I fall all over myself to please you?"

He watched in fascination as Lemon's eyes snapped with green fire. Her usually angelic face contorted into that of an Amazon warrior. He should have expected a pissed-off Lemon would be just as irresistible as the bright-eyed and wistful one. Maybe if he hadn't been so fascinated by her transformation, he might have noticed her intent.

The squished dough of what once had been a sticky bun hit him square in the face. The sugary coating clung to his face for a second before rolling off his nose and landing in a heap at his feet.

Lemon stood ramrod straight. Her fists curled into tight balls at her sides. Her breathing, shallow and ragged, broke through the otherwise silent surroundings. He could see the rapid rise and fall of her chest and knew she was struggling to gain control of her temper.

With one finger, he swiped the glaze remnant from under his eye, popping the gooey mess into his mouth. "Mmmm, thanks for breakfast."

Yet again, she surprised him. With hurtling speed, Lemon charged at him. For a second, he thought about letting her attack him so that he could see what she would do, but thousands of years of survival instincts can't be undone in a quest for curiosity. In a smooth movement, he bent, catching his shoulder in her middle. When he straightened, Lemon dangled over his back. Her slender hands beat against his back.

The best part of a studio apartment was that no matter where you stood, you were no more than ten steps from the bed. Once he was close enough, he tossed Lemon down with a satisfying bounce. Then, before she could wiggle from the bed, Jace pounced on top of her. His fingers dug into her taunt inner thighs, a self-satisfied grin breaking across his face at her squealing laughter.

"Stop," Lemon screeched as she struggled to push his tormenting hands away.

With a laugh, Jace asked, "Do you yield?"

"Yes. Please, yes. I give up." She gasped, "I give up."

Jace braced his hands on either side of her hips. Looking down at her tussled hair and cheeky grin, he felt a sharp stab of desire tighten his gut. Something must have shown on his face because Lemon's smile faded as a shadow of uncertainty clouded her expression. The delicate pink tip of her tongue darted over her bottom lip, and he couldn't help but watch its fleeting retreat.

"Was it just my imagination, or did you come looking for a fight?" He asked, in part, to cover his reaction and distract himself from what he wanted.

Lemon pinched her lips, her cheeks turning pink. "I guess I did."

"Care to tell me why? Maybe I missed something, but I thought we had parted on fairly good terms Monday."

"No, you didn't miss something. I wasn't mad at you. I just needed to take out my frustration on someone, and you were an easy target. If Berry had been around, I would have gone after him, but since he wasn't, you seemed like a suitable alternative."

Jace's expression darkened. The idea of being considered the same as her brother didn't sit well with him. "What got you all riled up?"

"Nothing important."

"I don't think so," he said as he brushed a clump of her hair back from her face. "You stormed into my apartment. Remember. The least you can do is tell me what set you off."

With a heavy sigh, Lemon met his gaze. The connection sent a jolt through his heart. "It was my mother. She said something that got under my skin."

"What did she say?"

"Boy, you know how to gnaw on that bone, don't you?"

Jace ignored her bristling tone. His thumb stroked the underside of her jaw. He probably should have removed his hand from her face, but the sensation of his fingertips brushing against her velvety skin left him unable to break the connection. "What did she say?" He asked again in a strained voice.

Lemon continued to surprise him. His vivacious and exuberant star was crying, and he didn't know what to do about it. He brushed a tear away with the pad of his thumb. Her lashes fluttered against the glistening moisture.

"It doesn't matter." Her voice shattered the silence, but her words broke his heart.

"Obviously, it does. Are you sure you don't want to talk about it?"

Even as she nodded, he felt a pang of regret. If only she trusted him enough to share her secrets. But then again, he wasn't staying. It was better this way. It was better for him to feel the ache of her absence than for her to be miserable with him. Yet for a fleeting moment, his heart wondered wistfully, what if?

He hovered over her, painfully aware of the soft bed under them. Sugar and cinnamon swirled around him, and the distinct scent he was coming to recognize as her. Her expression softened with emotion that made her appear touchable. At that moment, he wanted nothing more than to sink into her. To feel her arms curl around his neck as she held him close.

His gaze lingered on her parted lips. For one second, two seconds, then one more. With a groan, he rolled off her. Unfortunately, he'd miscalculated how close they were to the edge and kept rolling. Jace hit the ground with a bone-jarring thud.

Lemon's face appeared over the edge of the mattress. Her eyes were once again sparkling with mischief. "Real smooth, Jace." She said with a sly wink.

Then, as if to add insult to injury, she began to laugh. When he glared up at her, she only laughed harder. It wasn't until he threw his arm over his eyes and groaned that her laughter cut off.

"Are you hurt?" she whispered breathlessly overhead. Then Jace felt the silky end of her hair tickle his neck. "Jace?" she said more urgently, shaking his body. "What's wrong?"

"Oh, you mean something other than my wounded pride?" He asked, dropping his arm.

Lemon shoved him, and he grinned. "You're fine." She muttered, rolling her eyes. With both hands braced on his chest, she pushed herself up. He thought about pulling her back down again, wondering what she would do if he rolled her underneath him once more. Would her mouth curl into an inviting smile? Would she welcome a kiss, a touch?

He pushed the thought aside, bracing his head against the vinyl floor. Jace counted to ten, taking deep breaths as he pushed back the heat of his desire. When he was sure he wouldn't do anything crazy, he opened his eyes in time to see Lemon pause at the door. Her hand braced on the doorjamb. She turned back to him, "I almost forgot. Did you eat half of a sticky bun this morning in the kitchen?"

He probably shouldn't be surprised anymore, but he found himself once again shocked by the unexpected things Lemon said and did. "Nope. If I ever were to snitch a sticky bun, you can bet I would finish it."

"Fair enough."

Lemon pushed open the door to the kitchen and went straight to the sink. She flipped on the water and began to scrub her hands with more zeal than necessary. It wasn't until her hands were red and tingling that she shut the water off and toweled them dry.

Evelyn walked in from the back door, her gaze fixed on nothing. "There you are. Well, was it Jace?"

"Hmmm?" Lemon mumbled, her attention still focused far away.

Her mother smacked her arm. "Did Jace eat the sticky bun?"

"Oh, ah, no." Lemon struggled to regain her focus. "I don't know who ate it."

"So strange."

"It is."

"Are you missing an earring?" Her mother asked, her fingers brushing Lemon's hair back.

"Am I?" Lemon lifted a hand and was startled only to feel her ear lobe. Her eyes lifted to the ceiling. "I must have forgotten to put the other one on this morning." With a quick flip of the clasp, Lemon slipped the other earring out of the hole and set it on the counter next to the coin she had yet to bring home to her father.

Evelyn turned to lift another tray of cookies, ready to carry them to the front. She paused before asking, "By the way, what was going on up there? I heard the loudest crashing noise. It sounded like something heavy hit the floor."

Lemon blushed, letting her eyes fall away. "It was nothing. Jace dropped a book."

"It must have been some book."

"It was." Lemon couldn't agree more. Jace was becoming a problem. One in which she didn't yet know how to navigate.

Chapter Twelve

THURSDAY, DECEMBER 11TH

An idea is simply the first glimmer of something extraordinary waiting to unfold.

It was her best idea yet. Lemon had spent the past few days pondering Berry's predicament. As much as it tickled her to see her brother floundering like a fish out of water, she couldn't let it go on much longer. She had never seen him like this before, and to be honest, it was bordering on embarrassing.

If she had to listen to one more door slam, she might just lose it. Even with Berry being obnoxious, Lemon still found it much easier to think about his problems than to face her own. As she lay in bed last night, deliberately shifting her focus away from her jobless future, a bulb sparked in her mind. Lemon did not doubt that Mia found Berry attractive. Given the Frost family genes, it was implausible for others not to find them appealing. No, the problem with Mia ran much deeper. For whatever reason, the girl was afraid to take that step with Berry.

Not that Lemon couldn't understand Mia's hesitation. Although, it wasn't as if Berry was asking for a lifelong commitment. He only wanted a date, one single night out with her. What was the big deal?

But that was neither here nor there. The first issue was getting Mia to agree to a date, and that was where Lemon could help. The plan was simple. Berry would give Mia a coupon for a free cinnamon roll and hot chocolate from Frosted. At this stage, Lemon would be able to advocate on behalf of her brother and, with any luck, sway Mia into considering Berry.

Berry had been skeptical as if her idea wasn't fantastic. When he'd scoffed her off at first, Lemon struggled to resist the urge to dump her soup over his head. In the blink of an eye, their family dinner had turned into a battleground. It took her mother's calming voice to restore order.

"Why don't you give Lemon's idea a chance?" Evelyn asked while placing a restraining hand on Lemon's arm. Her mother was good. She always had a way of knowing where Lemon's thoughts were headed.

"What am I supposed to say?"

"You don't have to say anything. If you're embarrassed, just slip it into Mia's papers or purse. The whole point is to get Mia into the bakery, you idiot." Lemon ground the end of her spoon into the tabletop for a fleeting moment, picturing it as Berry's face. She'd worked on the dumb coupon for a couple of hours after work. The least he could do was pretend to be grateful for her efforts.

Berry stared sullenly at his mother, then Lemon. "Fine." He grumbled, pushing away from the table and storming to his room.

After the house settled from the force of his door slamming, Lemon mused. "I hope, once we get Berry a date with Mia, the doors won't suffer from such poor treatment anymore."

Evelyn chuckled, "You think it will be that simple?"

"Don't you?" Lemon wondered, her conviction wavering as doubt started to cloud her perception of the situation. "It isn't like this is once in a lifetime, love. Besides, when has Berry ever been interested in anything for longer than a few months?"

"What makes you think it will be over that quickly?"

Lemon turned her startled eyes to her mother. "You don't? You think this might have staying power?"

"I don't know. But if you remember, your father and I met in high school and have been together ever since."

"Yeah, but that isn't the norm. What makes you think Berry would be willing to make that kind of commitment? Especially when he is looking at four years away at college."

"She's a smart girl. It doesn't mean they couldn't wind up at the same college."

Lemon snorted, absently shuffling the contents of her soup bowl. "If you say so."

As if to dismiss the subject entirely, Evelyn turned her attention to William. "Dear, what did you think of the coin Lemon saved for you?"

William lifted his eyes at the sound of Evelyn's endearment, looking from Lemon to Evelyn and back again. "What coin? I don't remember her giving me a new coin. Is it meant to be added to my collection?"

"It was," Lemon muttered, silently cursing her mother for bringing it up.

"Was?" her parents said in unison.

"Well, you see, that's the problem. I had the coin and my earring—" she explained, turning to Evelyn, "you remember my earring?"

"Yes, the one from yesterday. Wasn't it gold and dangled?"

"Yep, that's the one –"

"Will you get back to my coin, please?" Her father grumbled, interrupting Lemon. "You can talk about jewelry later."

"Sorry, Dad." Lemons said, making a face. "But this is all tied together, I promise. So anyway. Yesterday, when I locked up for the night, I forgot again to grab the coin, but also, this time, I accidentally left my earring behind." At her father's impatient expression, Lemon hurried the story along. "Anyway, this morning, when I opened Frosted, I made sure to grab my earring and the silver coin. But I couldn't find them. They weren't where I had left them. And believe me, I looked *everywhere*. I moved the dish and checked the sink drain to see if someone had accidentally knocked it over."

"You lost them?" Evelyn asked, her expression incredulous.

"Not on purpose, Mama. I swear, I left them in the dish next to the sink. When I checked this morning, the dish was empty. Honestly, I hoped you had taken them home for me."

"I didn't."

"Yes, that is becoming clear."

"So, there isn't a coin?" Her father asked, sounding mildly perturbed.

"I'm sorry, Dad. What stinks is that it was my favorite set of earrings. I won't ever be able to replace them."

"At least you still have the other one."

Even though her mother meant well, Lemon felt a twinge of something yet to be identified. She knew exactly where at least one earring was, but she hadn't mustered the courage to face Jace again. Which, in light of their date or non-date Saturday night, was bound to make things awkward. She had hoped he would have brought the earring down with him when he'd opened The End for the day, but he didn't. Nor did he stop in for his usual sticky bun. Lemon tried to ignore the unreasonable disappointment. He didn't owe them his business; it was his right to buy what he wanted when he wanted.

Then, as the pattern repeated itself today, Lemon found herself unsure of what to think. Since she returned home, Jace had come to the bakery side every day. Seeing him had become a cherished and comforting habit in her life. It was as if she couldn't consider the day complete without some form of interaction with him.

Boy, did that make her world spin? Since when had Jace become such an integral aspect of her life? Lemon frowned at the table as her parents spoke around her. Her thoughts were so distant from the conversation they might have been in another zip code.

"What are you going to do about it?" Her father's sharp demand brought her focus back to the table and the heated expression of her parents.

"What would you like me to do about it?" Evelyn rose, her face flush. "I'm going for a walk." She exclaimed, tossing her crumpled napkin onto the table before turning to leave.

"Dad," Lemon asked hesitantly, "What was that about? What's wrong with Mom?" It was hard not to be curious about their disagreement. Her parents rarely fought. In all the years she'd spent at home, she could only remember a handful of instances where her parents engaged in heated arguments that resulted in one or both withdrawing to different sections of the house. Maybe thinking of her parents as soul mates was disillusioning, but she did. It had been a source of pride for her. How many times had her friends cried about divorced parents? That kind of heartache had never been a concern for her, because, despite everything, Lemon knew that her parents loved each other.

The shadow of worry on her father's face made her stomach clench. When he spoke, his strained voice had Lemon looking in concern. "It's nothing. No, that's not true. It is something. Something I'm not sure your mother will ever be able to get over."

"What, Dad? Please tell me what's going on. Is it you and Mom? Did you argue, and Mom won't let it go?"

"No, nothing like that." William rubbed his hands over his face. "It's so dumb. That a simple mistake would have the power to haunt her for the rest of her life, but the way she's carrying on, I think it might."

Lemon hovered over dread and hysteria. She wanted to know what was going on with her mother. Why had her father been acting so strange since she came home?

Yet, as he spoke, she worried if ignorance wasn't the best. She didn't want her opinions of her parents to change. She loved her fond memories, and the thought of compromising them turned her stomach. Lemon knew what came out of her father's mouth next had the power to cripple her. She almost stopped him. Practically begged him not to tell her. Right until he said the word, cookies.

"I'm sorry. Are you telling me that all of this," Lemon dramatically waved her arms around, "is because Mom screwed up a batch of cookies?" She couldn't keep the incredulous tone from her voice, nor did she want to. In fact, she felt her temper rise. To think, she had spent countless hours wondering what was going on, and all this time, it was about some dumb cookies.

"Well, what did you think it would be about?"

"Not cookies!"

"You've got to understand. Your mother has never liked to be embarrassed. She has always taken extra care to taste everything she bakes before selling it. But we had been busy that week, and she hadn't tasted one batch of chocolate chip cookies. Unfortunately, it was part of the ten dozen she had promised the school for their bake sale."

"Oh." Lemon knew this would not be good. It had all started and ended with the school bake sale. It was the one time when her mother shined and her rival Karen Whitting, the PTSO president, gnashed her teeth in jealousy.

"Yeah. By the time your mother heard about her mistake, Karen had made a point of labeling all the bakery cookies as inedible. Even though it was only a few dozen that had been messed up."

"She was always such a witch." Lemon hissed. Leave it to the horrid woman to turn a minor accident into something terrible. "But how were the cookies messed up? Surely, it couldn't have been that bad. I have eaten countless cookies that were a far cry from Mama's, but they were always edible."

"It was the salt."

"The salt?"

"Somehow, your mother added too much salt to the recipe. I was told later that Burt Whitting had taken a bite of one of your mother's cookies and had a fit of coughs. Then Karen, in all her righteous anger, snatched the cookie from his hand and tried a small bite, which she spat out onto the ground. The whole town talked about it for weeks. In all honesty, they still do. I think some have lost trust in your mother's baking skills."

"But sales have been fine. Granted, the chocolate chip cookies don't sell as well, but everything has done well enough."

William shook his head, turning his glass in his hand. "That's only because you came back. If you hadn't, we might have needed to close the bakery."

"I don't believe it! Just over one batch of cookies?"

"I suppose it's Karen's doing. She claimed your mother was trying to sabotage the bake sale."

"But that's outrageous!" Lemon sputtered. "Mama has supported that bake sale since I was in grade school."

"Yeah, well, now your mother wants to move. But with Berry almost finished with high school, we can't. Not now, anyway."

"But Dad, this is our home. You can't honestly be thinking of giving it up?"

Her father gave her a pointed look. "Sweetheart, for the woman I love, there isn't anything I wouldn't do."

Chapter Thirteen

Friday, December 12th

The virtue of patience is not without its constraints.

That was it. She'd had enough. Lemon shoved the door leading to the front of the bakery open. The force slammed the hollowed-out wood into the wall with a resounding thud. "Mama," she called out, "It's happened again."

Evelyn bid goodbye to a mother with a toddler in a stroller before turning. "Really Lemon. That wasn't very professional of you. To storm in that way, why it was as if you were throwing a tantrum."

Lemon's emerald eyes snapped with ire. "Maybe I wouldn't carry on, as you say if someone would stop eating our sticky buns."

"What on earth are you talking about?"

"The sticky buns, Mama," Lemon shoved two half-eaten pastries under her mother's nose. "Will you just look at these? And that's not all. I swear there is at least another whole one missing as well."

"That's ridiculous. Why would anyone steal a sticky bun from the kitchen? How would they even get in there? The back door is locked, and the only other way is through that door."

Lemon stalked to the garbage, dropping the remnants of the sweet treats into the bin. "I'm not claiming it makes sense. Trust me, this is beyond ridiculous, but the fact remains, someone is eating the sticky buns."

Her mother remained unimpressed by her tirade. She moved around the small prep area as though they were talking of nothing more interesting than the weather. "True," she said pensively, "but I seem to recall having this very same conversation with you a few days ago. It is just as true then as it is now. Aside from you and me, Jace is the only other person who could have access to the kitchen. And you said so yourself, it wasn't him. Where does that leave us?"

Where indeed? Lemon couldn't understand why her mother wasn't more upset by the missing food. If nothing else, she should at least be concerned that someone was sneaking around the bakery without either of them realizing it. Then her eyes widened. "Mama, you don't think it's possible whoever has been stealing sticky buns also stole the coin and my earring?"

That got Evelyn's attention. She turned around, her face reflecting the concern in her eyes. "Have the drawers been off?"

"No, thankfully. But who's to say that won't change? I mean, what if this guy gets bolder?"

"Lemon," Evelyn grabbed her hands, clasping them tautly between her own. "I think you should tell Jace. Maybe he can keep an eye out at night. You know. If he sees anything suspicious, he can report it."

"I don't know if that's such a good idea, Mama. I mean, what if he tries to stop the person and gets hurt?"

"He wouldn't be that foolish. Just tell him to call the police."

Somehow, Lemon found herself wandering through the bookstore. Instead of taking the direct line to the counter, she wove through the row of shelves, pausing occasionally to pick up a book whose title caught her eye.

She hadn't spoken to Jace since that day up in his apartment. Maybe that was why she felt like her feet were blocks of cement hindering her steps. But she couldn't seem to bustle up enough courage to face him again. Which was silly. This was Jace, after all. So what if they rolled around together in his bed? It didn't have to change anything. Did it?

While she mused over that, Lemon failed to notice someone was behind her until a hand suddenly rested on her shoulder. She shrieked, spinning around, and bumped into the shelf behind her. The force sent a shudder through the bookcase. Books rained down on her head, smacking her on the head and shoulders before landing solidly on the floor around her feet.

"Ough. Owe. Och." Lemon groaned.

"Are you all right?" Jace asked, dipping to pick up a handful of books.

"Yes. I'm fine." Lemon sank to her knees, thinking to help him. However, once she got down to the ground, the tight space made it hard to move. Every time she reached for a book, Jace seemed to reach for the same one. Their hands continued to bump into each other with a chorus of apologies. When they finally picked up the last of the books, Lemon stood. Her face burned as she muttered, "Sorry, I knocked your product over."

"It was my fault. I thought you heard me behind you."

The conversation fell off. Lemon couldn't seem to remember how to breathe properly. Her pulse leaping in her neck, she struggled to recall why she crossed over the invisible boundary they both had erected.

"How are you?" Jace asked in a husky whisper.

"I'm fine. You?" Lemon whispered in return, though she wasn't sure why it felt necessary. Even in a bookstore, there seemed to be an unspoken rule to keep voices low, creating a hushed atmosphere similar to that of a library.

"Fine."

With the niceties done, the conversation slipped back into silence, their gazes locked, the weight of unspoken words hanging between them. Her eyes swept over his face, taking in every nuance as if she hadn't seen him in years. The strange part was, in a way, it felt like an eternity since she had last seen him. Until now, she hadn't even been aware of how much she missed him.

When he spoke again, his voice sounded strained, as if speaking had somehow become a chore in the last ten seconds. "Did you need something? Or were you looking for something new to read?"

"Oh, yes, I do. My mother wanted me to ask if you had noticed any strange people hanging around the bakery after hours."

His dark brow dipped into a frown. "No, why do you ask?"

Lemon laughed, though she didn't know why. "It's silly. Really. Someone has been stealing sticky buns, and we also had a rare coin, and one of my earrings went missing, too."

The corner of his mouth twitched. "Just one earring? They didn't want them both?"

Heat flooded her cheeks. "Uh, I lost the other one. In your bed, I think. You haven't seen it, have you?"

"No, sorry. But I wasn't looking, either."

"Would you mind? Or I could go look if it's easier?"

"No," Jace said abruptly, startling her. "Sorry, it's a mess up there right now. I'll look tonight."

"Okay. Thanks." Lemon said, smiling brightly.

"Back to this sticky bandit."

Lemon laughed. "What about them?"

"What do you want me to do if I see anyone suspicious sneaking around?"

"Call the police, duh."

"Oh, I thought you might have wanted me to catch them in the act."

Her mouth dropped open in horror. "Absolutely not. You could get hurt."

"I don't suppose you would be equally concerned about someone like Brian getting injured. Would you?"

"What does Brian have to do with this?"

"Nothing. Forget I said anything."

Despite her confusion over his unexpected expression of pain, Lemon felt compelled to address the matter. Lemon laid a hand on his arm without considering the reason behind it. The warmth of his skin sent a tingling sensation through her fingers. "I want you to call the police, not because I don't think you could handle yourself, but because I don't think I could live with myself if anything happened to you."

The corner of his mouth curved into a half-smile that she found irrationally charming. "So, you are worried about me?"

"I suppose you could say that."

"There's no supposing about it. That's what you said. Lemon Frost is worried about boring old Jace Torte."

With a frown, she dropped her hand, "I never said you were boring."

"Yeah, but you never said I wasn't either."

"You're impossible." She muttered. As she turned to leave, Jace caught her hand.

"Before you go. I wanted to ask you about tomorrow night."

Panic flared from nowhere, scorching a path up her throat. As she gasped, she tightly gripped his shirt in her fist. "You aren't canceling on me, are you?"

"No, no, nothing like that." He rested his hands on her shoulders, lightly rubbing the tension from them. "I was just wondering if you wanted to get dinner, you know, before the dance."

"Oh. I hadn't thought about that." Her hand relaxed as she considered dinner. Her eyes lifted to his, sparkling with an awakened hope. "Where did you have in mind?"

"Honestly, I hadn't thought too much about where we would go. I was more concerned with getting consent from you first." He said with a wry grin.

"Well, I guess you better hop to it. Oh, and by the way, I'm wearing green in case you want to match."

"What kind of green?"

"Dark," she said, trailing a finger down his chest. Then she looked up at him through her eyelashes. "Like you said, it makes my eyes stand out."

Jace sat at the counter, his computer in front of him. He was in deep trouble. He had known it from the beginning. If he wasn't careful, Lemon Frost would shatter his heart.

He fingered the gold loop of the earring Lemon had lost in his apartment, on *his* bed. She had given him the perfect opportunity to return it. He'd been carrying the thing in his pocket for the past two days, expecting to give it back to her. But when the moment came, he couldn't do it. His hand had closed around it in his pocket, and there it stayed.

With a bitter laugh, he held the earring in front of him, watching the light play off its smooth surface. He wasn't far off from acting the part of a stalker. With a flick of his wrist, the earring was once more tucked into the palm of his hand.

His eyes returned to the computer screen, and he hit the reserve button, sealing the decision with a click of the mouse. This was his chance to make an impression. If he played his cards right, Lemon would see more in him than merely a nerdy boy from high school who worked in a bookstore.

A young, fresh-faced teenager walked into the bakery, her eyes darting around inquisitively. "Can I help you?" Lemon asked from behind the display case.

"Yes. I got this coupon from a friend and wanted to see if I could use it?" She said, laying a small scrap of paper next to the register.

Lemon's gaze sharpened. When the girl first came in, Lemon hadn't bothered to get a good look at her, thinking she was just another customer. However, now that she knew this was Mia, the one who had Berry tied up in knots, she was dying to see what it was that made him desperate.

From what she could see, there wasn't much that made her stand apart. Lemon supposed she was pretty enough, her warm and inviting dark eyes adding to her overall appeal. Lemon had to give her brother credit. He was right about her hair. It was simply beautiful; its dark, rich color almost resembling black, falling in loose curls down her back. Her petite frame was so similar to Lemon's she wouldn't have been surprised to find they wore the same size.

With a hand outstretched, Lemon said, "Hi, I'm Lemon. I used to live here, but it's been a while. I came back for the holidays."

The girl took Lemon's hand. "Mia. I moved here a year ago." She said in a voice smooth as honey.

"You move from the south?"

Mia smiled. "Yeah, I can't hide it in my voice, can I?"

"No, but nor do I think you should. It's nice to hear accents. Gives others the feeling of traveling without actually having to leave home."

With a laugh, Mia's smile widened. "Well, in that case."

Lemon swept up the coupon, pretending to read it even though she already knew what it said. After all, she had made the thing special just for this girl. The problem was, now that she got here, how was she going to bring up Berry without being obvious?

"How do you like Harper High?" Lemon asked as she slid open the glass panel. She half listened to Mia's reply, already guessing what she would say. With the spatula, she lifted one of the oversized cinnamon rolls. "For here or to go?"

Mia over her shoulder. "For here would be great."

This was working out great. Lemon tried to contain her excitement. "Have you made any friends?"

"No, not really." Mia scrunched her nose. "I haven't been able to crack through the established groups yet. Truthfully, I am not even sure if I want to."

"Oh, I'm sorry to hear that. High school can be a tough time."

"You're telling me. Try adding into it a brain that outshines the majority of your classmates.

Lemon gave her an incredulous look. "I am having a hard time believing boys aren't lining up around the block to ask you out."

"Well, believe it."

While handing Mia the cinnamon roll and hot chocolate piled high with whipped cream, she asked. "So, I take it you aren't going to the winter formal tomorrow night?" Color flooded Mia's checks, which made Lemon curious. Either Mia was embarrassed because she turned Berry down and worried that Lemon would know about it. Or perhaps it was because Berry had asked her, and now she regretted her decision. Whichever the cause, Lemon could hardly wait to find out. "From the expression on your face, am I to assume you are going?"

"No." Mia sighed. "I was asked, but I turned him down."

"Why?"

"I don't know. It's hard to explain. He's the type of guy who could break your heart, and I don't know how to keep my emotions causal. Do you know what I mean?"

Lemon's eyebrows shot up, her eyes widening. Although Mia looked young, she seemed to have an old soul, the kind that loved deeply and forever. Coming from one who knew Berry well, Lemon believed Mia had every reason to remain cautious because even though she loved her brother, she couldn't promise Mia that Berry wouldn't break her heart.

It troubled Lemon how Mia's words so hit close to home. Wasn't she worried about the very same thing? Her eyes moved to the opening between her bakery and the bookstore, her brow furrowed with worry. How simple it would be to put her worries aside and just let things happen. Maybe if she were younger. Maybe if her heart didn't already feel trampled on, there were too many maybes to ease her mind. With resignation, she muttered, "More and more every day." With Mia's puzzled look, Lemon said, "Never mind."

Chapter Fourteen

Saturday, December 13th

Surprises are often found in the most unusual places.

J ace struggled to stand still, not to pace the floor to dispel some of his rising agitation. He looked at his watch once more, wondering what was taking her so long. He told her yesterday that he would pick her up at six. Yet, here it was, six-fifteen, and still no sign of her. While his dating experiences in high school had been limited, and he hadn't bothered going to any of the dances, even so, they were adults now. Certainly, Lemon could manage her time well enough to be ready when he was expected to arrive.

Evelyn came down the stairs with a flourish only a previously crowned prom queen could manage. "Lemon will be right down. She had an issue with her hair slipping from its pins, but I think we got it taken care of now."

"Thank you for checking on her. I was beginning to worry she'd changed her mind." Jace admitted with a rueful grin.

"Nonsense. Lemon hasn't stopped talking about the dance all week. Why, when we went shopping for a dress, she'd been adamant that we find a green one. Of course, I love her in the soft mint color, but she said only dark would do."

It didn't mean anything. Jace told himself over and over again. So what? She got a green dress. It wasn't for him. Lemon probably wanted to look her best. That was all there was to it. Yet, his heart refused to settle in his chest.

"I'll admit I was surprised when she said she was going with you. I thought she would've taken up with Brian again. But who knows? It's so hard to keep up with these types of things."

"Lemon was going with Brian at first, but he had to cancel," Jace admitted, his inner glow fading.

"Oh, that makes sense." Evelyn laid a hand on his arm. "It was so nice of you to offer to fill in. And going the extra mile and taking her to dinner. So kind of you."

"Yeah, well, that's me, the nice guy."

Evelyn smiled brightly. "Yes, it is, which reminds me. How is your mother? The last time I saw her, she seemed to be doing so much better. I hope that is still the case."

"Mom's great. The treatment seems to be working. Brynlee and the boys are staying up at the house through the holidays."

"That must be so nice for your mother."

"Yeah, she has been buzzing around, trying to get everything ready. I told her not to fuss. The boys wouldn't notice a difference, anyway. But mom never listens."

"Has she gotten the house ready for Christmas?"

"Not yet. Brynlee and the boys are going to take care of that for her." Jace's gaze swept across the foyer, absorbing the garland-laden banister, the grand wreath suspended above the entry table, and the assortment of nutcrackers in varying sizes on the desk. "Not that they would even be able to compare with what you've done."

Evelyn fairly preened with pleasure. "You are too sweet to notice."

"Too sweet to notice what?" Lemon asked from the top of the stairs. Her hand rested on top of the banister. Her eyes locked with his.

Lemon Frost was worth the wait.

She stole his breath away. As she began her slow descent, he started at the tips of her pale pink painted toes wrapped in sexy-as-hell black high heels. His gaze moved up to her tan, shapely legs peeking through a thigh-high slit.

The dress, a green so deep it resembled the lush leaves of the surrounding woods in Harper. Its silky fabric hugged her curves, which made him jealous. He found himself wishing his hands could rest so intimately against her soft skin.

When his eyes finally lifted to her face, he couldn't find the words to speak. He stood rooted to the floor, clumsy and awkward, as he held out a stargazer lily to slide onto her wrist.

Lemon's eyes widened, the green color standing out boldly. "You got me a corsage?"

Jace cleared his throat, his gaze falling away from hers as heat flooded his face. "Um, I thought you might like one. You don't have to wear it if you don't want to."

When his gaze shot up, he found her looking at him with a smile that melted his heart. His pulse jumped. He was in deep trouble. If she smiled like that at him again, he might lose his heart. Then what?

The corsage was simple in design, but when he slipped the black elastic band over her hand, it made her glow. Perhaps it was foolish, but he felt a fierce surge of possessiveness that left him desperate to hold on. He didn't know why or what he needed to do, but he couldn't let her slip away.

"Are you ready?" He asked his voice tight with emotion.

Lemon gave him a questioning look. "Yes."

"Wait!" Evelyn said, lifting her phone. "I need pictures."

"Oh, Mama. Is that necessary?"

"Yes." She said. "I know Jace isn't Brian, but you look stunning in that dress, and we have to have pictures of it."

"Mama!" Lemon gasped, her eyes lifting to Jace. "Taking pictures has nothing to do with who is taking me out tonight. I was only saying that because I'm not in high school anymore. Besides, I am happy to be going with Jace. After all, I'm the one who asked him."

"But only because Brian couldn't make it. Isn't that right, Jace?"

"Don't answer her," Lemon ordered. Then, turning back to her mother, she said, "Please take your picture so we can go."

After Lemon's mother so sweetly ruined any illusions Jace had for tonight, he didn't care to take any pictures. However, when Lemon slipped a slender arm around his back, he felt the subtle pull straight to his heart. He didn't look at Evelyn. His gaze remained on Lemon, who smiled beautifully for the camera.

"It looks like a gingerbread man threw up in here," Jace muttered over Lemon's head the minute they'd crossed through the doorway leading into the school gymnasium.

"Shhh. What if someone hears you?" She giggled, pinching his side, causing him to yelp.

"What was that for?" He growled in her ear. His arm held her tightly against his side.

Lemon told herself to relax, which had been far easier said than done. Jace had been a complete and utter surprise this evening. Everything she thought she knew about him seemed to be limited. As if she had only ever barely scratched the surface. Although she still didn't know him, she wanted to, with a burning desire she hadn't felt in a long time.

Even during that short time when she worked with Jeff, she had never experienced quite the same level of interest. It seemed like every question Jace answered only resulted in more questions. Questions that she desperately longed for answers to.

When they had first left her house, she'd been so mortified. She didn't have an answer for why her mother had said those things, but the evening had suffered as a result. It had taken him almost halfway through dinner to relax enough to start talking to her. Then he began to open up, and she saw a new side of him unfold before her eyes.

She found herself unable to stop touching him. At first, their arms had accidentally brushed against each other, igniting a spark of familiarity. Then she couldn't stop finding excuses to touch him, seeking that sensation time and again. Now, his arm was around her waist in a way that let everyone know they were together, and she loved it. Her heart was galloping at a pace she had no control over.

When her attention turned back to the dance decorations, she understood what Jace meant. The student council had gone a little overboard with the gumdrops. Not that it wasn't cute, but maybe a few less would have been a better option.

"Look." Lemon pointed to a group of people gathered by the DJ station. "I bet you that is where we need to check in." As she moved forward, Jace's arm slipped from her waist. She grabbed his hand and pulled him behind her. She walked toward the crowd, a puzzled frown on her face. It could have been her imagination, but she sensed Jace growing more distant. One minute, they had been laughing and joking; the next, he was quiet, his expression remote.

Lemon gave him a fleeting glance over her shoulder. Yep, he looked perturbed, but she couldn't imagine why. "Is something wrong?" She asked in a hushed voice, slowing their steps so they wouldn't be overheard.

"No, why?"

"I don't know. You seem distant all of a sudden."

"Sorry, just had a flood of bad memories, is all. I'll be fine."

Her brow drew together in concern. "Was high school terrible for you?"

"No." He said, his expression softening as he gently brushed a strand of hair away from her face.

Lemon felt the caress as tender as butterfly wings brushing her heart. She leaned in, her eyes dropping to his lips, anticipating a kiss that never came, much to her disappointment.

"Lemon, there you are," Mrs. Butternick said, waving exuberantly as she pushed her way forward. Her eyes went to Jace and then back to Lemon. "I thought you were coming with Brian."

The flash of anger came fast and hot. She was about to snap at the rude woman when Jace spoke first. "He had something come up. So, I am his replacement. A poor man's substitute, but beggars can't be choosers."

"Wai –" Lemon started to speak, but Jace squeezed her hand. She stayed quiet when she saw the intent look in his deep, chocolate eyes.

"Well, I'm glad for the help, even if it isn't the power couple." Mrs. Butternick continued.

She stiffened, a frown darkening her brow. Jace tightened his hand around hers, their palms melding together as she faced the growing challenge of staying silent.

"I was just letting everyone know what we expect. Make sure you keep an eye on all the kids. Make sure no one is dancing inappropriately. If there are any problems, call me or one of the three security officers we have working tonight. All right?"

"I think we can handle that," Jace said.

"Excellent. Now remember, any trouble at all, just holler. Okay?"

"You got it."

When Mrs. Butternick was far enough away, Lemon turned around, eyes narrowed. "Why did you stop me from correcting her?"

"Because it wouldn't have made a difference. She was only saying what everyone else is thinking."

Lemon shook her head, causing a silky strand to fall loose. "That isn't true."

"It is. And we both know it. Come on. Let's get a drink before all the kids show up."

As far as dances went, it was exactly what one would expect. Kids danced, girls giggled, and only one fight broke out. The evening only became truly memorable at the end of the night, thanks to a little bit of drama involving Berry.

When she spoke to him yesterday, explaining Mia's concern for his commitment to relationships, he surprised her with his calm reaction. Lemon had assumed that he would stay home since Mia had turned him down. To say she'd been shocked when he walked into the gym an hour ago with another girl's hand on his arm was an understatement. Not only was she surprised but also deeply disappointed. This was exactly why the Frost family had the reputation they did.

Lemon handed her drink to Jace and stalked toward Berry with fire in her eyes. She only spared his date a fleeting glance before zeroing in on him. "What about Mia?" she demanded, her hand fisted at her hips.

"Like you said. She thinks I'm not serious, and I'm tired of trying to convince her." He said with a shrug.

"So you're giving up?"

"Looks like."

"I can't believe this. After all the work I went through, you're just walking away."

Berry looked down at her, hurt and anger flashing in his eyes. "What do you want from me? I tried. Let it go."

Just as she was about to lay a comforting hand on his arm, he turned away. His footsteps echoed loudly as he stormed toward the dance floor, leaving both Lemon and his date behind.

"Berry?" Lemon called out, rushing after him. Only to be drawn up short when Berry stood toe to toe with a bruiser of a kid that Lemon didn't know.

"I can't believe you came to the dance with *him*." Berry spat out.

The boy, taking exception, shoved Berry. Which, in turn, gave Berry all the permission he needed. No one saw it coming. Especially not the boy. The punch was fast and solid. Doubling the boy over. Berry shoved him aside as he took a step forward, coming face to face with Mia.

"What the hell, Mia?"

"I can't believe you did that." Mia gasped as she tried to step around him to get to her date. But Berry stopped her, catching her around the waist and halting her. "Put me down!" Over the blaring music, Mia's voice could be heard as Berry led her to the corner of the gym.

Lemon spotted Mrs. Butternick and stepped in to intervene. While she may not know Berry's intentions, a part of her found the whole thing to be a bit romantic. She wasn't about to let anyone disrupt what was about to unfold. After all, the Frosts had a reputation to uphold.

"What's going on here?" Mrs. Butternick asked, looking at the boy holding his middle, groaning on the floor.

"I don't know. I just got here myself. Jace and I were too far away to see what had happened." Lemon explained, and she bent over to help Mrs. Butternick lift the boy from the floor.

"Are you all right, Chance?" Mrs. Butternick asked the boy, who nodded. "Well, let's get you to a chair, and you can tell me what happened."

Jace stopped behind her. His hand rested at her waist as he whispered in her ear. "You have a visitor."

Lemon turned questioningly. "What are you talking about?"

Jace nudged his head toward the side of the room. Lemon followed his gaze to the doors leading in from the parking lot, where Brian stood looking like a Grecian god in his dark suit.

"Awe crap." Lemon groaned.

With a wry grin, Jace said. "My sentiments exactly."

Chapter Fifteen

Sunday, December 14th

Awkward moments are often a shared experience.

Harper provided an amazing benefit by offering easy access to some of the finest slopes. The mere glimpse of snow-capped mountains instantly filled Lemon with a sense of holiday joy. Whenever she had the opportunity, she enthusiastically put on her skis and headed straight for her favorite ski runs.

Lemon idly kicked at the powdery snow with the tip of her boot, her impatience mounting as she waited at the base of the ski lift. Brian had run into a couple he'd been showing houses to. They had chosen one option and were now asking Brian to begin the paperwork. The size of the commission must have been substantial, judging by his megawatt smile.

Lemon bit back a sigh as she watched another chair take a skier away. She breathed in the crisp air, her nose burning from the bite. At that moment, all she craved was the exhilarating rush of her body hurtling down the mountainside.

When Brian had suggested they go snowboarding last night, she'd jumped at the chance. Back in high school, they spent countless weekends on the slopes, usually with their friends. They would spend the day snowboarding and stop for hot chocolate on the way home. It was a time she looked back fondly on now, even though she hadn't stayed in touch with them after graduating.

After leaving Harper to face the world alone, Lemon envisioned life continuing in a similar fashion. However, life had a way of throwing unexpected curveballs. Before she realized it, a month had gone by without texting her friends. Then, three and six, by the time she graduated from college, she'd made a new circle of friends and left her old ones to her memories.

Now that she was back home, the familiar memories resurfaced, weaving through her thoughts, with Brian at the forefront. He represented a tie to that former life. Even amidst the crowd of people, she easily found him. Covered from head to toe in winter gear, he still stood out. He'd always had that "it" factor. What initially attracted her to him in high school. Together, they had always made a striking pair; like gilded gods, everyone followed their lead. But that was high school when standing out and being the leader of the pack meant everything.

As an adult, she no longer wanted to be that person. She'd learned her lesson. Jeff had taught her that the rules changed. She sighed, knowing it was a lesson she would have gladly skipped. Although, maybe it was for the best. Coming home again hadn't been all that bad. She'd been able to spend time with her family and reconnect with people from her past, like Jace.

That had been the part that had taken her by surprise. When she came home wounded and needing time to heal, she never expected to see Jace. Nor experience the unsettling emotions that arose whenever he was near. Then, there was her unexpected disinterest with Brian. Not that he hadn't given it some effort, but it was almost as though he assumed that they would pick up where they'd left off. Which was increasingly more implausible to her. Brian was a big part of her past, and she had many fond memories. However, it was becoming clear that the past was where he needed to remain.

"Watch out!"

Someone yelled from behind. By the time Lemon turned her head around, it was already too late. A tiny blue blur crashed into the back of her legs. The force knocked

Lemon's feet out from under her. Being unprepared for the startling blow left her with no time to react. It came as no surprise when she wound up lying flat on her back, the soft snow beneath her cushioning her fall.

The azure sky loomed overhead in a spinning circle of confusion. Lemon lay still. Unable to find the strength or wherewithal to lift herself from the ground. As she lay on the frozen earth, she couldn't help but reflect on the string of unfortunate incidents that had been plaguing her of late. Silently taking stock of her body, her vision was suddenly blocked. A winter cap designed to mimic a polar bear snugly clung to the face of a young child whose rosy cheeks came into focus.

"Are you hurt?" A soft, worried voice whispered over her head.

"No. I think I'm okay." Lemon said with a smile, to which the little urchin rewarded her with a toothless grin. Not that she spent a ton of time with children, but she'd always assumed that when they lost teeth, it was a one-at-a-time kind of deal. Yet the young child appeared to be missing several, including his two front teeth. Her lips widened, revealing her own perfectly straight white teeth. "Are you all right?" Lemon asked, a bit breathlessly.

"Yes, I fell on you. Your coat is softer than my pillow?"

Lemon bit back a smile. Her coat was soft. She had purchased it specifically for its irresistibly downy texture.

It was an added bonus that it also kept her warm. "Glad I could help."

"Tyler, you all right, bud?" A man's voice broke through their conversation, drawing the boy's attention to a person to her left.

"Yes, the lady helped me."

Lemon was about to argue that point when another small face appeared in her field of vision. This one looked similar to the first, though a little younger. "Did she die?"

"No dummy," Tyler said, exasperated. "Her eyes are open."

"But dead people's eyes are open sometimes."

"No, they aren't Jackson. That's how you know they're dead. Because their eyes close."

For a moment, Lemon lay stunned, speechless. Even in her wildest dreams, she never imagined a conversation like this happening over her while she lay complacent in the snow.

Her beanie had failed to keep out the snow, leaving her hair soaked and her scalp feeling cold and damp. She needed to get up but wasn't sure how to manage it.

As the cold earth seeped into her body, she shivered and pondered her choices. Her first instinct was to call out to Brian, but she hesitated, unsure if he would hear her or even care about the predicament she was in. Okay, no, Brian. He was officially added to her list of utterly useless things, alongside yellow pens, fruit-flavored gum, and margarine.

With a boy crouched on the ground on either side of her shoulders, she could hardly move, let alone roll over. Though she could try to ask them to give her a little room, she doubted they would understand what she wanted.

Right as she was about to ask Tyler to pull on one of her arms, a new face joined the group, catching her by surprise. In fact, she couldn't remember the last time she had been quiet this surprised, a state that rendered her momentarily speechless.

Jace's brown eyes almost appeared black as his intent gaze swept over her body before returning to her face. "Are you okay?"

Her lips, numb from the cold, managed a barely audible "Yes. I'm fine."

He stretched out a hand, which she took gratefully. "Thank goodness you came over. I was beginning to think I'd be stuck on the cold ground for the rest of the day." Lemon said with a fake sense of courage despite her teeth chattering.

Her attempt to make light of the situation fell flat. She hadn't expected to see him so soon after the way they had left things last night. The beautiful evening they had shared came to a grinding halt when Brian made an unplanned appearance at the dance.

Every time she thought of how Brian had stood by the door smiling at her as though he were a knight come to save her made her blood boil. She'd been tempted to tell him she didn't need his company and send him on his way. Yet the politeness ingrained in her by her mother since birth stopped her. Before she had a chance to say anything, Jace had turned her over to Brian as if she were some ball to be passed. He seemed to think his responsibility towards her ended with Brian's presence. She had wanted to correct the misconception immediately, but Brian latched on to her arm as if he had the right.

In a nightmarish moment, she found herself caught between two men, one desperate to leave and the other disillusioned with his own importance. Lemon had wanted to scream out in frustration. Jace refused to stay put long enough for her to explain, while Brian constantly interrupted her attempts to persuade Jace to stay. In the end, Jace walked away, his expression cold as he turned his back on her.

Instead of spending the rest of the evening with Jace as she had planned, he treated her like a possession, giving her to Brian. The humiliation of being rejected so thoughtlessly was painful. It had come far too close to a similar hurt she'd believed she was starting to overcome, but last night shattered that illusion.

Despite experiencing a tangle of emotions, Lemon couldn't take her eyes off him. Her gaze swept over the harsh lines of his taut face. He didn't look happy to see her. Which she didn't particularly care about, Lemon assured herself. There were worse things than a man's disinterest. She was sure she could put a nice list together if she gave it enough thought.

Jace cupped her elbow in his palm, effortlessly lifting her off the ground. Snow sprinkled the earth as it cascaded from her jacket. His hand brushed against her back, the connection setting off an explosion along her nerve endings. When he spoke, it took all her energy to turn her focus away from his touch and listen to his words.

"Sorry, Tyler plowed into the way he did. I was just getting Jackson strapped into his snow boots when Tyler slipped away." Jace explained while his hand remained locked around her elbow. That one point of contact kept her tethered to him. Whether it was from sensory overload or maybe she hit her head and didn't remember it, Lemon couldn't stop herself from leaning toward him. As gravity pulled her body toward his chest, she realized either he'd accept her weight or let her fall on her face. Either way, she was helpless to stop the motion.

When his arm circled her waist, she let out a shaky sigh. Her face burrowed into the warmth of his neck. As if a switch had been flipped, an intense cold engulfed her, sending shivers down her spine.

He bit the tip of one of his gloved fingers, pulling it loose and letting it fall to the ground. With his hand bare, Jace brushed the hair from her face. Then, with one finger under her chin, he lifted her face to his. Her breath held, and for one exhilarating second, Lemon thought Jace would kiss her. When he didn't move closer, when his gaze remained locked with her eyes, she realized that had never been his intent. A faint bloom of heat flooded her cheeks, a warmth she welcomed even if it was from embarrassment.

"Are you sure you're all right?"

Lemon nodded. "I'm fine, just a little cold. My head got wet from lying in the snow for so long."

He gave her a sheepish look. "Yeah, well, that was probably my fault as well. I ran into Nicole Whitting, and it took me a minute to get past her."

Even though her mother often referred to Nicole as her nemesis, Lemon had never felt that way. A mild nuisance? Sure. But her nemesis felt a little strong. At least, that *had* been how she felt; now, she wasn't so sure. A sharp pang of jealousy twisted in her stomach. Lemon's eyes narrowed as she looked at the faces of people around them. "What did she want?"

"Nothing important."

"Well, she must have wanted something; otherwise, she would have said hi and let you walk past." Lemon's words were laced with a hint of bitterness that she couldn't shake off. Not that Jace had done anything wrong, but the sudden and unexpected surge of emotions caught her off guard. And like any reasonable acting adult, she lashed out at the person who she felt was responsible.

"Why do you care who I talk to or why?"

"I don't." She snapped, forcing herself to stand upright and away from him.

Jace frowned down at her. His expression turned dark and brooding.

"Uncle Jace, when are we going down the mountain?" The sound of Tyler's voice broke through the building tension.

"Right now," Jace answered, holding out a hand for each boy to take.

"Well, that answers one question I had."

"What was it?" Jace asked, raising a dark brow.

"I was wondering who the boys were to you. I hadn't heard you had any kids, but then again, I never did ask."

His lips twitched despite the obvious irritation that remained in his eyes. "They're my sister's boys. They are staying for the holidays since their dad is serving overseas right now."

"Yeah, daddy works on a big ship?"

Lemon sank to her knees. "Does he? What does he do on the big ship?"

"He helps the other people who are sick." Tyler declared, then turned his attention to Jace. "Isn't that right, Uncle Jace? Daddy helps people."

"He sure does."

Lemon watched the exchange, and her heart did a funny little flutter. Then Jace looked at her, and damned if her heart didn't flutter again. She stood up, brushing the snow from her legs to distract herself from the unexpected feeling.

"He's the Senior Medical Officer. He's supposed to be home in time for Brynlee to have her baby."

"Brynlee's pregnant?" Lemon asked with pleasure while a little stab of envy nicked her heart.

"Yeah. She's having a girl. Says she's done with three, and it's up to me to add more grandkids for Mom and Dad."

"Oh, and do you have any candidates in mind?" Lemon asked playfully, her voice betraying a mix of curiosity and apprehension.

Jace's face turned unreadable. His voice pitched so low she had to lean forward to hear his reply. "Maybe."

The one word shattered her heart. Lemon turned her face into the breeze, hoping the brisk wind would dry the tears that had sprung to her eyes.

"There you are," Brian said, coming up behind her. He rested a hand on her shoulder. She desperately wanted to push his hand aside, feeling the weight of him pressing down on her chest, suffocating her. Brian looked from her to Jace and then to the boys. "Everything, okay?"

A smile spread across Lemon's face as she turned to face him. "Yes. Are you ready?"

"Yes, sorry about that. They're a big client and have been dragging their feet about picking a place. It was only this morning that they finally decided to go with a house on Boulder Street."

"Congratulations," Lemon said with feeling. The homes on Boulder Street were unique and expensive. Despite making her wait for him, she understood the drive to succeed and could hardly blame him for wanting to follow through with such a promising deal.

Jace held out his hand, which Lemon noticed was gloved again. "Good for you. If you will excuse us," he said, taking his nephews by the hand. "I promised to take these boys down the mountain."

"Sure. Have fun," Brian said pleasantly.

"Be careful," Lemon called out, though she wasn't sure if Jace heard her. She frowned at his retreating back as she realized this was the second time Jace had left her with another man in as many days. Whether or not it was deliberate, she was determined to learn what his motives were because this newfound attraction couldn't be only one-sided, or could it?

Chapter Sixteen

MONDAY, DECEMBER 15TH

Regrets are best left to the foolish and impulsive.

J ace watched Berry gradually wearing down the sidewalk in front of the bookstore for the better part of twenty minutes before curiosity drove him outside. The biting cold air stung his face, causing him to swear under his breath. Jace frowned as he looked at the ominous clouds in the distance. The news had just announced a storm front expected to arrive within the next twenty-four hours. It would make for a miserable couple of days if it lived up to everyone's expectations.

With his hands tucked into his pockets for warmth, Jace called out to Berry. "You want to come inside where it's warm?"

Berry looked up in surprise. "Sure, man. Thanks."

Jace held open the door and was relieved to let it close solidly behind them, blocking out the biting breeze that nipped at their heels. "Want to tell me what that was all about?" Jace asked, nodding toward the sidewalk outside.

With an awkward shrug of his shoulders, Berry wandered around the front of the bookstore, picking up small items and putting them back down again. "I'm supposed to meet Mia here." He finally muttered, his gaze lifting momentarily before falling away again.

"Who's Mia?"

Berry's cheeks brightened with a ruddy hue. "She's the girl from the dance."

"Ah. The one whose date you punched?"

"Uh, yeah."

"Want to talk about it?" Jace couldn't believe he'd said the words. As if he could ever offer help in this area. High school, for him, had been an experience he had to get through. Not one to be relished or relived with fond memories. However, when Berry gave him such a hopeful look, he couldn't bring himself to rescind the offer.

"I guess. But don't tell Lemon." Berry clarified.

Jace stood in stunned silence. Why on earth would Berry be worried about him telling Lemon anything? What kind of relationship did he think they had? Jace, too bewildered to articulate his thoughts, simply nodded in response.

"Here's the thing. I only took Sheila to the dance because I knew Mia couldn't stand her, and for good reason. She's about as interesting as a fence post."

"Sheila was the girl in red, right?"

"Yeah. She's a looker, I'll give her that, but there comes a time in a man's life when looks can only take a person so far."

Jace struggled to keep his mouth straight. "Very astute."

"Yeah, well, my plan backfired. I didn't know Mia had agreed to go with Chance."

"So? You were there with the other girl. What difference did it make that Mia came with someone else, too?"

"Because Chance is me."

"What?"

"Chance, he is exactly what Mia says she doesn't like about me. He's what she said she wanted to avoid."

"And what exactly is that?"

Berry began to pace. "You see, the thing is, Chance is known for being a player. He's dated more than his fair share of girls from school, and he never gets attached. He's only looking for a good time. Nothing serious."

"I don't see what the big deal is. This is just high school."

"The problem is, Mia isn't like that. She's sensitive and trusting. If Chance told her he was only looking to be friends, she would believe him."

"You don't think he would be?"

Berry snorted. "Not in this life. Chance has only been interested in one thing, and this time, he can't have it." With Berry's eyes narrowed in determination, Jace caught a glimpse of the man he would become.

"It sounds like you two have it in for each other."

"No, not really," Berry admitted. "He's my best friend."

Jace released a low whistle. "And he went out with her knowing how you felt? That's some friend you've got there."

Berry ducked his head as color flooded his face. "Yeah, well, that might have been my fault. I didn't exactly tell him how I felt about Mia."

"How come?" Jace asked, his arms crossed over his chest as he watched the young man with growing interest.

"I don't know." Berry spun around, threading his fingers through his hair. "This was the first time I couldn't put a name to what I was feeling, and it was embarrassing. I genuinely care about what Mia thinks of me, and I don't like it."

"Yeah, I know that feeling." Jace clapped a friendly hand on Berry's shoulder. "Trust me, it doesn't get better with age."

"Wonderful," Berry muttered.

"Did you patch things up with Chance?"

"Yeah. He gets it. Though I promised him he could have a free cinnamon roll from Frosted every day for the rest of the year."

"That's some commitment. What did Lemon have to say about your generosity?"

"She won't care."

"You haven't told her yet, have you?"

"No." They shared a smile.

"It sounds like things are fine with your friend, so what's with the restless pacing?"

"Mia." Berry sighed. "She agreed to meet me here this afternoon. I figured neutral territory would be a good idea after the way I behaved the other night. You wouldn't believe what it took to convince her to come today. She kept looking over her shoulder like she was planning her escape route or something."

"You are meeting her here?" Jace asked. "I thought you didn't want Lemon to know."

"I don't. That's why I'm meeting her in the back of your store, you know, on the green couch."

"Oh, you mean here, here. I don't know if that's such a good idea."

"Come on, man. You gotta help me out. This is my last chance. Mia has already dropped me from her tutoring schedule. If I can't convince her, then that's it. My shot is over."

"Convince her of what?"

"That's the problem. I don't know. All I do know is when I think of never seeing her again, my stomach tightens, and this heavy feeling settles in my chest. Right here." Berry's clenched fist rested over his heart.

It was amazing how a kid could sum up exactly how he'd been feeling with a few words where he'd been tormenting himself for days. Jace didn't know whether to tell Berry to walk away while he could or leave him to stay the course. Either way, the boy was looking at heartache. "All right. Just no tears, okay? I don't want to have to deal with any of that."

"Sure, man. I'm not looking to make matters worse."

"We never are."

A harsh wind sent a chilling howl through the bakery. Lemon shivered in response and flipped the oven on. She'd already finished baking for the day but hadn't left yet. She couldn't. Not when too many mysteries remained unsolved.

She promised Berry to keep the bakery open an hour later than usual. He wanted to treat his study group to a few goodies while they used the bookstore to study. Lemon was surprised Berry didn't just use one of the tables in the bakery. Instead, he wanted to use the cozy seating in the back of the bookstore.

When Berry came in fifteen minutes earlier, she boxed up three sticky buns and prepared three hot chocolates piled high with whipped cream. Lemon had been surprised to see Jace at his side, offering to carry two of the hot chocolates. They had murmured a brief hello, but the silence that followed hung in the air.

She hated not knowing how to act around him. Jace had a way of turning her upside down and spinning her sideways. Not that they had ever had an easy relationship, but compared to now, she longed for what they had before.

However, now was not the time to dwell on things she couldn't control. No, she had much more important matters to handle. With unwavering determination, Lemon heaved her father's toolbox onto the counter. She'd reached her limit. It was time to end the mystery and find out once and for all who was stealing from the bakery. Even though her mother refused to give the matter its due attention, Lemon felt determined to solve this crime.

Although only about a hundred dollars worth of items had been taken, it still bothered Lemon. It was a matter of principle for her. Allowing this person to continue stealing felt like she was saying, "Sure, come on in and help yourself." Determined to put an end to it, she decided to take action. Lemon went online and ordered a simple wireless camera. According to the box, all it took was a nearby outlet for a hassle-free installation.

Tonight, she had one goal: to catch the thief.

She shouldn't be surprised that things rarely go as smoothly as one hopes. With each piece of the camera laid on the counter, Lemon was no closer to assembling it than she had been when she first opened the box. The directions may as well have been in German for all the good they were doing her. Resigned, she let her head fall onto the countertop and rolled her forehead on the cold surface.

"Need help?" Jace asked from the doorway, making her scream in surprise.

"Don't do that!" She snapped, pressing a hand to her racing heart.

Jace smiled, "Sorry." He crossed the kitchen, his nearness causing her heart to race and her senses to heighten. His eyes swept over the assorted pieces she had set into a grid. "Are you assembling a camera?"

She eyed him warily. "Yes, but not for the front. I want it set up back here."

"Worried the staff is eating too many cookies?" Jace joked, and maybe if she wasn't feeling so beaten by life, she might have been able to laugh. However, given the current situation, her only remedy was to break down and cry. When she looked at Jace, her tear-blurred vision wasn't enough to hide the horror on his face. "Hey," he said, patting her awkwardly on the shoulder. "It's okay. I'll help you. Don't cry."

Lemon tried, but once the storm clouds rolled in, she couldn't stop her tears from falling. "Lemon, it'll be okay," Jace whispered against her hair as he tucked her into his arms. She let herself ease into his solid frame. Her cheek rested against the soft woven sweater.

He rocked her, swaying from side to side as he continued to whisper sweet words of encouragement. His hand slid up her neck to burrow into her hair. She could feel his fingers stroking the tender skin, sending a shiver down her spine.

The tide of tears subsided almost as soon as they had sprung. Now, she had an awkward predicament. If she lifted her face, she knew her makeup would have run, and her eyes would resemble that of a raccoon. Although she found it unexpectedly delightful, she couldn't stay pressed against his chest. She released a shaky breath, and Jace gathered her in.

She jumped at the sharp shrill of her phone ringing. Lemon bit back a groan when Jace let his arms fall away. Her lips formed a slight pout as she turned to her purse, digging around until she pulled her phone free.

"Hi, Mama. Yes, I'm still at the bakery. I'll just be a little longer." Her eyes lifted to Jace. "No, Mama. I'm not alone. Jace is with me. Yes, I'll tell him. Okay, see you soon." Lemon gingerly placed her phone down as if it were a delicate teacup, giving the task more care than it needed. However, she couldn't shake the feeling of being exposed and vulnerable. Neither of which made her happy. "Mama wanted me to remind you of our Christmas party on Saturday." She managed to say, even though she hadn't yet lifted her gaze.

"Right, the Frost Christmas Party. It has been quite some time since I last attended one." He said, then his gaze sharpened. "Does your dad still hang the mistletoe in the doorway?"

"Yes." Lemon felt a surge of warmth on her face, betraying her thoughts through her flushed cheeks. She hadn't thought of that particular Christmas party for years. Not since she had started dating Brian. It had been her eighth grade year. All the neighbors, including Jace and his family, had come to the party as usual.

In all the years that their families had done business together, Jace and she had never tried to form a friendship. Maybe it was the two-and-a-half-year age gap between them, but they had always stayed out of each other's way. Except for that one Christmas when she found herself under the mistletoe with Jace. She had tried to laugh it off, but something had changed in his dark eyes, and her laugh died in her throat. He hadn't said a word, merely dipping his head, brushing his lips over her cheek in a light caress.

She remembered now how she had struggled to fall asleep that night. Her mind could not forget the second their lips connected, changing everything for her. For the next few weeks, Lemon had intentionally put herself in Jace's path. Only he didn't ever seem to notice her. Then she met Brian, and her attention turned.

"Why do you ask?" Her eyes widened once the words were out. She hadn't meant to ask him that. Her heart raced, unsure if she could handle his reply.

His hooded eyes held hers. "I've always been a fan of mistletoes."

Heat flooded her face, warming her to the center. She couldn't tell if he was purposefully saying these things to get a rise from her or if he was speaking generally. Instead of commenting, her hands picked up a piece of the camera. She pretended to be deeply focused and ignored him completely, which became impossible when his hands covered hers. His lips quirked into a smile far too alluring for her peace of mind. "Those don't go together."

"How can you tell?"

"It's easy. If they don't look like they belong together, the chance is they probably don't. At that point, it's best to set the piece aside and try a different one."

Something in his manner made her suspicious as if he were talking about something other than camera parts. "What if I think they could go together? Maybe if they are flipped or given a little more time."

"It's doubtful. If they didn't fit the first time. They probably won't fit this time."

His somber words caused Lemon's mind to whirl, her brows knitting together in confusion. "That's too bad. Some of the best pairs come from unlikely matches."

Jace lifted an eyebrow. "Oh really? For example?"

"For example?" She asked, her heart racing, but she wasn't entirely sure why.

"Yeah," He said, leaning against the counter. "I want you to give me one example of unlikely things coming together to make a great pairing."

After a moment, Lemon smiled, her face shining with victory. "Peanut butter and jelly."

Chapter Seventeen

TUESDAY, DECEMBER 16TH

The best opportunities may slip away if one waits too long to seize them.

The storm was coming.

Lemon flipped the bakery sign to close and pulled down the shade, shutting out the flurry of snowflakes dancing in the air. The sun had long since disappeared behind the heavy gray clouds, leaving a gloomy ambiance that made her shiver. Perhaps it was the weather, but a sense of melancholy had weighed on her since she woke up to the incessant buzzing of her alarm.

Lemon couldn't pinpoint a specific reason for her sudden bleak outlook, merely that she felt the mood weighing heavily on her. When Berry was eight or nine, they would play a game when it was too cold to go outside. He would run around the house, grabbing every blanket he could find and throwing them on top of her. She would lie on the floor still and wait for Berry to come close enough for her to grab him. They would roll in the soft tangle of blankets, laughing and tickling each other. Today, the weight of her mood reminded her of those blankets piled on top of her, except she couldn't figure out how to lift them off of herself.

Her thoughts returned to yesterday, the words Jace said echoing in her mind. *If they didn't fit the first time. They probably won't fit this time.* No matter how often she reminded herself they had been talking about the camera, it didn't make a difference. Maybe it had been the distance in his voice or the guardedness in his expression, but it was as if he were subtly suggesting to her that they wouldn't work. The idea of them, her and him, having a relationship seemed completely out of the realm of possibility. She scoffed, vigorously wiping down the tables in the small eating area. She didn't remember suggesting they should give it a try. Lemon carried the tray of napkins on her hip, scowling at the adjoining doorway.

The bakery had fallen silent. After enduring an hour of upbeat Christmas music blaring from the speakers,

Lemon had finally decided to switch it off, plunging the bakery into an uncommon stillness. Given her gloomy mood, the last thing she desired was to be surrounded by anything cheerful.

The swirling winds outside howled through the empty room. Her soft-soled steps sliced through the quiet, yet the stillness did nothing to ease the growing ache in her heart. Tears sprang to her eyes, but she quickly blinked them away. Now wasn't the time to give in to her emotions. She had too much to do, and she knew with every tick of the clock what little time she had left was slipping away.

The original forecast predicted moderate snowfall for the next few days, nothing new for Harper, especially this time of year. However, within the last few hours, things had taken a drastic turn for the worse.

People had scurried past the bakery in a frenzy of panic, rushing to bolster their supplies. Not that the system was supposed to tarry, but these things had a way of lasting longer than expected. There were those few staples that became necessary: water, food, and heat.

Lemon still couldn't fathom why her mother unfailingly succumbed to hysteria whenever the possibility of a blizzard arose, especially since she'd lived in Harper all her life. Yet, she did. The moment she had ended the call with Berry, who informed her that he was coming home due to school cancellation, her mother went into a frenzy of panic.

"I need to pick up some supplies," her mother had said while throwing on her coat. "I want you to close up the bakery. Put everything away like we do when we go on vacation."

"But Mama, the storm is supposed to blow over by tomorrow." Lemon had argued following her mother's whirlwind path.

"Lemon," her mother's sharp retort, still came as a shock. "I don't need your opinion right now. Do as I ask. I want you home in three hours. Three," she said, holding up three fingers. "Do you hear me?" With that, she had dashed out the door, the open sign swinging behind her.

The three hours her mother had initially allotted her had long since elapsed. Contrary to her mother's wishes, Lemon had kept the store open. Foolish, she now knew, but at the time, she had expected not everyone would have the same reaction to a minor snowstorm.

Six years away had a way of clouding and distorting one's memories. The snow storms from her youth had become winter wonderlands filled with snowmen and ski trips. Never once did she remember feeling afraid. Yet, when she peered out at the darkened sky where snow flurries speckled the air, she couldn't help but wonder if maybe she'd been more clueless than she'd thought.

With a resigned sigh, Lemon yielded to the inevitable. She took one last walk through the front of the bakery. It may not be necessary, but she checked the locks and ensured all the blinds were fully closed. She turned to look at the dark interior. The sight of the empty glass display pierced her heart, evoking a sense of loneliness. She wrapped her arms around herself as if to dispel the starkness. The cold from outside sent a chill over her skin. She rubbed her arms in a futile attempt to dispel the sudden rise in goosebumps.

Feeling disheartened, Lemon made her way back to the kitchen, determined to finish the task as her mother had asked of her. With eyes intent on cleaning for the week, the task became daunting. Even though she'd cleaned the kitchen hundreds of times, a sense of urgency created a rising panic within her.

Her phone chimed, making her jump in alarm. She snatched it off the counter. "Hi, Mama."

"Where are you? Are you on your way?" Evelyn's voice trembled with barely contained hysteria.

"Not yet, Mama. I am still cleaning the kitchen."

"Leave it. Just come home."

"I can't leave this. What if we get bugs?" Just the thought was enough to make her do her yucky bug dance. "Give me an hour, then I'll be able to head home."

"Lemon. You don't have an hour. You need to leave now."

"Why? What's happened?"

"The ... it...wor...th...y...say."

"Mama?" Lemon frowned, pulling her phone away from her ear. "Mama, can you hear me?" A soft ding sounded, and Lemon knew the call dropped. She hit her mother's picture, groaning when nothing happened. Her fingers tapped restlessly against the metal counter. She could hop in her car and leave now. She'd be home in thirty minutes. Yet, even as she considered doing that, a feeling of ill ease crawled up her neck.

No, she couldn't leave. But if she didn't, what would she do for the night? Granted, the bakery had food and ovens for warmth, but she couldn't sleep here. There weren't any blankets or pillows. She had to go home. There wasn't any other option.

Her phone's shrill alarm, blaring with a weather alert, made the decision for her.

Jace locked into place the last of the weather guards. His parents had installed this last precautionary measure after a rock had gone through the window during a particularly nasty hail storm. With the shattered glass and high-speed winds, there had been enough damage to make things uncomfortable for a while. His father didn't want to suffer another loss like that again, so they installed three steel according covers to the outside. Once locked into place, the windows were shielded from the harsh elements. The one blocking the door was the trickiest. He had to secure it, then run to the back of the bookstore to get inside.

He fought the last latch, kicking it until it flipped, and he was able to get the lock secured. The snow fell sideways, pelting him in the face and his bare hands. He rubbed them together, blowing on them, but it didn't help. It was too blasted cold outside. Jace looked at the dark front of Frosted with a mixture of relief and regret. It looked like Lemon made it out just in time. His gaze lifted to the heavy cloud cover. With a shiver, he jogged to the back. His frozen fingers numbly searched for the keys that should have been in his front pocket.

Jace swore as his fingers dug into every pocket, only to come up empty. Panic began to tighten in his chest as he tried to think of what he could do. He turned in a circle, his eyes landing on Lemon's car parked next to his truck. His brows furrowed as he looked at Frosted's closed door. With a silent curse, he stepped up to the door and beat at it with unneeded force.

He could barely hear the jingle of the door knob above the wind howling around him. With the biting cold seeping into his bones, he huddled against the building, his gaze focused on the narrow opening. A pair of misty green eyes peaked at him through the crack, then widened as recognition set in.

"Jace," Lemon gasped. Opening the door, she grabbed a handful of his coat, pulling him inside. "What are you doing outside?" She asked, slamming the door shut against the whistling wind.

"I lost my key and couldn't get back into The End. What are you still doing here?" He could tell she'd been crying. Her eyes were wet beneath her lashes, and a salty track ran down the side of one cheek. He couldn't stop himself from brushing a finger across the trail. "Have you been crying?" He asked, his face darkening with worry.

Her lip trembled, and he worried she might start crying again. Damn, he shouldn't have said anything. Jace let his hand fall back to his side and busied himself with taking off his coat. "What are you still doing here, Lemon?" When he spoke, his voice was harsh and mirrored the intensity of his feelings.

"I meant to leave before the storm got here, but I missed my chance. Now I'm stuck here for the night, and I don't know what I am going to do." Lemon sniffled, her lips quivering.

Jace groaned. He reached out, pulling her into the comfort of his arms. She yelped at the chill of his body but didn't pull away. He threaded his fingers through her hair and, for a moment, allowed himself to imagine a life where he could do just that any time he wanted to. With her head nestled under his chin, he closed his eyes and inhaled deeply, savoring her delicate fragrance.

"You can stay with me." The words were out of his mouth before he could stop them. He couldn't do this. A whole night alone with Lemon was something out of his wildest fantasies or perhaps his worst nightmare. He expected her to object or offer another alternative, like sleeping in the bookstore. It wasn't the most comfortable place, but the couches weren't bad. He'd take a nap on one or two of them himself. But she didn't say any of that; she didn't say anything. His eyebrows drew together as he looked down at her bent head. "Well?" He asked, with a bite to his tone.

"Okay."

She uttered a single word, a word that could render him helpless. His heart pounded against his rib cage, yet he managed to suppress the surge of unexpected panic. "Okay. Do you need help down here, or are you ready to go upstairs?"

Lemon slipped from his arms, shutting off the one light still on, and with her purse in her hand, she said, "I'm ready now."

The walk up the stairs was done in silence. Only the creaks of the hollow steps broke the quiet. Jace led the way, with Lemon close behind. He gave a furtive glance over his shoulder once, but Lemon gave no clue to her feelings about the sudden change in events. It was on the tip of his tongue to ask if she was certain she wanted to stay with him, but he swallowed the words. If she didn't stay with him, what would she do? It wasn't like she could simply drive home.

At the top of the stairs, his hand turning the knob, he remembered what his apartment looked like. Heat shot up his neck and flared high in his cheeks.

"What's wrong?" Lemon asked. She had wedged her body next to his on the narrow landing.

He looked over his shoulder at her and wondered how honest he should be. "Um, last week was kind of crazy for me." He could see from the confused expression on her face she didn't understand what he was trying to say. "I didn't have a lot of time to pick up."

"Oh, that doesn't matter." She smiled, her hand on his shoulder.

His gaze locked onto her slightly curved lips before clearing his throat. Jace shook his head, turning back to the door. It swung open, and he groaned. He had hoped it wasn't as bad as he remembered, but unfortunately, it was worse.

Clothes, both dirty and clean, were flung over the couch, chair, and bed. Shoes and socks lay haphazardly on the floor, creating a scene of disarray. No surface was clean. His color deepened as he stepped aside to let Lemon pass. He watched her walk around, stopping at his table. She looked at him. "Can I put my purse here?"

"Uh, sure. Let me get some of this out of your way." He swept his sketches and files off the table and stuffed them into his portfolio, which he left leaning against the back of the couch. With her hands free, she went to the kitchen, lifting a ceramic mug from the strainer by the sink. "Do you have any hot chocolate?"

Jace smiled, his heartbeat settling marginally. He opened a cupboard and set a box on the counter. "Help yourself."

Lemon lifted a package to her teeth and tore along the edge. His stomach tightened as he watched with helpless infatuation. "Do you want some?"

"No. I'm okay."

She held the mug cradled between her hands, lifting it to her lips. Blowing lightly over the surface, her eyes lifted to his. If he didn't know any better, he would have sworn she was intentionally trying to seduce him. However, now that he thought about it, could sipping hot chocolate be considered seductive? His eyes darkened as he watched her parted mouth close around the steaming liquid. Yes. Yes, it absolutely could.

In an act of self-preservation, Jace left the kitchen. He sat on the couch, picked up the remote, and turned on the TV. "Feel like watching anything?"

"Something funny. Maybe a Christmas movie." Lemon sank onto the couch next to him. The heat of her body burned him through his clothes as the sweet and spicy scent of her circled around him. Glancing at her from the corner of his eye, he bit back a curse. Granted, his furniture was designed for small spaces, but this sofa had three cushions, which meant that three people could sit comfortably on it. Or, in their case, two people could sit at either end, and the middle cushion would become the neutral zone. So why, then, did Lemon decide that the center cushion was the perfect spot to sit?

Jace glared at the narrow space separating them. She was sitting so close that she was practically sitting on his lap. His skin flashed hot and cold as his imagination ran wild.

"Is something wrong?" Lemon asked, taking another sip of her cocoa.

The sound of her voice jerked him out of his fantasy. "No. Why do you ask?"

"No reason. You just haven't picked a movie yet."

"Oh, right." Gathering himself, he scrolled through the options until the power went out. He sat in stunned silence.

The fire he'd lit earlier cast a warm glow throughout the apartment, providing just enough light to keep him painfully aware of Lemon's every movement. She licked the edge of her mug, her eyes peering at him over the rim. "Now, what do you want to do?"

Jace felt the jolt from that lick all the way to his center. He jumped from the couch and went to his nightstand, cursing when he stubbed his toe on the corner of the bed. He stood there with his back to Lemon, his mind racing to think of something they could do that didn't involve his heart being shattered when this winter rendezvous ended.

He turned to her, the heat of the flames warming his back. "I've got Battleship."

Chapter Eighteen

Wednesday, December 17th

Comfort can be found in the mundane.

L emon sat crossed-legged in front of the crackling fire. The heat from the flames enveloped her in a cozy embrace. Holding a bent wire hanger between her hands, she left it hovering over the glowing embers. The sweet scent of toasted marshmallows floated through the air.

When she checked her phone a few minutes earlier, the glowing screen illuminated her face, confirming it was well past midnight. It had been ten hours, ten hours since she climbed the stairs and embarked on what could be the strangest and most unexpected night of her life. Lemon gazed into the flickering yellow flames, her mind struggling to make sense of it all. She couldn't quite grasp that she was here, now, with Jace.

Jace Torte, the boy in high school who was more likely to be found with his nose pressed against the screen of a computer, absorbed in the virtual world rather than the social one Lemon frequented. The same boy she had flirted shamelessly with when she was in the eighth grade, and he had been a sophomore. She could still hear the backhanded brush-off he had given her when she tried to steer him under the mistletoe at her parents' Christmas party.

"Why are you laughing?" Jace asked. His shoulder brushed against hers as he worked his melted marshmallow off his haphazardly made skewer.

She chose to ignore the sudden flutter of wings in her belly and said, "I was just remembering that Christmas when I tried to get you under the mistletoe." Her face lit up bright as the star on the town Christmas tree.

Jace choked, grabbing his drink. A trail of water slipped from the corner of his mouth, leaving a glistening path down his corded neck. Lemon watched the silent progress with a strange fascination. "What?" He strangled out. His eyes widened with confusion and, if she wasn't mistaken, disbelief.

"Oh, common on. There is absolutely no way I will believe that you have no recollection of the most humiliating experience I had at my parent's annual Christmas party."

The incredulous look he gave her ignited a wild urge to do something outlandish and impulsive, such as throw herself onto him and kiss his pouty lips. Maybe if she did, he would roll her over and run his fingers through her hair. Maybe he would trail kisses from her eyes to the tip of her nose, all the while telling her how wonderful he thought she was, maybe when pigs fly. She snorted, shaking the disturbing images from her head.

"Lemon, I can honestly say I have no idea what you are talking about. I don't care how old I was. If you had ever suggested we should stand under the mistletoe together, I would have been there in a heartbeat with my eyes closed and lips puckered."

She experienced a sudden wave, but it was sadly fleeting. If only he had stopped there, she could have had something to hold on to. However, her excitement faded as he added, "Of course, any girl who asked to meet me under the mistletoe would have been welcome with open arms. Well, maybe not *any* girl. But you know what I mean," Jace said, his voice laced with a playful tone and his lips forming a lazy grin.

There was no rational reason for her to have the sudden and unmistakable ache of disappointment. So what if she wasn't his exclusive desire? It didn't matter, she told herself. Yet somehow, the words rang hollow.

With a forced smile, Lemon sweetly reminded him, "We were in the living room. You had on the gray sweater your grandmother had knitted for you. I had questioned why you'd been embarrassed to wear it, to which you had replied. 'It's not that it's homemade, but the heart she stitched at the bottom.'" Sure enough, the embarrassing shape had been perfectly knitted into the pattern with exquisite care. The tiny pink heart, measuring only about two inches, had managed to make his face glow with embarrassment.

Lemon could see the faint glimmer of memory sparked in the dark rings of his eyes. "Wait, you aren't talking about how you wanted me to look at your computer?"

Color rose to her cheeks. "Yes." She admitted with a laugh. "It was the only thing I could think of to get you to walk through the same doorway with me."

Jace threw his head back and laughed. "Lemon, if you wanted me to stand under the mistletoe with you. All you had to do was tell me. I would have gladly followed you anywhere."

Lemon stared in utter amazement, then frowned. "That's not true. I specifically asked you to come look at my computer, and you told me to figure it out for myself."

"Yeah, well, that's because I thought you really just wanted me to look at your computer."

"It's too bad."

"What is?"

"That night. At that party, I had a huge crush on you. But you brushed me aside, and I moved on. Makes you wonder what high school would have been like for both of us if we had kissed under the mistletoe that night."

Jace scoffed. "Nothing would have changed. I was no more than a passing fancy. You would have moved on the minute you found someone more interesting, like Brian."

Lemon found herself momentarily at a loss for words. Sitting on the floor beside a man she had assumed had a basic understanding of her, she was now faced with the reality that he was completely clueless. All this time, she had believed that he knew her and simply didn't care. How many times had she passed by him in high school, waving hello only to be ignored? She had always assumed that he wasn't interested in her, but the truth was far worse. Jace didn't know her at all.

A seething rage set in, burning from the inside out. She dropped her marshmallow into the fire, ignoring the hiss of flames licking up the melting mess. Instead, her complete focus turned to the idiot lounging on the floor, completely oblivious to the volcanic fury boiling in her veins. She rose to her feet in a jerky, abrupt movement. Her hands fisted on her hips. She towered over him. "You don't know a thing about me, do you?"

It hurt more than she expected. They grew up together. With their parents' shops being so closely linked, there had been countless days where they had spent playing while waiting for closing time. All this time, all those memories. Were they false? Did she create a smoke screen without realizing it?

"I know exactly who you are." He reached behind him, pulling a pillow from the couch and stacking it behind his head. With hooded eyes, he stared up at her, his intense gaze making her squirm. "Don't kid yourself. You wouldn't have liked my kisses anymore then than you would now."

Well, wasn't that straight talk? Heat flooded her face, and damned if she didn't look away from him. Lemon had begun the conversation full of righteous anger, but it had turned sideways on her, taking her to a place she wasn't brave enough to go.

The sorry truth was that she had been thinking a lot about that long-ago Christmas party and wondering where she would be now if she had shared that kiss with Jace. Not that she had any intention of revealing her thoughts to him. There were simply things that were better left unsaid. But one thing she couldn't tolerate was this misconception he held about her. She couldn't bear to have him think badly of her, not even for a moment.

"Whether or not I would enjoy your kisses isn't the point. The point of this conversation is that you seem to think I am shallow."

Jace shook his head. "Not shallow. Just temporary."

"Temporary? What exactly is that supposed to mean?"

"It's simple." He said, rising to his feet. Reaching his full height, he towered over her, making her acutely aware of the size difference between them. Lemon had to tilt her head upward to meet his gaze, her neck straining slightly. The fire cast his face into a rough contrast, making his features seem stern and unbendable. "When the road gets rough, you move on. There's nothing wrong with it. I don't personally care to form relationships with people I can't count on."

The threat of tears welled up in her eyes, causing her nose to tingle. She refused to turn away, even when the sound of his words circled dizzily in her mind. "I am not a quitter." She growled between her tightly clasped teeth.

"No?" He asked, his brow lifting in amusement. "Care to explain what happened to this great job you had in L.A.? Or why you dumped Brian when you left for school, despite telling everyone that you were going to make the long-distance thing work? Or how about the bakery?"

"What about it?" Lemon demanded, too angry to defend herself on the other accusations he laid at her feet.

"Everyone knows your parents wanted to give the place to you, but you've been too wrapped up in your own life to notice or even care."

"That's not true."

"What part?"

"None of it!"

"Really." Skepticism flickered in his eyes as he lifted a dark eyebrow. "Then explain it to me because where I stand, you are as you always have been."

She could defend herself. Explain to him that what he thought was true about her was lies, but she didn't. A part of her wanted to let him sit with his misconception, and one day, he would look back on this night and realize what a serious mistake he had made, even as she stood facing him. Her hands fisted, and a tear slipped from her lashes. She wanted to scream. To curse at him for believing the worst about her when he should have known better.

What she didn't want was for him to see her tears, to know he had the power to make her cry. But it was too late. Too late for her, at least.

"Shit," Jace muttered, running his fingers through his hair. "I didn't mean any of that stuff that I said to you." His eyes dropped to the dying embers. "I'm sorry."

The next hour was spent in silence. Lemon didn't know what to say or how to act. She had foolishly believed that she and Jace shared a mutual respect and fondness for each other. How wrong she was!

Jace wandered around the apartment, letting the fire die until only the tempting orange glow of embers remained. As the wind howled outside the window, a deep chill settled in the air, causing her to shiver. Lemon looked at the couch and grimaced. The last thing she wanted was to have to curl up on the small thing. Her gaze turned to the bathroom. If only there were hot water so she could take a shower, but then she'd have to put her clothes back on, which didn't sound appealing at all.

She watched Jace pace the limited confines of his living room area. The guarded look on his face had remained since his apology; what she wouldn't give to know what he was thinking. If only the conversation hadn't abruptly shifted to a topic they were both unprepared for. There were times like this when she wished she could turn back the clock. She wouldn't go back years. Too many great things had happened in her life to make drastic changes like that. However, a few hours could make all the difference. She wouldn't change being caught in the storm or being stranded with him. No, the only thing she would take back was sharing that memory with him. Oh, what a fool she'd been, and to think she had harbored the hope Jace would make a move, perhaps altering the basis of their relationship.

"You feel like a shower?" Jace's voice suddenly broke through her melancholy, causing her to startle in surprise. With a hand pressed over her rapidly beating heart, Lemon narrowed her eyes. "Did you have to do that?"

"Do what?"

"Scare me. Jeez, sometimes you are such a creeper."

Jace's face darkened, his eyes hardening. "Pardon me. I'm sorry I creep you out."

Lemon rose from the chair, her emerald eyes flashing. "I didn't say you creeped me out. I only asked why you felt it was necessary to scare me that way."

"Well, excuse me. Sorry to bother you. Serves me right for offering the prom queen a shower." With a disgusted shake of his head, Jace stomped away.

Her gaze followed his taunt shoulders as he made his way to the kitchen. With his arms braced on the counter, his muscles tensed and bulged. Lemon couldn't shake off the lingering pain caused by his brutally honest words. It may be juvenile, but she couldn't shake the urge to inflict the same pain on him that he had caused her. "I can't imagine why you'd think I would ever want a cold shower, especially since your already frigid behavior has left a noticeable nip in the air. Unless, of course, that was your aim all along." Warming to her tirade, Lemon stormed up to Jace, stopping when they were a breath apart. "It all makes sense now." She said, with her head slightly tilted. She studied him with fresh eyes. "You are trying to keep me at a safe distance, aren't you?"

Jace leaned against the kitchen counter, his feet crossed at the ankle. Despite his effort to appear unphased by her observation, she could see his muscles tense beneath his shirt. There had been a slight flicker of alarm in his eyes that made her smile brightly. She poked him in the chest with her red glittered nail. "I think I will take that shower. Do you have something I could borrow?" Looking down at her wrinkled top. "I don't think I could stand to put this back on to sleep in."

"Sure." He muttered. When he pushed away from the counter, Lemon didn't step away. Instead, she stood firmly in his path, causing the full force of his body to collide with hers in a breathless moment before he hurriedly maneuvered around her. She heard his sharp intake of air and wanted to laugh. He *did* want her. Probably even liked her. All this time, he'd been saying things to throw her off, but he wanted her. If she had been alone, she would have started dancing. Lemon refrained from displaying her joy, fully aware that Jace would be offended by it.

"Here, you can try these." Jace handed her a neatly folded pair of plaid pajama bottoms and a threadbare green t-shirt that looked as if it would disintegrate with one more washing. When she reached out to take the clothes from him, her fingers tangled with his in a heart-stopping moment. Lemon shuddered from the sudden spark of desire that curled around her belly. "Oh, by the way. The water heater is run on gas, so there's plenty of hot water."

"Are you kidding?" Lemon exclaimed. She'd been preparing for a freezing shower, but what a surprise. "Don't worry if you don't see me for an hour or two." She said jokingly. After setting her clothes on the small expanse of counter space in the bathroom, she turned back to Jace, who hovered at the door. She swallowed audibly, her heart thundering at the intent look on his face. "Ah,

Jace." Lemon strangled out. "What should I do for light? I don't suppose you have a flashlight or maybe a candle lying around anywhere?"

His smile was fleeting, but it warmed her faster than the flames from the dimming fire. "Yeah, I think I've got a candle somewhere." He disappeared for a moment and was back in the doorway. He passed over a candle he'd lit, which she took with shaky hands.

"Thanks."

"No problem."

"Jace?"

"Yeah?"

She wanted to ask him if he liked her. More than anything, she needed to know if he cared, even if it was only a little. Yet, she couldn't bring the words out. Lemon stared at him, her question lodged in her throat. She shook her head. "Never mind," and closed the door on his quizzical expression.

Chapter Nineteen

THURSDAY, DECEMBER 18TH

The unexpected can become something worth waiting for.

A s swiftly as it came, the storm made its way through, leaving in its wake a thick layer of soft, white snow. By yesterday afternoon, the streets had been cleared. However, towering mounds of snow, reaching nearly five feet in height, adorned the sidewalks, making shopping a nearly impossible task. Luckily, Lemon had managed to return home in time for dinner. Her mother, overwhelmed with relief, embraced her tightly, tears welling up in her eyes.

Naturally, her parents were curious about how her night with Jace had gone. Was he nice? Did he feed her? Did he make her uncomfortable? She answered honestly but vaguely. Those hours with Jace had been a bittersweet combination of joy and despair. Yet, what mattered most was that they belonged to her alone, and she refused to share them- not even with her parents.

Despite her heart's unwillingness to accept the truth, she knew there was no future for her and Jace. They just couldn't seem to get the timing right. This realization drove her to cling to every fragment of memory she could gather.

She supposed it was silly to think in such a way, especially since he had never once given her any signs that he was interested. But there was no denying his disinterest now, she thought gloomily, not after spending the night together in bed, with the faint flickering light throwing the room into a romantic light.

At first, when he'd offered to share the bed, she'd panicked, thinking he might want to become more intimate with her. She didn't oppose their relationship evolving, but she preferred a slower and less drastic rate of change. It had been as if he'd known where her thoughts were going because he'd said. "It'll be too cold in here for you or me to sleep on the couch. If you're comfortable with it, we can share the bed. If you want to put them between us, I've got some extra pillows."

She'd smiled. "No, I don't think that will be necessary."

He gave her a fleeting smile before pulling the blankets back. "I added a few blankets to the bed while you showered," he explained. "I'm not sure how cold it will get in here, but I don't want you to wake up cold."

"I'm sure this will be fine."

He shifted his weight as if he didn't know whether to climb in or wait for her to go first. Lemon hesitated but pushed her sudden bout of shyness aside. "Do you care if I take the left side?" She asked, her voice betraying a hint of nervousness as she tried to overcome the awkwardness.

"No."

It had taken them a few minutes to adjust to each other and the sharing of the mattress top, but once she'd found a comfortable spot, she'd looked over her shoulder at him. Lemon took in his damp hair, which almost looked black, and the musky scent of his freshly washed body in one long sweep. A wave of desire crashed over her, leaving her breathless. She bit her lip. Her gaze fell to his mouth. She yearned to know what it would feel like to have his lips pressed against hers. Would his warm breath make her tremble with need? If she turned to face him if she lifted her face toward his, would he kiss her? Lemon shuddered, wishing she were brave enough to find out.

"Thank you." She whispered.

"For what?" He asked, his gruff voice electrifying her nerve endings.

"For everything." She said before turning back to face the dark bank of windows. Her future felt as bleak as the whirling snow on the blistering winter night.

She should have kissed him. Stupidly, she'd missed her chance and woken to find the bed empty and Jace nowhere in sight. After changing back into her clothes from the day before, she'd gone in search of him and found him in the bookstore, restocking shelves of books. It was something that could have waited another day or two. It hurt to realize he'd rather be stocking shelves than cocooned in a warm bed with her.

Well, that was that.

She'd spent the night with Jace. A fantasy she had shamelessly held for years. In some ways, it had surpassed her wildest dreams. Yet ultimately, she'd still come out the loser, with a broken heart and shattered hope.

Her mother had suggested they leave Frosted closed for an extra day, but Lemon refused to. She needed to work. Needed to have something to keep her distracted. At the very least, she would be able to catch a glimpse of Jace.

The door's chime jingled, causing Lemon to turn and greet the customer, only to be brought up short. Not only had Jace come through the doorway, his dark hair curling slightly over his brow, but he wasn't alone. Two boys raced up to the counter. Their mitten-covered hands pressed against the glass as their eyes widened.

"I want the tree, Mommy!"

"I want a snowflake!"

"It's my turn first." The taller boy shoved his brother aside, causing the smaller boy to stumble over his shoes. He fell to the ground, letting out a wail loud enough to rattle the glass.

Lemon was just about to intervene when a woman came inside. She wore a winter coat that stood out with its vibrant teal blue color and a hood lined with fluffy fur. The stab of jealousy came swiftly. Lemon sucked in a breath as she struggled to control her emotions. However, as the woman pushed her hood back, Lemon's feelings of envy melted away, leaving her feeling foolish.

A smile spread across her face as she circled the counter. "Brynlee! I can't believe how fabulous you look."

Brynlee gave her a weak smile. Her dark hair fell over her shoulders as she slipped her coat off. She wore the exhausted look of a mother who had been up all night caring for her little ones. "Ha, not hardly. You are the one who looks wonderful! When I heard you were back in town, I had to come see you."

"I'm so glad you did. How are you?"

Brynlee stuck out her round belly. "I am so ready to be done. I swear I get bigger with each pregnancy."

"Oh, bosh. You look beautiful. Do you know what you're having?"

"A girl." Brynlee beamed, her eyes alight with pleasure.

"That's wonderful. Do you have any names picked out?"

"Not yet." A shadow of pain flitted through her eyes. "We're waiting until Shawn is home on leave before we pick out a name."

Lemon eyed Brynlee's protruding belly. "I hope he is coming home soon."

"Not soon enough." Jace cut in. Effectively bringing her attention back to him.

"Don't start." Brynlee began, only to be cut off by her son's urgent tugging.

"I want a cookie, Mommy."

Brynlee looked down at her son, brushing her fingers through his hair. "Sure, baby. Which one do you want?"

"The snowman!"

"I thought you wanted the tree, Tyler," Jace said, a smile playing at his mouth.

"No, I want the snowman. Pleeease." He begged, jumping up and down.

"Yes, of course. What about you, Jackson? Do you want a cookie?"

"Uhuh."

"Tell Lemon which one, and she'll get it for you," Jace told the toddler. His eyes locked on hers, holding her prisoner under his unwavering gaze.

When she finally turned away, she felt stripped bare, her emotions raw and vulnerable. Lemon's legs trembled as she awkwardly walked around the counter. She slid the glass door open, reaching in for the tray of cookies. Smiling at the boys, she said, "That was one snowman and one snowflake." Thankfully, her memory hadn't suffered as she managed to recall what Jackson had asked for initially.

"I love cookies!" Tyler proclaimed around a mouthful.

"Me, me!" Jackson stretched out his tiny fist, the other holding what remained of his snowflake cookie.

Brynlee laughed, "No, Jackson. One is enough."

"No, me!" Jackson squawked.

Jace leaned over the display case. His eyes twinkling with merriment. "It looks like you have a new fan, Lemon."

"I think you mean Frosted has a new fan," Lemon replied, a faint blush covering her cheeks. She watched the boys devour their cookies because meeting Jace's gaze seemed impossible. Before she had time to think better of it, she asked the boys, "Would you like to help me frost cookies tomorrow?"

Tyler immediately turned to his mother. "Can I, Mommy?"

Instead of answering, Brynlee gave Lemon a perplexed look. "Are you sure you want to do that?"

"Yes," she said, surprised to mean it. "It'll be in the afternoon. I have to make five dozen for my parents' Christmas party."

Brynlee continued to look doubtful. "I don't think you understand what you are agreeing to."

"It'll be fun," Lemon assured her, though with less enthusiasm than when she had started.

"Don't worry, sis, I'll bring the boys. You can take some time for yourself." Jace cut in, his face softening as he touched Brynlee's shoulder.

"Only if you're sure."

"Absolutely," Lemon said with a smile.

"Oh, all right. Boys, how would you like to help Uncle Jace and Lemon frost cookies tomorrow?" Brynlee asked, laughing.

The boys cheered, and their joyous voices rang in Lemon's ears. She smiled until her gaze met Jace's, and then her pulse leaped in a flurry of panic.

Oh no, what had she gotten herself into?

Chapter Twenty

Friday, December 19th

Chaos is subjectively tolerable.

J ace walked into bedlam. Although it was probably more accurate to say that his parents' home had turned into a whirlwind of small children prepared and capable of bringing three adults to their knees. Scattered across the floor were discarded toys interspersed with his mother's treasured wooden carved nativity set. It took the skills of a seasoned spy to navigate the minefield from the front door to the living room, where he could hear Jackson's screeching cries.

Even as he made his way across the floor, his eyes scouted for clear placement of his feet. He wondered if maybe this state of crazed behavior wasn't, in fact, a family-shared psychosis.

All day, he had wondered what he'd been thinking. Agreeing to spend more time with Lemon, was he mad? As if the other night hadn't been enough. As if sharing a bed with her hadn't been more than enough.

It had been the longest night of his life, lying only a few inches from her. He'd started on his back, staring up at the ceiling and wondering if a person could lose their mind from wanting. Only when he noticed a slight alteration in her breathing did he shift his position to lie on his side. In her sleep, Lemon had turned to face him, and he found himself captivated.

She'd looked beautiful. With her pink lips parted and her face flushed from sleep. Her hand rested palm up next to her face. Ever so lightly, Jace trailed a finger down her silky skin. He wanted to press his mouth there. He wanted a lot of things concerning Lemon, but none of them were ever going to happen.

For what seemed like hours, he watched her, his body aching with a need and his heart breaking with regret. Maybe if she hadn't been so beautiful. Maybe if she hadn't been used to a life of popularity. Maybe if he hadn't been such a coward.

He'd fallen asleep with the growing list of maybes circling his mind.

Damn, he hadn't intended to offer to bring his nephews. But when Lemon had asked Brynlee if she wanted a break, he could see how much she longed for it. Brynlee's life was tough. With Shawn away a lot and her ever-growing family, Brynlee often lived the life of a single mother. That was why she was staying at home for the holidays. Their parents had insisted she come when they learned Shawn wouldn't make it home for Christmas. If nothing else, Brynlee deserved to have a little time for herself.

The only problem with this was that Lemon was included in the package, and he desperately wanted to put some distance between them. He'd worked hard to create the illusion that he didn't like her. And so far, it was working. Then he paused, his mind recalling that random memory of her parents' Christmas party years earlier.

He remembered that night. He'd been standing in a corner, keeping to himself as usual. Large groups had never been his thing, and even though his parents made him attend Frost's annual Christmas party, he refused to do more than sulk in a corner.

However, his eyes always managed to find Lemon in a crowd. She often wore a holiday dress. That year, it had been a deep forest green. Her eyes had glimmered against the bold backdrop. The Christmas lights hanging overhead had made her hair glitter like starlight. The one thing he didn't recall was Lemon trying to get him under the mistletoe. If he would have known that was her intent, he wouldn't have brushed her off as he had. Though he wasn't sure how much he believed her story.

"Uncle Jace," Tyler screamed, running full tilt toward him. The little man didn't care about the obstacles in his path. He just ran over them. "Are we leaving now? I want to make a snowman. Do you think Lemon will let me make a snowman?"

Jace perched the boy on his hip, smiling down at him as he ruffled his hair. "I'm sure she will."

"You'll ask her, won't you? I got to do a snowman."

"Sure." He easily agreed to the request, setting Tyler back to the ground. Jackson stood at his side, his chubby little fingers tugging on the hem of his shirt. Jace leaned down, hoisting him up into the air. Jackson squealed, his face glowing with excitement. "How about you, buddy? Are you ready to go frost some cookies?"

"Yes!" Jackson shouted from the air.

"All right, let's go find your mother."

"Why?" Tyler asked, a frown darkening his face. "She isn't coming, Uncle Jace."

"I know, but don't you think she wants to say goodbye to you?"

The sudden frown receded into a glowing smile. "Oh, okay." Taking Jace's free hand, Tyler tugged on his arm. "Come on, she's this way."

Jace let his nephew lead him, wondering once again what he was getting himself into.

Tyler pulled on the bakery door. His small muscles straining to open it. "It's stuck." He grunted, looking up at Jace with disappointed eyes.

"Here, let me try." Jace gave the handle a firm jerk. Sure enough, the door was locked. He cupped his hands around his eyes, peering into the bakery window. He couldn't see anything beyond the front area, and what he could see wasn't promising. A quick look at his nephews' upturned faces had him cursing under his breath.

This was just like Lemon. She may be the life of the party, but when it came down to it, she wasn't dependable. He reached into his pocket, digging out his phone. His fingers swiped through his contacts until he found her number. After the first ring, he hung up and walked to The End Bookstore door. With jerky movements, he forced the key into the lock.

"Come on, boys," he said, holding the door open for them.

"Are we going to pick out a book, Uncle Jace?" Tyler asked as he hurried inside, heading straight to the children's books section.

Jace watched Jackson trail after his brother at a more sedate pace. "Why don't you two look the books over while I see if I can find Lemon." He didn't expect an answer, nor did he get one, but they weren't fighting, and the way he saw it, that was a win.

Now that the boys were occupied, he focused his fiery gaze on the closed door. With deliberate motions, Jace opened the double doors, letting them swing wide. He passed by the counter and went straight through to the back of the bakery, where he came to a startling halt. His eyes widened in surprise as he stumbled on Lemon in a rather awkward position.

Lemon stood on the metal counter, her legs spread as she straddled the industrial sink. She was bent slightly, giving him an unobstructed view of her round bottom gloved in snug-fitting denim jeans. She muttered to herself, but he couldn't decipher her words as her voice was muffled. Probably due to her head being shoved towards the back of a high-hung shelf. Her arms were swinging wildly about. Jace deftly ducked in the nick of time as a tin measuring cup hurtled towards him.

"Lose something?" She yelped, a solid thump followed by a string of words that made him wince as a smile spread across his face.

"Jace!" Lemon yelled. With a slight flush coloring her cheeks, she turned to meet his gaze. As her hair fell loose from its tie, it created a golden veil that obscured most of her face. "You scared the hell out of me." She accused, throwing another measuring cup at him.

He knocked the cup away as he moved toward the counter. He was drawn to her, even if he didn't want to admit it to himself. "What are you doing up there?"

"I got them this time. You'll see." She spun around, dropping from the counter. In her hands was the small camera he'd helped her assemble.

"Who exactly is it you think you've managed to catch?"

She waved the camera in his face. Her eyes sparkled with triumph. "Whoever has been stealing. I set a trap last night, and I am sure I caught them in the act. Want to watch it with me?"

Jace almost invited her upstairs, but a soft thump from the bookstore reminded him he had a responsibility beyond himself. "What about the cookies?"

"What cookies? I already put the leftovers away."

He gritted his teeth, fighting the urge to scold her. She couldn't help who she was, even if he wished she could. Instead, he counted to five and started again. "No, I mean, the cookies you told Tyler and Jackson could help you decorate. Don't you remember?"

Lemon tilted her head to the side, a look of blank confusion on her face. "Who are Tyler and Jackson?"

Jace could feel his patience slipping. It took another count to five to be able to speak through clenched teeth. "My nephews." He growled.

Then she laughed. Not a light giggle or a playful chuckle. No, she wrapped her slender arms around her waist and bent over, howling with merriment. She made such a ruckus both Jackson and Tyler came skidding into the kitchen, each demanding to know what was so funny.

"I have no idea," Jace said, staring at Lemon as if she'd lost her mind. "What's so funny?" He demanded when she gave no indication of settling down.

"Your face." She gasped.

Tyler and Jackson looked at him. Their brows furrowed as they struggled to see the humor.

Not caring to be on display as some kind of sideshow, Jace scowled at her. "What's wrong with my face?"

She shook her head, wiping the tears from her eyes. He had hoped she was managing to get a hold of herself. However, when she looked up at him, she started laughing again. What was worse, the boys joined in. At least Lemon didn't point at him while laughing. Jace glared at his nephews. "Traitors." He accused, fully aware that they had no clue what he meant. Frustrated, he turned to leave, intending to go somewhere else, but Lemon caught hold of his arm.

"Wait." she pleaded, holding his forearm clasped between her hands. "I'm sorry. I didn't mean to hurt your feelings." She said, her lips forming a ridiculously alluring pout.

He forcibly tore his eyes away, honing in on her forehead instead. "You didn't hurt my feelings."

"Didn't I?" She asked, lifting a pale brow. "Wait, Jace. Please. I'm only teasing."

"Teasing? About what exactly? Do I have something on my face?"

"Come on, Jace. You should know me better than to think I would forget you were bringing your nephews over today. I have the cookies ready to go on the prep table." She explained, leading him to the three trays with different-shaped Christmas cookies.

"Snowman!" Tyler exclaimed, climbing onto one of the stools she had set up beforehand.

"Me too! Me too!" Jackson cried, holding his arms up to Jace.

"Here you are, buddy." Jace set Jackson down next to Tyler.

"Okay, boys, who want to frost some cookies?"

Both boys practically danced in their chairs.

"Okay, okay," Lemon said with a chuckle. "Here are the rules." After a few groans and moans, they quieted down enough to listen. Lemon held up a finger. "First, no licking. Second, the frosting only goes on the cookies. And the third and final rule, you must have fun."

The resounding cheer made Jace smile, his eyes meeting Lemon's over the heads of the boys. After she got them settled, Lemon pulled Jace aside. "So, what do you think?" She asked, her eyes alight with glee.

For a moment, Jace forgot what they were talking about. He struggled to pull his gaze away from her. When he finally looked at his nephews, he smothered a laugh. The boys were having a grand time actively breaking the first two rules. "I think your rules were a bit pointless." He admitted, a smile more tender than he meant to show her tilted the corners of his mouth.

"No, what do you think about watching my video?"

"Oh, yeah, that could be fun. Do you want to watch it while the boys are frosting?"

Lemon shook her head, shaking loose the few remaining strands, her tie falling to the floor. "I was thinking I could wait until you took the boys home. Then we could watch it upstairs."

Jace swallowed, his face burning. "Uh, sure. I can do that." His eyes lifted to the ceiling and the room that lay above it. Already, his apartment had changed into his own personal torment. If he hadn't figured out how to separate himself from Lemon when it came time to leave, his heart might not make it with him.

Lemon tucked her legs onto the sofa, laying the blanket Jace had given her over herself. She couldn't decide if it was Jace or learning the identity of the thief that was making her heart race, but the feeling was unsettling.

"Are you ready?" Jace asked, sitting next to her.

She noticed that he always maintained a little space. Not much, but enough to prevent contact. Unfortunately for her, contact was something she was beginning to crave more than air to breathe. "Yes." She sighed, wondering what he would do if she shifted just enough so that her arm would brush ever so lightly against his.

"All right, here we go."

The black screen scrambled, then turned white before a dimly lit picture of the kitchen appeared. Lemon sat in absolute silence. All thoughts of shifting her position, taking a back seat as she waited for the image of the villain to appear.

"Maybe we could watch it at a higher speed and slow down when we see something?" Jace suggested, and she had to agree with him.

Like a scurrying rat, Lemon watched herself dash around the kitchen and out into the shop area as a cartoon character hyped on some special juice. She watched herself make the cookie dough, then leave the kitchen before coming back and rolling the dough out on the counter. Then, the video stopped.

"Hey," she sat up. "What happened? Did the camera stop recording?"

"No, I stopped it."

"Why?"

"Didn't you see that?"

"See what?"

Jace rewound the video, playing the part where she stood at the counter mixing the cookies. "This is me making cookies. What's the big deal about that?"

"No, shhh," Jace said, pointing back to the television. "Be patient. Just watch."

Together, they leaned forward. Lemon held her breath. Although she didn't know why. Then Jace hollered, making her jump. "What?" She snapped.

"There." He said, pointing to a blur above the shelf.

"What is that?" Lemon asked. Moving the blanket aside, she sat directly in front of the TV. Then she saw it. A small creature ran along the shelf, knocking over a salt shaker as it scurried past, carrying a large portion of a sticky bun held between its teeth.

Lemon sat back on her heels. Her mouth hung open, but no sounds managed to come out. "Was that.." she began, then stopped, shaking her head and trying again. "Was that a raccoon?"

"I believe it was."

"But, how? Why?"

"I don't know, but we should probably check out the attic."

"Oh my, you don't think they live here, do you?"

"Probably."

This wasn't good. Having any kind of pest living in the bakery wasn't good for business. Nor was having one that liked to steal more than food. Then, Lemon's eyes focused on a blur across the screen, running her fingers along the trail when a sudden and horrific thought occurred to her. "Oh, no," she gasped, jumping to her feet. "That damn pest added a fourth of a cup of salt to my sugar cookies."

Chapter Twenty-One
Saturday, December 20th

The spirit of the holidays resides in one's mindset.

T he house was teeming with friends and neighbors donning festive attire and radiant smiles. The sound of Christmas carols floated over the mingling flood of voices. A fire crackled in the fireplace where her mother hung the stockings she used when entertaining. The real stockings, the ones that would be filled to overflowing on Christmas morning, were tucked away under a bed upstairs.

Lemon stood by the fire, relishing the comforting heat as it enveloped her legs. Usually, it wasn't quite this cold for their annual Christmas party, but the storm that had blown through earlier in the week had brought with it a lingering chill. Every time someone came through the front door, a draft swept through the room, causing goosebumps to run up her legs.When the door opened again, Lemon moaned, rubbing her hands together as a shiver racked her body.

Overall, her cocktail dresses were perfect for social events. The long sleeves provided warmth for her arms, while the shorter skirt allowed for comfortable airflow. However, she was beginning to regret her choice this year. She probably would have been better off wearing the same dress she'd worn to the winter formal. Except, Jace had already seen her in that dress, and his reaction had been underwhelming. Now she was freezing, waiting for Jace, who had yet to make an appearance.

She watched the entrance, hopefully when the wind rushed in.Her face collapsed in disappointment when Nicole Whitting walked in. Not that Harper was all that small of a town anymore, but her family's circle of friends included the Whittings, even if she couldn't stand the family. With narrowed eyes, Lemon watched Nicole smile and greet everyone she came across as if everyone was there to see her.

"I see Nicole has made an appearance," Brian whispered in her ear, startling her. She pumped her head into his chin.

"Sorry, I didn't mean to scare you." He smiled, his eyes crinkling at the corners.

"No, it was my fault. I was just thinking."

"Here, I brought you some of the punch you love so much."Brian handed her a clear plastic cup filled with the green frothy liquid.

"Thanks," she murmured, taking the drink even though she didn't want it. Her stomach had been in knots all day, and the thought of putting anything in her mouth caused the knots to tighten. "See anyone worth talking to?" Lemon asked, her eyes sweeping over the familiar faces.

Brian hovered at her side. Every time he breathed, her arm brushed against the buttons of his shirt. She could feel his warm breath gently caress her ear as he dipped his head closer. "Other than you?" he asked, his voice taking on a hint of wistfulness, mirroring their past relationship. Back then, that change in timbre would make her quiver in delight, but now it failed to arouse any response.

She turned her head, about to ask him if there wasn't some client who needed his attention more than her, when his mouth caught hers. She sucked in a startled breath, jerking back. "What are you doing?" She hissed.

Brian smiled, clearly oblivious to how upset he'd made her."I thought it was about time that we kissed again. I'll admit, I had forgotten how much I enjoy the taste of you." When she felt his arm slip around her waist, a chill wrapped around her legs. She pushed a hand against his chest as he leaned over her and turned her face away in time to connect with a pair of dark, glittering eyes.

Lemon watched helplessly as Jace spun on a heel and turned away. She wanted to call out to him, but she didn't want to make a scene. With her temper simmering just below boiling, she turned to Brian. "Brian, I don't mean to disappoint you, and I know this won't in any way hurt your feelings,but I'm not interested in you that way. Not anymore."

Even as she spoke, he continued to smile, brushing a strand of hair behind her ear. "That's because we haven't had a chance to spend anytime together."

"No. I don't need or want to spend any more time with you.Things were great in high school. We got along well, but that was high school.I'm a different person now, and so are you."

He laughed, actually laughed at her. Lemon could only stare in dazed disbelief. It was beyond her comprehension how she had ever believed he was kind and considerate. Especially when he found her attempt to sever things so amusing.

"Brian, this isn't going to happen." She said again, hoping her words would sink in.

Instead of agreeing with her, he bent and gave her an abrupt kiss. "I'm going to check out the refreshments table. Care to join me?"

"No." Lemon snapped, smacking his hand away. "And here," she said, shoving her cup of punch back at him. "I don't want your drink either."

She spun on her heel, storming away from the spot where she'd been waiting impatiently for Jace to arrive, only to have it ruined by Brian. *Brian*, she wanted to scream. All of her plans for the evening seemed to be slipping through her fingers. But she wasn't going to give up. Even if it took every ounce of willpower she had, she was going to get Jace under the mistletoe tonight.

He should just leave.

Jace wandered through the crowd of people, nodding when someone greeted him but not stopping to converse. He hadn't even wanted to come tonight, not after having spent the last few days with Lemon as he had. The tide had shifted on their relationship, and he couldn't go back to the way things had been.

That was the tricky part about having feelings for someone who was supposed to be a friend. Inevitably, there would come a time when the lines would blur, and he had reached that point. Maybe if he didn't know how she smelled after a hot shower with a mixture of herself and his soap on her skin. Perhaps he could have slipped back into the neutral zone if he hadn't lain awake so he could watch her sleep, fantasizing about what it would be like to kiss her, hold her. Maybe then it wouldn't feel like a six-inch dagger was protruding from his chest where the hurt of seeing her back with Brian had torn through him.

Dammit! He didn't belong here. He needed to go back home where it was safe. Where women were a pleasant distraction but didn't have the power to cripple him. Yet, he couldn't help but wonder if he could go back to what he had been. Would he be able to take a woman out on a date, all the while knowing it would go nowhere? Was it fair to lead them along when his heart was no longer his to give?

"Jace, you made it," Evelyn exclaimed, pulling him into a hug.

The sound of Lemon's mother jerked him out of his reverie and back into reality- a reality he wanted to escape.

"Yep," he said, smiling, though he knew nothing could touch the emotionless hole of his eyes.

"How's your mother?" She asked, her eyes darkening with concern.

"She's getting better every day. It's helped to have Brynlee home for a spell. Her boys have done a great job of keeping my mother occupied."

"I'm sure they have." Evelyn laughed. "I don't know if I am looking forward to being a grandma or dreading the day."

"When the time comes, you'll love it."

"You think so?"

Lemon rushed in. "Mama, you found Jace."

Jace looked down at her. Surprised to find her sandwiched to his side. She grabbed his hand, lacing her fingers with his. He scowled. "I didn't realize I was hiding." He said, tugging slightly on his captured hand only to have Lemon tighten her grip. When he looked down at her, she smiled,but it didn't reach her eyes. She looked tired. He wasn't surprised. After realizing the sugar cookies for the party were inedible, they'd worked on a new batch, but she hadn't left the bakery until well after midnight. Yet still, she managed to come in the next morning right on time.

"Did you tell your mother about the video?" He asked with a smile. She'd been so proud of herself for solving the mystery.

She shook her head at the same time her mother asked, "What video?"

"Nothing, Mama. Jace showed me a funny clip of a bear in the forest. It was cute, but nothing you would be interested in."

Jace looked down at her, puzzled. Then, she completely distracted him by sliding her hand up the inside of his arm and tugging him away. He followed meekly behind her, more curious than not to know where she was taking him and why. When they started up the stairs, he hesitated. Lemon turned to him and whispered, "I don't want anyone to overhear our conversation.Upstairs is the only place where there won't be anyone."

He nodded, but only reluctantly. Jace had never been upstairs. Even though he'd been to Lemon's house countless times over the years, he had never been permitted to leave the bottom floor. His eyes followed the trail of pictures marking Lemon and Berry's life. He couldn't deny the Frosts were a good-looking family. He imagined they were the type of people who Greek gods were envisioned after.

Lemon led him down a dark hallway, passing three doors until she reached one that stood shut in the back corner. With a flick of her wrist,the door swung open, and she shoved him inside. Well, at least she tried. His blasted curiosity is what allowed her to succeed.

With one wide sweep, he took in the details of her room. To say he was surprised would be an understatement. He had fully expected to see trophies and photos documenting her high school days, but there wasn't any of that anywhere. Her room, in a sense, mirrored his perception of her: clean,fresh, and sweet.

When he turned back around, he almost knocked her over. His hands shot out, catching her by the waist. Through the thin, silky fabric of her dress, he could feel her heat. In a moment of weakness, Jace allowed his thumbs to gently graze along her hip bones. Then he let go as if seared by a hot pan. The urge to pull her up against him was almost more than he could resist.

"What did you want to tell me?" He managed to ask. His voice was gruff from the strain of continuing to deny himself something he desperately desired.

"What?" She looked dazed. Her face flushed. Then her eyes cleared, and she said, "Oh, right. Don't tell my mother about the raccoons."

"Why not? You will have to deal with it eventually."

"True, but I don't want her to worry. I'm going to take care of it for her, then let her know it was the raccoons that sabotaged her."

"Your mother was sabotaged? I don't know Lemon. That is pretty elevated thinking for some vermin to plot against your mother."

Lemon punched him. He bent in half and let out a grunt as if her gentle fist caused pain. When she gasped, reaching for him, her eyes full with worry, he smiled. "You are the absolute worst!" Lemon cried. "I thought I hurt you."

"Not likely with your tiny arms." Jace held up her hand, trying to ignore the tingle in his fingertips.

She pulled her arm away, shoving him. "My arms are not tiny."

"So you say." His grin widened, his eyes lighting up with joy.

Lemon stepped toward him, her lips parted. Panic flared in him as he froze, unable to move forward or run away, although both options had merit. His heart thrummed in his chest, his pulse leaping in his neck. As if under a spell, he felt himself being drawn towards her, unable to break free from the invisible force.

The crash of a door broke the spell. They sprang apart in surprise. Lemon frowned, her brows pulled down in concern. "What on earth?" she began, walking toward the open door but stopped abruptly. She spun around and pushed him back a step.

"What is it?" Jace asked, only to have her fingers pressed against his mouth. "What's wrong?" He whispered, his lips tingling from the contact.

"Shhh," she said. "Just wait."

Jace felt silly standing in her room with Lemon's fingers still pressed against his mouth. He wondered what she would do if he kissed each fingertip or maybe slipped one finger between his teeth and bit down.

"Berry, open the door." A girl's voice cut into his musing and pulled him back into the room. Lemon met his eyes, and she mouthed, *Mia*.

He nodded. It was the girl Berry had met in the bookstore.When they'd left, he thought they had managed to work out whatever was between them, but evidently, they hadn't.

"Just forget it, Mia," Berry muttered, his voice muffled by the closed door.

"I had, but it seems you haven't. We have to talk about this. Remember? You're the one who said you could handle this kind of relationship."

Handle what? Lemon mouthed.

Jace shrugged.

"Please, Berry. It's not what you think. I wasn't kissing him."

"Right, that's why he was all over you."

"No, Berry. Listen. He was just teasing you."

The sound of Berry's door hitting the wall rattled Lemon's room.

"The hell you say!"

"What did you expect? After the way you hit him at the dance."

"He deserved it."

"No, he didn't, and you know it. Maybe if you worked on communicating, you wouldn't fly off the handle."

The sudden silence was abrupt. Lemon looked up at him and blushed. Her hand fell away from his mouth. Berry's conversation with Mia brought back vivid images of Lemon kissing Brian, reigniting all the pain and jealousy. He couldn't look at her. He worried that if he did, she would see the hurt she'd caused, and he couldn't bear for her to know.

"Do you think it's safe to leave?" He whispered.

Lemon peeked around the doorway. "Nope. They're kissing."She said with a giggle.

"Great. So what, we are stuck here until they finish?"

Lemon's green eyes darkened in a flash of hurt. "You feel like you're stuck here? You don't like being with me?"

Jace swore, running a hand through his hair. "No. That isn't what I meant."

Lemon looked at the floor, color flooding her face. "Jace, if we were standing under a mistletoe, would you kiss me?" When she finished the question, she faced him boldly as if daring him to lie.

He reached out, brushing her hair back over her shoulder."Lemon, we would never find ourselves in that sort of situation, so I don't see how me answering the question would make any difference."

Once the words left his mouth and he saw her expression change, he didn't wait. He turned to the doorway and walked through, leaving Lemon crushed and deflated behind him. Berry and Mia were still locked together, and he didn't care. He walked by them without sparing them more than a disinterested glance.

He had to get out of there- out of this house, out of this town- before it was too late.

Chapter Twenty-Two

SUNDAY, DECEMBER 21ST

Kind deeds are never a waste.

L emon woke up to a thick layer of freshly fallen snow outside. The cold air made her nose cold. She pulled her blanket up to her face and let out a sigh, enjoying the warmth of her cozy down blanket. She snuggled for a few more moments before reluctantly throwing it aside and getting out of bed.

Last night, instead of falling into bed like her body wanted to, she sat at her desk and pulled out a sheet of paper. On it, she wrote a list of things she wanted to do. None of these were things anyone would find on a typical to-do list. For her, the list was not merely about getting things done. No, she was set on doing things that would improve her character.

After Jace stormed away last night, Lemon had much to consider. One thing in particular kept nagging at her. She wasn't sure if it was her perception or if he thought it, but Lemon kept getting the impression that Jace didn't believe she was a good person.

The initial realization was hard, and it hurt. However, it made Lemon look at herself, her life, and her attitude. She found herself wondering if maybe he was right. Was she a bad person? Sure, she was kind. Anyone who came into the bakery was always greeted with a smile and a friendly hello. She never intentionally was rude to anyone, even when they wore on her nerves, but that wasn't the same.

She could sense that Jace saw her as a privileged, high-maintenance, conceited woman. Sure, she might have moments of being self-centered, but what he didn't know was she was so much more than that. She cared about others more than Jace believed she did, and she was determined to show him. Lemon hoped he would realize that her beauty was just the tip of the iceberg and there was so much more to discover.

Her list transformed into a strategic plan to alter Jace's perception of her. She stood at her desk, staring down at the piece of paper, even though she already knew what it said. There were five things. Five things that if she could make happen in the next few days, maybe Jace would see her. See beyond the image she portrayed to the world and see who she was underneath it all. Perhaps, then, their relationship could evolve into something more than just friendship.

It was fascinating how a simple list ignited a newfound sense of motivation in her. Something she hadn't felt in quite a while. She now possessed a sense of purpose, a burning desire to accomplish something extraordinary, and she was determined to make it happen. With enthusiasm, she fairly bounced down the stairs, eager to start despite not yet having a clear plan of action.

As she entered the kitchen, the aroma of freshly cooked bacon made her stomach growl. A smile spread across her face when she saw her mother hovering over the stove. Lemon wrapped her arm around her mother's waist and gave her a quick hug. "Good morning, Mama."

Evelyn smiled, her eyes bright and cheerful. "Are you hungry?"

"For bacon? Absolutely. Can I help?"

"I was going to mix up a batch of pancake batter if you want to get that started?"

"Sure." Lemon moved to the cabinets, pulling out a glass bowl. She moved around the kitchen with familiarity. Along the counter sat flour, sugar, baking powder, and oil. With the ease of a routine well established, she added the ingredients, one after another. The measurements were stored in her memory. The only problem with tasks that didn't require one's full attention was that the mind would wander. Then, inevitably, a question would slip out that was better left unasked.

"Mama, do you think I'm a good person?" As soon as the question slipped out, she regretted it. It was on the tip of her tongue to play it off as a joke. Yet, when her mother answered, Lemon stilled.

"Of course, you're a good person. Just look at all the wonderful things you've done with your life. You were a cheerleader and prom queen. You graduated with a degree in culinary arts. You interned at a five-star restaurant. Yes, I'd say you are a very accomplished person."

Hearing her mother proudly recite a litany of her achievements as evidence of her virtuous acts made her blood run cold. Surely there was more to her than being a prom queen? She whisked at the egg white with more vigor than the task required. "But Mama, I've done good deeds too. Right?"

Evelyn gave Lemon a searching glance. "What's this all about? Did someone say something to you last night at the party?"

"No. I just was thinking, and I couldn't remember a time when I did something purely for the sake of being kind."

"That's not true! You do kind things all the time. Just look at how you have helped me with the bakery."

"I don't think that counts."

"Why not?"

"Well, you are family, for starters."

"Bosh. You are a good person. No one expects you to lay out a list to prove it."

Maybe someone did. Lemon thought gloomily. If her mother couldn't provide an example of a good deed. "What did you do with the leftovers from the party last night?"

"I put everything in the refrigerator. Why?"

Lemon set the pancake batter next to the cooktop and leaned against the counter. "Nothing; I just thought I could take some over to the Tortes later today."

"Oh, how come?"

"Well, since Nancy and Robert couldn't come last night, you know how much they love your cooking. Then there's Brynlee and the boys. I just figured that they might appreciate not having to cook a meal." Lemon shrugged away her explanation. Heat flooded her cheeks, and she struggled to meet her mother's gaze.

The silence stretched in the room. Only sizzling bacon kept the weight from bearing down. When her mother spoke, Lemon could tell she was confused by her sudden desire to do something out of character. "If that's what you want. Heaven knows we don't need all that food."

"Thanks, Mama." Lemon let out the breath she hadn't even realized she'd been holding. Just hearing her mother's consent felt incredible, as if she had received an official seal of approval. Already, she was making a dent on her list, and when she delivered the food to the Tortes, she could cross off number three, *helping someone without being asked.*

Lemon shut the car door, juggling the three foil pans in her arms. The sidewalk had been cleared of snow, but a thin layer of ice made it treacherous to walk on. With each step she took, Lemon made sure her boot had traction. The last thing she wanted was to end up on her back, covered in six different appetizers.

Little did she realize the true struggle lay in navigating the three slippery cement steps leading to the front door. The slick concrete caught her off guard, and she yelped when her foot slid to the side. Her hand shot out, making a mad grab for the railing. After teetering to the side, she managed to find her center. Thankfully, all those years spent on cheer were still paying off. She let out a shaky laugh, straightening herself.

The Tortes front door held an extravagant Christmas wreath swathed in red and gold ribbons. She stood in front of the festive decoration. With her hand poised over the doorbell, the door swung open, and Jackson, or maybe it was Tyler, rushed out.

He didn't stop.

Nope, he didn't need to stop because Lemon stopped him all without his help. Seeing as he ran full tilt into her. Her oversized coat offered some protection, but it wasn't enough to keep her from taking a step back after the impact. Regrettably, her foot came down on empty space, causing her to stumble and collide with the step below. Unprepared for the motion, Lemon lost all ability to recover her balance. She clutched the foil pans to her chest and let gravity take her.

When she hit the ground, the air left her body. For a full minute, she lay motionless, staring at the clear blue sky. Lemon wondered if this would be the last image she had before she died. Amazingly, the foil pans remained clasped against her chest. At the very least, the Tortes could still enjoy their meal.

Once her brain unscrambled, and she could begin to feel again, Lemon had a strange sense of déjà vu. Especially when a cute little cherub face wearing a bright red jacket suddenly appeared in her line of sight.

"Do you have an owie?" Jackson asked, popping a finger into his mouth.

His worried expression made her rush to assure him. Lemon shook her head slightly. "No. I'm okay."

"I'm sorry I hit you." He leaned closer, his nose almost touching hers. "You aren't going to tell my mommy, are you?"

Lemon smiled. Even though it hurt too, which was strange, seeing as she didn't land on her face, nonetheless, it did hurt. She worried every part of her body would ache tomorrow. "No, Jackson. I won't tell your mom. Now move back so I can get up." Instead of just sitting straight up, Lemon did an awkward roll to the side, bracing herself on her elbow. The motion made her dizzy, but if she closed her eyes, it wasn't so bad.

"Are you here to see Uncle Jace?"

"No, I was just dropping off some food for your grandma."

"Grandma's sick."

Lemon's smile faltered. That was precisely the kind of talk she avoided. She never knew what to say in situations like these. Even if she was talking to a small child. "I know, honey." She said gently. "Maybe a treat will help her feel better."

Jackson eyed her suspiciously. "What kind of treat?"

"Let's see. I believe there are some sugar cookies and a couple of cinnamon rolls in one of these pans."

"Cookies?" Jackson asked, his eyes glimmering with hope.

"Yes, but you have to share with your grandma."

"I'll go tell her right now."

"Wait!" Lemon made a grab for his coat sleeve but missed, and, like a shot, the boy was gone. Sighing, Lemon rested against the freezing concrete, wondering how she came to this pass. This is what she got for trying to do something nice. With a grumble, Lemon eased herself awkwardly into a sitting position. She looked dumbly at the foil in pans in her hands, trying to decide how she was going to get up with her arms full of food.

"Need help?" Jace asked from the doorway.

Lemon's head snapped up, her eyes widening in surprise. She hadn't realized that he was there. Though she supposed it made sense. Like Frosted, The End was always closed on Sundays. He stood with his shoulder braced against the door jab, a half-smile teasing his mouth. His arms were crossed loosely over his chest, the sleeves of his shirt pushed back over his forearms, revealing corded muscle. The pulsating wave of desire that ran through her had become a sensation she knew all too well, something she had come to expect.

She felt her body flush despite sitting on the cold earth. Her heart clenched with fear. Fear of failing. A deep, unmovable dread lodged in her throat and made it hard to speak. When she managed to push the words out, they came tight and strained. "Sure." She said with a weak smile. "If you don't mind?"

He tilted his head as if trying to come to an understanding. "Why would I mind?"

She shrugged, dropping her gaze to the foil pans in her arms. Tears stinging her eyes, she took a shaky breath. Now was most definitely not the time to lose it. When his booted feet came into view, Lemon looked up, reasonably confident she had successfully hidden her anguish from him.

"What's wrong?" He asked abruptly, dropping down beside her. His lean hands ran over her hair and down her arms. His expression was taut with worry.

Her body trembled, but not from the cold. She couldn't even feel it now. Her sole attention was on his hands as he stroked gently over her.

"You must be freezing," he said, lifting her and the foil pans simultaneously. "Let's get you inside where you can warm up."

Lemon gasped, her arm looping around his neck as he carried her inside. Although she loved being in his arms, she felt a bit foolish being carried when she was perfectly capable of walking. "Jace, I can walk." She began, but her voice died off with the hooded look he gave her. Surprised and a little confused, she fell silent and let him carry her, all the while studying the hard lines of his profile.

When he was almost to the door, Lemon whispered in his ear, "Are you mad?"

The corner of his mouth twitched. "No." His eyes dropped to her for a second. "Why do you ask?"

In his arms, she took the opportunity to study him intently, with no inhibitions. Her eyes ate up every nuance as a starved animal desperate to survive. She ran a finger along the dipped line in his brow. "You have a line here when you are angry."

He looked down at her again, a puzzled expression relaxing the line she had touched. "I do?"

"Yes, didn't you know that?"

"No, I didn't."

He set her down in front of the fireplace, where golden flames danced on a log. The heat came as a shock. Her body shivered against the wave of warmth.

Jace took the foil pans from her arms. "What's this?"

Heat flooded her cheeks. Lemon didn't know why her desire to share brought on a wave of uncertainty. Yet, an unsettling urge to explain had her mustering all her courage to face him. "I thought your mother might enjoy some of the leftovers from the party last night. You know, since she wasn't able to come."

His gaze dropped to the pans in his arms, then lifted to meet hers. The confusion and surprise evident in his eyes infuriated her. Her eyes narrowed. "What? You don't think I'm capable of doing something nice? Is it so inconceivable that the prom queen has a heart?" She snapped.

"I don't remember saying anything," Jace said, his mouth tightening.

"Yeah, well, your face speaks with exclamation points!" Lemon stood panting, her blood boiling as she glared at him. Then, just as quickly as it rose, her anger simmered and cooled. She rubbed a hand to her aching head, rubbing her temple. "I'm sorry. Will you tell your mother I said hi?"

Silence stretched between them. Her courage wilted. Deflated, she made to leave but stopped when his hand caught hers. She lifted her eyes to his.

His voice, deep and roughened, said, "Thanks, Lemon. I will."

He let his hand drop, and she moved toward the door. Every step away from him tore at her heart, leaving her aching and unable to heal. Since when did falling in love feel so hopeless?

Chapter Twenty-Three

MONDAY, DECEMBER 22ND

The pursuit of happiness leads to joyful experiences.

With the turn of the weather, The End's business had slowed considerably. No one seemed brave enough to venture outside when the gray sky hung low and white flakes swirled in the air.

Jace hadn't seen a soul pass by in the last two hours. He debated closing early but figured it didn't much matter. He could work just as easily in the bookstore as he could in his apartment.

His final project for the year was almost complete, with just a few last-minute details left to take care of. However, he had difficulty staying focused long enough to finish any of it.

No matter how many times he woke the screen of his laptop, inevitably, it would go dark again. Instead of finalizing details of his design, he would find himself straining to hear any stray sounds from the bakery. His gaze would linger on the adjoining door as if he could will Lemon to appear.

The woman was driving him mad. She wasn't acting like herself. First, with the food she'd dropped off yesterday unexpectedly. Then he heard she'd made extra sticky buns earlier this morning for the county deputies. Not that either of those things was bad. He just never knew her to be concerned with others.

No, frowning into the screen, that didn't sound right. It wasn't that she was mean or thoughtless; it was just that Lemon walked around with an almost absentmindedness. It was as though her head was permanently in the clouds, and nothing would or could bring her down. She went about her business without a care in the world. This was one of her most endearing qualities, the way she could look at the world and smile.

Still, she was like any other female. A scary spider would make her scream, and bugs of any variety would have her running to the next room. He smiled, recalling the time she'd seen a beetle on the floor next to the bathroom. She sounded like an offended hen screeching as she hopped from foot to foot. She'd called for him. A warmth spread through him as the memory flooded his senses.

He'd forgotten about that, but now the memory had resurfaced, and so had the details. He'd been stocking books in the back for his mother when Lemon had let out a squeal, and then she'd cried for him. His name had been unmistakable.

At first, he'd thought something was wrong. When he tore around the corner, his heart pounding inside his chest, he'd almost run her over. She'd thrown herself into his arms and cried on his shoulder. Her words tumbled out in an incoherent stream of sounds, but he'd managed to string enough words together to realize she wasn't hurt.

Nope, the whole hysterics had been because a rather small black beetle had found its way into the bakery. Being a teenage boy at the time, he'd laughed. Laughed at her, at himself, and most of all at the beetle. Lemon hadn't taken kindly to his merriment. She'd shoved his shoulder and glared at him. As he took the bug outside, she muttered a barely audible thank you and refused to acknowledge him for the rest of the day.

Reflecting on it now, he deeply regretted his laughter. If he could do it over again, he would have held her in his arms, whispering reassurances of how he wouldn't ever let anything upset her. He would slay dragons for her, and maybe if she let him, he would take care of her, always. Unfortunately, that moment had passed, and it had been wasted on an impulsive pup who had no business taking care of Lemon. However, that boy was now a man, and he was in a position where he could help her with her new pest problem. If she was willing to accept it.

Yet, when she realized raccoons were living in the bakery, he expected her to demand the raccoons be captured and removed. Days had passed, and she still had yet to do anything. The few times he had brought it up, she'd become visibly upset. Once, he swore he saw tears shimmering in her eyes. Jace couldn't explain it.

He ran his fingers idly over the keyboard, tapping against the loose space bar. He should probably see about getting it fixed, he thought with disinterest. What he wanted was to fix Lemon's problem, or any of her problems, for that matter. Anything that would allow him to get back into her good graces, a place he hadn't been in since high school. When he'd been too blind and foolish to recognize what was being offered. Jace signed, pushing away from his computer. If only time travel was an option. He would pay a visit to his younger self and kick him in the ass for being so blind. Then he'd make damn sure when Lemon made her move at that Christmas party so many years ago, he'd follow her.

He shuddered with regret. To think he could already know what it was to kiss Lemon, to hold her, to know that she was his. The mere thought of it seemed absurd and unfathomable. What does one do when their lifelong desire is finally fulfilled? Fortunately, he hadn't experienced it yet, but if it ever did happen, he'd have to come up with a new pursuit. He imagined it would have something to do with Lemon. It seemed he was destined to be linked with her. On some level, at least.

A sharp crash broke the silence, making his body jolt in surprise. Just as he rose to his feet, Lemon's scream rent the air, and like a time not too long in the past, he ran toward the sound. His heart slammed against his ribs as he vaulted over the display counter. He shoved the hinged door open with such force it slammed against the wall. His dark eyes burned like coals as they swept the kitchen. He found Lemon almost immediately. If he hadn't seen her, her bellow of outrage would have given her position away. She was on her knees, her palms braced against the cold tile floor. Her face rested on the floor as she looked under a row of large shelves holding supplies necessary for making sweet foods sweeter.

"Come back here, you dirty rotten thief!" Lemon yelled, throwing a slender arm under the shelving unit. She swept the floor in a wide arc. "Dammit!"

Jace stood behind her, taking in her position and the clear angst in her voice. Any idiot could sum up what was going on to a point. He sank down next to her hip. "Everything okay?" He asked, a smile tugging at his lips.

Lemon glared at him over her shoulder. "No, does it look like everything is okay?"

He laughed. He couldn't help it. Even after knowing Lemon would be mad as a hornet, he couldn't help himself. Lemon crawling on the floor, chasing after a tiny critter, would stick with him forever.

"Why is it that when I find a situation to be difficult, your response is always to laugh at me?" She challenged, sitting on her heels. Her hands propped on her thighs. Even disheveled, with her hair hanging over her eye, she looked beautiful. Jace wasn't sure if there was ever a time when she wouldn't look beautiful to him. She was and would always be his muse.

He couldn't seem to help himself. He reached his hand out, pushing the loose hair behind her ear before he even realized what he was doing. His eyes locked with hers, and for one burning moment, the air between them sizzled and filled with all the things he wanted to say to do but didn't dare to act upon.

Lemon's gaze fell away first. He didn't know what that meant or even if he should care. Jace cleared his throat, his eyes falling away as if continuing to stare at her would reveal feelings he wasn't ready to acknowledge. "What's the matter, Lemon?" He finally managed to ask. His voice was gruffer than he meant for it to be. "You scared the shit out of me, screaming the way you were."

He watched with subtle amusement as color flooded her cheeks. "Sorry," Lemon muttered, dipping her head so he could only see the tip of her nose through the curtain of her hair. "The raccoons stole my ring."

His eyebrows rose with his surprise. He looked around the kitchen but couldn't see any betraying movements. "It's the middle of the day."

"I know that," she snapped. Rising to her feet, she stomped to the sink, washing her hands with the commercial-grade soap. Jace winced, watching her lather up her delicate skin. He didn't understand why they insisted on using the stuff. He always figured soap was soap. The sheer strength of that stuff could easily strip the paint off a car. "Why do you use that stuff?" Jace asked.

Lemon gave him a puzzled look. "What stuff?"

"The soap. It's awful. I swear it could eat the stain off wood."

"Hardly," Lemon said with a laugh. Then she shrugged, resuming her task. "It's the stuff my mother buys. Seeing how it's her bakery, I use what she prefers."

"Is it what you used when you were in L.A.?"

She smiled. "No, it was a five-star restaurant. The chef was temperamental and insisted on soap with aloe to keep them from drying out."

"Did it?" Jace asked and elaborated with Lemon's perplexed expression. "Did it keep your hands from drying out?"

Lemon looked at her palms, then flipped them over. "Yes, I suppose it did. I hadn't noticed before, but this stuff hasn't been doing me any favors." She admitted with a grimace.

"What was the kind you used before?" Jace asked, frowning at her hands.

She tilted her head, her expression reflecting her confusion. "I think the brand was called Ella-vate. It was a white bottle with a tree silhouette on the label."

Jace nodded but didn't say anything more on the subject. He leaned against the counter, his hands braced against the cool metal surface. "How did the raccoon get your ring?" He asked, remembering what had brought him into the bakery, to begin with.

Her sudden blush left him puzzled. He couldn't imagine what she would feel embarrassed about now. Jace watched her nervous behavior with growing fascination.

I took it off because I was going to knead some dough. You can't believe the dreadful task of extracting dough from every tiny crevice. She pointed to a dish next to the sink. "I put my jewelry there so it doesn't fall into the drain. When I dumped the dough onto the counter, I heard a faint clinking sound and turned in time to see the blasted raccoon run across the back of the sink with my ring in its mouth."

"Did you see where it went?"

"No, I lost it under the shelving. It disappeared toward the back wall."

Jace pushed away from the counter and walked along the shelving unit until he reached the last unit against the back wall. He stretched out on the floor, his face resting against the tile. Pulling his phone from his back pocket, he turned on the flashlight, shining it along the bottom of the shelf that ran parallel to the floor. Evelyn certainly kept the bakery spotless. There were only a few dust bunnies accumulating near the baseboard, probably because it was challenging to clean that particular spot. Other than that, the floor was immaculate. The raccoon was nowhere to be seen, but there was a hidden hole in the shadowed corner just above the baseboard.

Jace pushed away from the floor, his muscles bunching as he lifted himself from the ground. He gave Lemon a fleeting glance before turning to the shelf, giving the unit a testing pull. He felt the give in the wood and tugged again. This time, with the intent of moving it. Despite its frivolous occupants, the unit itself was deceptively heavy. He grunted under the strain but managed to move the piece enough to see behind it. The light from overhead cast the hole into a dark contrast.

"Check this out." He said, pushing the shelf further out of the way. He moved back so Lemon could squeeze up next to him. However, having her so close might not have been the wisest decision. Her sweet scent had his head swimming. His fingers tightened on the shelf to keep himself from sinking his hand into her hair. He wanted to bury his face in her silky locks, nuzzle her neck, and inhale deeply. He longed to discover if filling his lungs with the essence of her would ease the painful emptiness in his chest.

"What is it?" Lemon asked, pressing closer to him.

His pulse leaped with pleasure. He let his hand rest on her waist. It was a friendly gesture, he assured himself. This was something any good friend would do when trying to help them see. And wasn't that what he wanted to help her with?

"Right there," he whispered against her ear. The fine blonde strands of her hair tickled his lip. He inched closer, pressing his chest against her back. The warmth of her body, her soul, melted the coldness inside of him. "The hole. Do you see it?"

She shivered. He felt her betraying ripple against him and wondered at the cause. Was she excited? Was her heart racing like his? Did she feel the same exultation just from being close to each other?

She turned in the tight space, her front brushing against him, alighting a shock of pleasure. "Do you think the raccoon lives in the wall?"

"Perhaps." He said, his voice sounded tight and harsh to his ears. "The only way to know for sure is to take a look."

"How do we do that?"

"You'll need to call in a professional."

"You can't do it?" Lemon asked, her face turned up to his.

He could lean down and kiss her. She was so close to him it wouldn't be hard. In less than a heartbeat, he would discover the feeling of her lips pressed intimately against his, to feel her warm breath mingling with his. Instead, he snapped at her. His frustration boiled until all that remained was his sizzling temper. "No, I can't do it. In case you missed it. I'm a graphic designer. I don't crawl into tight places looking for pests for my pain in the ass, neighbor."

Her smile, once vibrant and warm, was swept away by the wave of his hurtful words, leaving behind only a broken expression. A shadow darkened her green eyes, making them shimmer a rich emerald. He felt like a cad. His frazzled temper dissipated as quickly as it had sparked. His mouth once more landed him in a mess he couldn't easily get out of. The kicker was none of the things he had said were true. He didn't even know why he'd said them in the first place. Lemon meant the world to him, more even. The last thing he wanted was to be the one to extinguish the glow in her eyes.

"Look. I'm sorry. I didn't mean that." He began, but she was already working her way out of the tight corner.

"You're right. I shouldn't have assumed you would help me."

"No. Dammit. That isn't it." Jace said with frustration. "I don't know why I said what I did." Lie. He knew exactly what had caused his sudden flare of fury. "I can take a look. Let me go lock up The End first."

Lemon shook her head. Her eyes looked mysteriously misty. "No. It's okay. I'll manage."

"Lemon," Jace began, but he stopped. His throat tightened at the single tear sliding down her cheek. He took a tentative step forward, but she stepped back. Her hand was outstretched. "No, Jace. I've got it. Sorry to have bothered you."

His shoulders slumped as he turned to leave. Jace walked through the adjoining doors, turning back once more. Lemon no longer looked like she was about to cry, which relieved him. But she didn't look happy either. The glowing joy of her was missing, and he ached over its absence. "Are you sure you don't want my help?"

Her lips curled into the smile she used when greeting strangers, and he felt the stab of realization. "No. I'll manage."

Resigned, and with no other option, he continued to walk away. He came to an abrupt stop when he heard the sound of the adjoining doors locking shut. The hole in his chest expanded with a chilling purpose.

Chapter Twenty-Four

TUESDAY DECEMBER 23RD

Just because something used to work doesn't mean it still will.

L emon turned right, then left. The mirror's reflection of her elf costume confirmed what she already knew. The costume still fit. In a moment of weakness, her mother had asked if she would be willing to be Santa's helper for one shift, something she hadn't done since high school. The question had come after a long day, and Lemon had been tired. Before she had time to think better of it, she'd agreed to work the third shift on the Tuesday before Christmas.

She didn't know if she should be pleased or disgusted that her body still resembled that of a teenage girl. The costume was made of wool. The green-dyed skirt fell in dramatic ruffles just above her knees. She had red and white candy-stripped stockings pulled up to her thighs; the material was surprisingly warm, which was good because tonight was particularly cold. The tips of her golden shoes curled at the toes that rang with each step she took. Her green wool coat, with its large gold buttons showcasing a joyful Santa Claus, concealed a button-up shirt. The shirt had candy cane stripes and a thick red ruffle encircling the collar. Perched on top of her freshly curled hair sat a green cone-shaped hat. The tip curving over from the weight of a larger gold bell.

Even though it wasn't necessary, Lemon still went further by dusting her cheeks and eyelids with gold glitter and gluing tiny stars along her cheekbones. She slathered on a coat of high gloss candy apple red lip gloss. She stepped back, her eyes examining every detail of her outfit. Even in the harsh light of her bedroom, she had to admit she still could truly embody Candy Cane, her elf persona. The only thing left was to apply the pointy ears. Made with moldable plastic, the pieces perched easily on her ears after she added the washable adhesive. It was the same glue she used for the stars. As long as she refrained from sudden jolts or excessive perspiration, the ears would remain in position for the entire four-hour shift.

"Lemon, are you about ready? We've got to go," her mother yelled up the stairs. Lemon sighed, looking at herself once more before turning to the door. She could do this. After all, it was only four hours. Then, she would be home again.

Then, she would have to make a decision.

The holidays were almost over, and she had to decide what was next. Her stomach clenched, but she ignored the tightening coil of dread. Now wasn't the time. Later, she could lie in misery as her life continued to happen around her. For now, she was Candy Cane, and the children needed to give Santa their Christmas lists because who wanted to wake up to no presents under the Christmas tree.

Two hours in, and the line hadn't seemed to shrink at all. Lemon gave the elf Lollypop a grimace. Lollypop, whose real name was Jill, a senior at Harper High, looked equally strained as Lemon felt. Whether it was because Christmas was only a couple of days away or perhaps children were more demanding these days, Lemon's patience was quickly dissipating.

With the sun sinking below the horizon an hour ago, the temperature had dropped dramatically. It was fortunate most of the line to see Santa was snaked through the temporary structure. Even though the walls weren't thick, they still helped to protect those waiting from the harsh elements. Already, there was talk of another storm system set to blow through. No one said it out loud, but everyone was praying it would hit the day after Christmas. It would be a miracle, but one that Lemon would be grateful for.

Lollypop shivered, "Two more hours." She whined as she had for the last hour and a half. Lemon was sure she wouldn't need a clock for the rest of the night, given Jill's insistence on whispering in her ear every fifteen minutes about the remaining time on the clock.

"Thank you, Lollypop," Lemon said between clenched teeth. Part of the guidelines for working as an elf in Santa's workshop was to only address the elves by their elf names. If anyone was ever caught not adhering to this rule or the other four hard fast ones, the person would be excused and not permitted back.

At least the city council, who funded Santa's workshop every year, made the rule easy to remember. They had them hanging on the wall in a gold frame written in fanciful writing.

1. *Only smiling faces should greet Santa's visitors. Names make the experience magical. Don't forget to use them.*

2. *Naughty or Nice, all children deserve a turn.*

3. *Elves are helpful and will only share merriment with visitors.*

4. *Kind words and actions help all to have a good time.*

Lemon figured there must have been an issue at some point. Otherwise, she couldn't understand why the city council had been so specific about elf behavior and tolerating obnoxious children. Still, Lemon toyed with the idea of breaking a rule. At least then, she wouldn't endure hours of fighting with naughty children while parents stood clumped together talking. Yet if she did it, it would be the only thing she was remembered for: Candy Cane, the rule breaker.

At the jolly ho of Santa, Lemon grabbed the next family and brought them forward. She smiled as she explained how the pictures worked. The routine was almost instinctual at this point. She moved them through the room, allowing the children to watch the train run around the space on its raised tracks. Then they giggled at the tumbling dinosaurs and spinning tops.

Colorful Christmas lights hung from the ceiling, casting an exciting glow of color in the small space. Lemon's eyes sparkled with delight as she pointed out the toys she knew would capture the children's interest.

"Which brings us to the man running all this, Santa Claus," Lemon said with a sweeping motion.

The two kids, Lemon imagined, were on the younger side of school age, squealed, racing forward. The boy pushed his sister out of his way to climb on Santa's lap first. Meanwhile, the little girl sat on the floor, crying around a mouth full of fingers.

It was a struggle to hold on to her smile. Her patience was paper thin. The night was seemingly endless. She would listen for Santa to sing out "Ho, ho, ho," then grab the next family. On and on, it went in an endless cycle of children passing through. Some were happy, some were upset, and the parents always were impatient. Twice, a dad tried to slip her a business card, asking if a private session was an option. Meanwhile, the wife and children were actively distracted by the animated toys. Lemon smiled sweetly and slipped their card back into their palm.

Jill's latest reminder of the time made Lemon sigh with relief: fifteen minutes to go. The outer doors had been shut from any additional families, hoping to sneak in under the last remaining minutes. The only ones left were those waiting in the coiled line. Granted, it might take a bit longer to get everyone through to see Santa, but the end was in sight.

Lemon hummed happily with the song playing in the background despite having heard it countless times this evening. Suddenly, checking Santa's list to discover who was naughty or nice wasn't such an annoying task. At the familiar chant from Santa, Lemon turned to greet the next family. Her smile froze on her face.

Her thoughts became as scrambled as the eggs she had eaten for breakfast. She couldn't remember what she was supposed to do. The three faces smiling expectantly back at her took her completely off guard. She hadn't seen Jace since he made her cry yesterday. Nor had she intended to see him anytime soon. Her plans to show him she was a good person had blown up in her face.

She realized now that she had been foolish to believe he would ever see her as anything but a forgotten prom queen. She had failed miserably, and the shame and disappointment were still reflected on her face. As heat flooded her cheeks, she couldn't muster the courage to look him in the eye.

"Lemon!" Tyler shouted, running forward and throwing his arms around her legs.

Lemon teetered but found her balance. She smiled down at him. "Hi, Tyler. Are you excited to see Santa?"

Tyler nodded, his angelic face brightening with his smile.

Jackson came up, tugging on her hand. "Me too." He exclaimed before sticking his finger back into his mouth.

"You too?" She grinned. "Well, let's get you to him," Lemon said, walking them through the toy shop, pausing when the boys shrieked. Tyler and Jackson followed the train, only to stop when the dinosaurs flipped in front of them. With so much to see, the boys turned in circles, unable to stay with any one thing.

"This is cool," Jace said from behind her. She stiffened but didn't move away. She was determined not to let him sense the ache in her chest his careless words had caused.

"They do a good job setting it up. It's the city council's pride and joy." She felt his finger flick her earring. "I didn't know you were still playing an elf." He whispered next to her ear. His warm breath brushed against her neck in a titillating sensation.

"Only upon request," Lemon said, stepping away from him. He was too close. Why was he acting this way? Flirting as if nothing had changed, wreaking havoc on her nerves.

"Really? Is that anyone's request?"

Lemon darted a startled look at his face, but he looked bored. She shouldn't have jumped to conclusions. It was only because those two other men had made a pass at her that she was so sensitive now. Jace wasn't interested in her that way.

"I've been known to make appearances if the right request is made." She said brazenly. A strange inclination to challenge him, to make him squirm, urged her to be bold.

His eyes narrowed slightly, but then a smile eased his scowl. "I'm sure Brian made his fair share of requests."

Heat flooded her face. With her hands fisted at her side, she glared at Jace. "His request was denied," Lemon admitted. Not that it was any of Jace's business, but she had never worn the elf costume for anyone. She only donned the outfit when there was a need at Santa's workshop.

Jace lifted a brow. Whether the surprise was genuine or not, she didn't know. "Not able to ask the right way?"

"No. I just didn't like the person asking."

He stepped toward her. Lemon backed up. She didn't want him near her. Not when she was still reeling from the emotional upheaval he'd caused her. With each step forward he made, Lemon slid back until she bumped into the table with dancing figures skating on the ice. Her body trembled with excitement. Her eyes widened as she looked up into his shadowed face.

"And what would you do if the right person asked?" His low-pitched voice washed against her skin like a lover's caress.

She swallowed, unable to break away from the heat lying beneath the surface of his dark eyes. "I–" she began, but Tyler cut over her.

"Is it our turn to see Santa now?" Tyler asked, tugging on the sleeve of her costume.

Lemon yanked her gaze away, looking down at Tyler. "You bet it is." With one last fleeting look, Lemon led Jace, Tyler, and Jackson to Santa. She left them with Lollypop and smiled when he arched a brow at her. "I don't pick the names." She said over her shoulder, closing the doors behind her.

She let her body slump. Unable to support her shaking legs a moment longer. She rested her head against the closed door. All the while taking deep breaths. The man was driving her crazy, treating her as a person would a yo-yo. One minute, she was a nuisance to him. The next, he was playfully teasing her as if they were soulmates.

At least the holidays were almost over, and then she would be free. Free to live whatever version of her life she wanted to. To her, that sounded like the perfect solution.

Chapter Twenty-Five

WEDNESDAY, DECEMBER 24TH

The comfort of home can sometimes be challenging to attain.

C hristmas Eve was always one of the busiest days at Frosted. It seemed the whole town wanted either cinnamon rolls or sticky buns—sometimes both—for Christmas morning.

Lemon had come in an hour earlier in preparation for the rush in sales. She'd spent most of the morning with her arms buried in dough. Her fifth batch of cinnamon rolls were in the oven, while the next sat on the counter, rising.

If the day continued at this pace, she might collapse into a heap on the floor.

As she stood by the sink, she splashed water on her face while pressing a damp cloth against the back of her neck. The ovens had emitted so much heat that the kitchen area had become uncomfortably warm. She debated whether to open the back door. Outside, the freezing temperatures made it quite frigid. However, opening the door posed a reasonable risk of cooling the room too much, which could hinder the dough from rising properly. So, for now, the door remained closed.

Lemon spent most of her time working in the kitchen. Her mother would come back when she needed to restock, but otherwise, she spent the morning alone. They were only open half the day, closing at noon for the holiday, which Lemon couldn't be happier for. She needed a break. Not even on the most challenging nights in L.A. next to Jeff had she worked so hard.

Guilt began to eat away at her. It had started earlier when the doors to Frosted were unlocked, and a line of customers flooded the front. For six years, her mother had to work this rush alone. Well, not exactly. Lemon knew her father helped out when they knew a day was going to be busier than normal. But her dad wasn't a baker, and the amount of baking needed to cover this kind of rush was unbelievable.

Yet, somehow, her mother had managed and never said a word. How many times had she spent lounging around the house on Christmas Eve while her parents slaved away at the bakery? It had never even occurred to her to offer to help.

Maybe Jace wasn't far off. Could it be she lacked the ability to think of anyone but herself?

Lemon lifted a pan of sticky buns to her shoulder. The weight was wearing heavily on her. She would be better, she promised herself. No matter what came next, she would pay attention. She pushed the door open with her back, spinning around in time to see Jace handing her mother a red gift bag with a paper gingerbread man on the front.

"Hi, Jace." She said, forcing a smile.

"Hi, Lemon. How are you?"

"Fine, and you?"

"Fine." Jace turned his attention back to her mother. "Thanks, Evelyn. Merry Christmas."

"No problem. I'll see to it. Merry Christmas. Tell your mother I said hi. Will you?"

"Sure." Jace nodded to Lemon, leaving the bakery through the adjoining door.

"What's that?" Lemon asked, sliding the pan onto the counter.

"What's what, dear?" Evelyn asked, setting the gift bag under the counter.

"The gift, Mama. What else would I be asking about?"

"I don't know. That's why I asked." She said, moving to the back counter. "Oh good, more sticky buns. I just got a phone order for a dozen. Why don't you box them up for me?"

"Mama." Lemon whined, "Aren't you going to tell me what the gift is?"

"No, dear. It's none of your business."

Lemon walked over to where her mother had set the bag, intent on looking inside. She couldn't help the rise in curiosity. What could Jace possibly be giving her mother, and why?

"No, you don't." her mother stepped in front of her, swatting her hand away. "That is *my* gift, and it is going under the Christmas tree."

Lemon frowned. "Why won't you let me peak? Come on, I promise not to spoil the surprise."

"But if you peek, it will be. Now, let it alone until tomorrow. You can wait that long, can't you?"

"No," Lemon said, pouting. She was unaccustomed to not getting her way, and the sensation didn't sit well with her.

Evelyn laughed. "Hush now and quit that pouting. I need you to get those sticky buns boxed up and ready to go. Please."

With a resigned sigh, Lemon walked away. The curiosity might kill her, but apparently, no one was concerned about her plight.

Lemon stood outside of Jace's apartment, her hand hovering. She needed to get into the attic, but to her knowledge, the only way in was through the small opening above Jace's bathroom door. Suppressing her doubts, she took a deep breath and summoned the courage to knock. The resonating echo reverberated in her mind.

The door flew open. Lemon froze, her words stuck in her throat. Her mouth hung open as she stared at Jace's bare chest. Her heart raced at the unexpected but appreciated view. He had a deep blue towel hanging over his shoulders. Plaid pajama bottoms hung low on his hips. His feet were set snuggly in a pair of wool slippers. The smattering of shaving cream along his jaw and under his nose emitted a refreshing scent of mint. His dark eyes were filled with concern as he stared at her expectantly.

"I'm sorry to interrupt." Lemon squeezed out, her voice high-pitched and strained.

"Is everything okay?" He asked.

"What? Oh, yes. Sorry. I need to get in the attic, and I think the only access point is over your bathroom door."

His dark eyebrows pulled together. "Why do you need to get into the attic?"

"I think the raccoon is living up there, and the only way to confirm it is to climb up there and investigate."

"I don't think so," Jace said, lifting the corner of the towel to his jaw. His hands dabbed at his face almost absently, yet he managed to clear away any remaining shaving cream.

She watched his progress, almost forgetting why she was there. Then his words set in. "Wait just a minute. You can't tell me no. I wasn't asking permission. I need to get into the attic, and I need inside your apartment to do it."

"Yeah, and how do you expect to get up there? In case you missed it. I don't exactly have a ton of space in my apartment for a ladder."

"I brought the one from the bakery." Lemon lifted the one she had leaned against the wall.

Jace moved to grab the ladder. His bare skin brushed against her knuckles, sending a jolt of electricity zinging through her body, setting her nerves on fire. "What the hell, Jace?" Lemon yelled, jumping back as if he burned her.

He whipped his head around. "What?"

"I can't believe you answered your door dressed like that." She grossed, sweeping her hand down.

His eyebrows knit together, forming a scowl. "What's wrong with plaid?"

"Nothing. I mean, I wasn't talking about your pants."

"Well, they're the only thing I'm wearing..."

"Exactly!"

The corner of his mouth quirked in a way that melted her heart, and she stubbornly refused to allow him to distract her with his disarming smile. Her gaze shifted upward, fixating on the plain, white ceiling above her. The way she figured, the ceiling or the floor were her only safe places to look. However, to get to the floor, she would inevitably get another look at his impressively broad shoulders and excitingly flat stomach. Quite frankly, she wasn't sure she had the willpower to keep her eyes moving down, so up they went.

"I would have never figured you for a prude." Jace laughed. He actually laughed. Oh, how she hated it when he laughed at her. As if she were an idiot or some pathetic soul to be pitied. Her temper sizzled like water splashed on heated oil.

"I'm not a prude!" She argued, her gaze dropping back to his face, which was a mistake. Jace laughing, even if it was at her expense, was a sight worth seeing. His dark, brooding eyes lit with humor sparkled under the fluorescent glow. His usually stern mouth softened, causing his bottom lip to pout. She couldn't pull her eyes away from his mouth. All the years she'd spent wondering what it would be like to kiss him compounding on top of each other until she thought she would go crazy from it.

In a moment of complete insanity, she considered taking the step that would bring them chest to chest. She imagined her arms circling his neck, her lips pressed against his. What would he do? What would he say? Would he kiss her back? She wanted so much to know, but her courage had long since diminished. Life had taught her that bravery wouldn't protect her from heartache; it only intensified the pain.

Lemon closed her eyes. Her pulse thundered in her ears. When she opened them, she found herself ensnared in Jace's penetrating stare. Her heart leaped. Her breath catching. For one unbelievable second, she thought, hoped, he would decide for her. He would be the one to step closer, but the second passed, and neither of them moved.

Her voice trembled, but she forced herself to say, "I could have been anyone. A stranger. Your mother even."

"That's unlikely."

"How would you know? Unless you can see through walls."

His mouth twitched again. Damn him and his adorable dimples!

"Lemon." He said her name in such a condescending way she wanted to kick him in the shin. "I locked up downstairs. The only other way a person can get up here is if they page me from out back. Since you knocked on this door, I knew exactly who I was opening up to."

She wanted to ask why he hadn't put a shirt on if he knew she was at his door, but that was a question a person asked who was brave enough to hear the answer. And she already knew she wasn't brave. "Oh," was all she could muster, and it came out as a faint squeak rivaling the sound of any mouse.

Having made his point, and her knowing it, he took the ladder and carried it inside his apartment. She followed quietly behind him, unable to think of anything clever or cute to say.

Lemon hadn't been in his apartment since the storm. It was hard to believe it had been a week ago. So much has happened since then. Too many things were said. Not enough was discussed. Neither of them being completely honest with each other. Yet, those hours spent with Jace had been some of the best in her life. Tears stung her eyes when her gaze fell on the bed. In a foolish dash of whimsy, Lemon thought there may be a future for them. One that included marriage and children. Only those dreams, like so many others, faded until only a shimmer of hope dangled out of reach.

"Are you crying?" Jace's incredulous tone shook her out of her revive.

Heat shot to her face in an explosion of emotions. Instead of facing him, Lemon turned away. She let her lashes flutter, frantically beating away the moisture. "Don't be absurd. It's the smoke from the fire." She explained. The lie fell easily between them. He gave her a skeptical look but didn't push, to which she was grateful.

"Here." He set the A-frame ladder up, locking the joints into place. Then, he grabbed his shirt from the corner of the unmade bed, throwing it over his head. He slipped on his tennis shoes, not bothering with socks, and stepped onto the first rung.

"Wait. What are you doing?"

Jace's sigh could have blown out a flame. "What does it look like I'm doing? You want to know if the raccoon is in the attic, don't you?"

"Yes, but I don't want *you* to look. I'm going to do it."

He shook his head, stepping down and turning to face her. His hands resting on his hips, he glared down at her. "No, you are not. The last thing I need is for you to put a hole in my ceiling. Since you won't let a professional handle this, that leaves me. Doesn't it?"

Lemon's eyes narrowed until only a sliver of green remained visible. "Listen. I don't want you doing me any favors. You know, seeing how much of a 'pain-in-the-ass' you believe I am. Besides, I think I can handle crawling around in the attic without a big, strong man's help."

"So, you think I'm big and strong?" He asked with an unsettling gleam in his eye.

"No." She huffed. "That is not the *point.*" Lemon glared at him. "I am going up there. If you don't mind." She brushed past him. Her heart lurched when his hand caught her wrist. When she turned back to him, she schooled her features, determined not to let him see how much he affected her. "Yes?"

His thumb stroked the inside of her wrist, and her stomach fluttered. "Just wait. Let me grab a flashlight first." He muttered.

He was back within a minute, but this time, he let her climb the ladder first. With every step she took, Lemon was painfully aware of Jace behind her. This had to be bad for a person's health. Experiencing sporadic fluctuations in her heart rate was unsettling.

When she reached the attic access panel, Jace had scaled the ladder behind her, standing on the rung just below the one she was on. His body was pressed intimately against hers, his warmth seeping through her clothes, searing her skin. He reached past her, pushing the access open. Then his light flicked on.

"Up you go," He said against her ear. His breath tickled her skin.

With no other option, Lemon stepped up. Her head popped through the opening, and her eyes widened. She stifled the shriek bubbling up and dropped back down, bumping Jace in the process.

"What's wrong?" He asked. His hand latching onto her hip, steadying her.

"I found the raccoons."

"Racoons?"

Silently, she nodded. Her eyes widened in astonishment. "How many are we talking?"

Lemon swallowed. "I'm not sure. It was hard to know for certain."

"More than two?" Jace asked, his tone conveying his wavering patience.

She nodded.

"Lemon," Jace warned. His hand tightened on her hip. "Will you spit it out already?"

"Seven, maybe eight? I already told you I can't be sure. Some of them are small. They looked like little balls of fur."

"You mean there is a family of raccoons living in the attic?"

"Looks that way."

"Can we call pest control now?"

Lemon bit her lip. She couldn't explain it, but she just couldn't turn the animals in. For some reason, her mind kept conjuring images of them trapped in a cage, destined for euthanasia. "Let's just wait. Maybe they will leave on their own. You know, in the spring, when it's warmer."

When she sank down from the attic, she had turned, sitting on a step just above her feet, making them eye level. With him so close, she had to spread her legs, encasing him between her thighs. Despite the intimacy of their position, Lemon's thoughts were on the raccoon family. They needed a home, a place to belong. Somewhere safe and secure where they knew they would be loved and cared for. She didn't care that they were pests, that they had stolen from her and ruined countless cookies. This was their home. They deserved a home. She deserved a home.

Jace studied Lemon's face. He watched as worry and doubt flashed across her expression. It was then he understood. It wasn't the raccoons that she cared about so much as what they represented. Somehow, Lemon had come to believe she was a pest, someone forced on family and friends to be tolerated.

His heart clenched as he recalled the harsh words he had thrown at her. How many of those same hurtful words she had quoted back to him? He may not be the sole reason, but he could admit he held his fair share of the blame.

Before he could think better of it, he brushed her hair away from her face. His fingers tangled in its silky strands. Her eyes glistened with tears, and he winced, regretting the pain he had caused her once again.

When he spoke, his voice was thick. "Okay. We can wait."

Her weak smile broke his heart. Looking into her watery green eyes, he knew what he needed to do. Luckily, he knew just the man to help.

Chapter Twenty-Six

THURSDAY, DECEMBER 25TH

Magic is found, not in the season but in those whom you share it with.

As the Christmas tree shimmered in the dimly lit room, it filled the air with the invigorating scent of pine, creating a cozy and festive atmosphere. In the predawn hours, a tranquil silence settled over the house. Amid the absolute calm, the soft tick of the mantel clock resonated in the air.

Lemon crept toward the tree. She'd spent the night tossing and turning until she couldn't stand the pressure of not knowing a moment longer. Driven by curiosity, she left the comfort of her warm bed and ventured into the darkness until she found herself in the living room. The family tree illuminated and shimmered in its full glory, presenting a truly awe-inspiring sight.

She loved it.

So many memories were wrapped up around the Christmas tree.Half of the ornaments that adorned the branches were handmade by her and Berry during their school years. Her mother had lovingly preserved each one.

Lemon smiled at the lopsided gingerbread ornament she had made in the first grade. In her early artistic endeavor, she'd painted a crooked smile that arched higher on the right than the left. Googly eyes were carefully affixed, although she'd accidentally used too much glue on one,causing it to droop. She remembered how proud she'd been to give it to her mom on Christmas morning.

Beneath the tree, there were stacks of presents wrapped in festive paper and ribbons, exceeding what a family of four would typically need. However, her mother was determined to make this Christmas a truly memorable one.

Her mother had said last night it would be the last they had all together in this house. Which at the time made little sense, but the more Lemon considered her mother's words, understanding sank in. It wasn't just about spending Christmas together; it was also about Berry starting college.Their time together at this stage was ending. Her parents would be empty nesters. The future stretched out before them, devoid of any clear direction.Numerous possibilities seemed within reach, yet doubt and uncertainty hovered in the back of her mind.

Lemon sat cross-legged next to the gift she wanted desperately to look at. She glanced over her shoulder, her body relaxing at the silent house. As carefully as she could, Lemon lifted the red gift bag, placing it on her lap. She moved the white tissue paper aside until her hand found a cool, smooth surface. Similar to a proficient surgeon, she delicately removed the object from the bag without emitting any revealing noises.

The white bottle with a tree silhouette gleamed in the soft light. Stunned, she stared at the bottle. It was the soap she used at her old job. Only this time, when she thought of her days at Opal's, there was no pain.Only a warm glow of something new and brilliant.

Jace had bought her mother the soap. She tried to reason through the unexpected gift. When she slipped the soap back into the bag, her eye caught on a splash of green mixed with the remaining tissue paper. Her fingers slipped over the paper, sliding it out.

It was an envelope.

Jace had included a card.

Lemon turned the envelope over in her hand, weighing the consequences of reading the card before her mother did. She was astounded by how desperately she wanted to read it, but he'd sealed it, and if she broke the seal, her mother would know she had snooped. With a heavy heart, Lemon carefully slid the card back into the bag. There was no hope for it. She'd just have to wait until her mother opened the gift to know what his note said.

The trek back to her room was slow. Lost in thought, she didn't notice her mother coming toward her.

"I hope you weren't peaking at the presents." Her mother chided.

Lemon yelped, slapping a hand over her mouth to muffle the sound. "Mama! You scared the life out of me. What are you doing up?"

"I need to pull the cinnamon rolls out of the fridge if we want to have them freshly baked this morning."

"What time is it?" Lemon asked, confused. She could have sworn she'd only sat in front of the tree for a few minutes.

"It's almost seven," Evelyn said, turning the oven on as she opened the fridge, pulling out the pan of cinnamon rolls she had prepared last night.

"Seven?" Lemon blinked. She'd been up since five. Somehow, two hours had passed without her noticing. "Do you need help, Mama?"

Evelyn smiled, her eyes sleepy. "No. I can manage. Don't worry, I tested the dough already to make sure it tasted all right."

"Oh, Mama, I never worry about your baking tasting good."

"Yeah, you might be the only one." Evelyn's face tightened with pain.

Lemon wrapped her arms around her mother, pulling her into a tight embrace. "I'm sorry, Mama. I meant to tell you yesterday, but I forgot."Holding her mother at arm's length, she explained. "It wasn't your fault. The cookies, I mean. The bakery has raccoons. They roam around the kitchen and knock things over. They ruined a batch of cookies I made, too."

Her mother gave her a perplexed look. "What are you talking about? We do not have raccoons in the bakery. I think I would have noticed."

"How? You've been so busy, and they wander more at night than during the day."

"How do you know raccoons are to blame?"

"I caught them on camera, and Jace and I found them in the attic above his apartment."

"Oh, my. What are we going to do?"

"Don't worry. I'll take care of it after Christmas."

"I should hope so. I doubt anyone would want to buy any of our cookies if they knew we had a pest problem."

"They're not pests." Lemon snapped. "Sorry. I didn't mean to get testy. I'm just tired. Don't worry, Mama. I've got it."

Evelyn's expression darkened with concern. "You should go back to bed. Berry won't be up for another couple of hours yet."

"Are you sure?"

"Yes, go."

With that, Lemon found herself back in bed. Unfortunately, her warm sheets were cold again. Her mind automatically returned to the red gift bag with white tissue paper and a green envelope. The note consumed her thoughts as she slowly drifted off to sleep.

Lemon jerked awake. The sound of a text message alert jarring her out of her sleep. With a groan, she rolled over and reached for her phone, squinting at the blinding brightness of the screen. The clock revealed it was almost nine. Berry would be up soon, and with him, everyone would be ready for presents.

With her phone in hand, Lemon fell back onto her pillow. She opened her messages, expecting the text to be from friends in Los Angeles. Yet, to her surprise, it wasn't. She stared at her phone in shock.

The text was from Jace. Her hand trembled as his message filled her screen.

Merry Christmas. I hope I didn't wake you. My nephews had us up hours ago. I tried to wait, but evidently, the excitement of Christmas morning was contagious. I left something for you outside of Frosted. It's in the back near the park. You can't miss it. Hopefully, you will have time to see it before we come for dinner tonight. Not sure if your mother told you, but she invited the whole lot of us over. Which is a relief because Brynlee is ready to pull her hair out, and Mom isn't up to fixing dinner for a large group yet. If it had been left to me and Dad, we would have ordered a pizza. Anyway, I hope you have a good Christmas. I'll see you tonight.

Lemon reread the message again and then once more. Her heart racing by the time she finished. Wide awake, she rolled out of bed and threw on her clothes. She was out of the door in under five minutes, only pausing long enough to tell her mother where she was going.

She left her mother sputtering in surprise as she ran to her car. The drive to Frosted was made in record time. Thankfully, the roads were still clear. The threat of snow still hung in the air but had yet to follow through.

After parking in the back, Lemon got out of her car and walked toward the park. On the ground were red arrows. She smiled, following the trail until it stopped at the base of a cluster of trees bordering the parking lot and forested park area beyond. At first, she didn't see anything. Then, a slight moment drew her eye to the dense shrubbery at the base of the trees. Nestled inside was a miniature house painted green with a small opening. Inside, she could see two black masks peaking through the dim interior. Her eyes blurred.

Jace made them a home.

She couldn't believe it. A warmth spread through her body,filling her heart almost to bursting. If he had been there, she would have kissed him. She was so happy; she didn't bother brushing the tears that slipped down her cheeks aside. Just when she thought she knew him. When she believed she had an accurate picture of the man he was, he would do something so incredible that it shook her to the depths of her being.

He was the one person she had never seen coming. Jace had stolen her heart, her whole heart. Something that no one else had managed to do. Only she didn't know what to do with her newly discovered feelings.

Lemon silently drove home, deliberately taking the scenic route to delay her arrival. She knew well that a barrage of questions awaited her, and she wanted nothing to do with it. She didn't want to feign interest,not when she was standing at a critical point in her life.

When she walked through the door, she found her family at the kitchen table, laughing over cinnamon rolls. They stopped when she came in. Her mother held up a plate. Lemon smiled weakly. Unable to muster the energy to pretend she was happy.

"Everything okay?" Her mother asked.

"Of course. Why wouldn't it be?"

"Well, you lit out of here so fast I assumed there was an issue."

"No issue. Now, tell me. What are you all laughing at?"

Lemon listened to her father retell the same old stories. Only half listening. Her mind returned time and again to the raccoon home Jace built for her. There was no mistaking the gesture. He had made it clear he wanted them removed, that they were nothing more than a hassle. It was she who wanted to save them. The house he built had been for her.

As they gathered around the family tree, Lemon's eyes remained fixated on the vibrant red bag. When her mother lifted the gift, Lemon's brow furrowed at the sight of it hanging from her fingers.

"This one is yours." Her mother said, dangling a red gift bag in her face with a wicked gleam in her eyes.

Lemon took the bag, her eyes widening. "For me? I thought Jace gave this to you."

"I know." Her mother admitted with a smile. "Now, open it. I have been dying to know what he got you."

Not having to hide her actions this time, Lemon let the tissue paper fly as she tossed it out of the bag. The white puffs floated down around her shoulders. She pulled out the soap, holding it up for everyone to see.

"It's soap." Her mother sang out, her voice filled with a hint of disappointment.

Lemon smiled. "You don't understand. This is the stuff I used when I worked with Jeff. Jace asked me about it after watching me wash my hands at Frosted. It does wonders for the skin. Trust me, your hands will be thanking you."

"Let me see it." Her mother grumbled, but Lemon didn't mind.It was the best gift. Thoughtful, expensive, what more could a girl hope for? She handed the bottle over and turned her attention back to the bag. Her hand anxiously rummaged through the bag, desperate to find the awaited card.

Her hand quivered, pulling the envelope out. Everything Jace did seemed to carry a different meaning now. As she read his card, her eyes clouded.

"What does the card say?" Evelyn asked, swatting at Berry for taking a present before it was his turn.

Lemon read the card aloud, her voice only cracking once, but she felt every word.

Lemon,

This past month with you has been enlightening. My only regret is not having longer to spend with you. I hope you like the soap. No one should have to suffer while washing their hands, especially you. Now, every time you use the soap, you will be able to think of me. Merry Christmas Lemon.I hope you get everything you wanted for Christmas.

Jace.

"What a lovely letter. Although now I'm not sure I want to follow a gift that had such an overwhelming impact on you."

"Don't be silly, Mama. Jace's gift is hardly anything special." Even as she said the words, she knew they couldn't be farther from the truth. To her, both of his gifts meant more to her than anything she had ever received.

Evelyn gave her a skeptical look. "If you say so." Then, with a sigh, she handed Lemon a small box. It was incredibly light, barely weighing anything, and when she shook it, not even a whisper of sound escaped. She slipped the bow off before lifting the lid. Inside, she found a lone key with the word "Frosted" stamped at the top.

Lemon looked at her mother and then at her father. Her face clearly displayed a look of confusion.

"It's yours if you want it." Her father said, his eyes sparkling with delight.

"What do you mean, it's mine? What is?"

"Frosted. It's all yours. That is if you want to keep it. Your mother and I want to travel before we die, and if she keeps working at the bakery, we won't ever make it out past the town lines."

"But, Daddy. I can't accept this."

"Sure you can. This has always been the plan, you know. You get the bakery. Berry gets the house. Of course, you understand we are welcome any time we are in the area."

Lemon laughed. She threw her arms around her father's neck, jumping up and down. "Yes!" She squealed, pulling her mother into a hug. It didn't seem possible, but the day just kept getting better and better.

Dinner passed in a flurry of activity. Her mother's invitation extended not only to Jace and his family but also to Mia and her family. The dining room buzzed with the clatter of plates and the hum of conversation. The children gleefully played with the toys Evelyn had thoughtfully bought for each of them.

Country Christmas music played in the background as Lemon wove her way through the crowd, stopping in front of Jace. She smiled up at him, her eyes sparkling with joy. "Thank you for my gifts." Looking into his face, she felt her heart swell with a rush of love, making her breath catch in her throat.

He smiled, his eyes betraying a hint of sorrow, but she couldn't understand the reason. "What did you think of the raccoons' new home?"

"I loved it!" Her excitement overflowed, and she couldn't stop herself from gushing. "It's amazing. I can't believe you made them a home. You don't think they will sneak back into the attic?"

"I'm sure." He said, rubbing a strand of her hair between his fingers. "I closed the hole they had used to get in. As long as their new home stays warm enough, they should be content."

Her stomach danced with butterflies as the warm, intoxicating scent of his skin enveloped her. "You gave me three amazing gifts this year. I wish I had something more I could offer you than a few words."

Jace tilted his head, his expression reflecting his confusion. "Three? I only gave you two."

Lemon shook her head and smiled. "No, you gave me three. The first was the soap. It was a thoughtful gift from a man who remembered what kind I used after one conversation. The second was the raccoon home. This gift was not only considerate but also selfless. You take my breath away." She confessed. "Did you know that?"

"No, Lemon. I didn't know that." He spoke with a gruff voice that sent shivers down her spine.

"The third," she paused, her eyes flickering with uncertainty, yet she mustered the courage to maintain eye contact. "The third gift was one neither of us expected. You gave me back my courage. And with it, I want to give you my present." She took a deep breath, then told him what was in her heart. "I love you, Jace. During these past few weeks, you've been my guiding light, helping me understand my true self and what I desire most in this life. But I realized something: nothing I strive for in the future carries any worth unless you are a part of it. You have my heart, my whole heart. No one has ever managed to hold all of it, but you have. I love you."

"Lemon," he whispered, resting his forehead against hers. His hands pulled her into the warmth of his embrace. "I love you, too."

They stood together as if they could hold on to the moment. Neither of them moving. Lemon glowed in the pleasure of his touch. The man she loved, who loved her back. Tears filled her eyes, but she blinked them away. She didn't want to cry, didn't want to ruin this moment even though they were tears of joy.

Lemon clasped his hand, stepping backward a step. Jace followed with ease, prompting her to step back again. When her next step brought her under the mistletoe, she stopped. "Jace?"

"Yes?"

She smiled, her eyes shimmering with anticipation. "I've finally got you under the mistletoe."

He looked up. A smile slowly formed at the corners of his mouth, brightening his eyes with happiness. "So you have," he said, his arm snaking around her waist as he pulled her close. "I suppose it's only right for me to give you a kiss."

Lemon licked her lips, anticipation making her sound breathy. "It is the only honorable thing to do. After all, no one wants to be the Scrooge of the party."

"No, we don't want that." He murmured. Bringing his head lower until their lips met, and she melted. Lemon wanted to cry out with relief. All she could think was, finally.

Later, snuggled on the couch, Lemon rested her head on Jace's shoulder. She traced the back of his hand as she hummed along to the Christmas carols playing.

Her mind danced with blissful happiness, her heart brimming with hope. Not that they had talked about any serious commitments, but Lemon knew they were coming. Maybe by next Christmas, she would have a ring on her finger, and she would be -. Her thoughts came to a grinding halt. She bolted up, turning to Jace with a horrified look.

"What's wrong?" Jace asked, his brow furrowed.

"You have to take my last name," Lemon announced. "It's the only option."

Jace grimaced. "I'm sorry. I have to do what now?"

"You have to be a Frost."

"What are you talking about?"

"When we get married," she began, "I want you to be Frost."

He did not bat an eye at her announcement of their pending marriage, which warmed her heart. Instead, he sank into the couch cushion, seemingly unconcerned about the weight of their conversation. "Because?"

"*Because* if you don't, that means I will be a Torte."

"And that's a bad thing."

Lemon fixed him with a fierce glare, accusation in her eyes. "It is when your name will be Lemon Torte!"

She stared in abject horror as Jace laughed, his head thrown back, tears streaming down his cheeks. Lemon folded her arms, her bottom lip protruding. It infuriated her whenever he found amusement at her expense. As she tried to scoot away from him, he wrapped an arm around her waist, tucking her firmly back into his side.

After regaining control of his mirth, he brushed away astray tear, a mischievous glimmer appearing in his eye. "How about we go on a date first, then we can talk about rings and last names?"

Lemon smiled. That sounded like an excellent plan to her.

Excerpt from Snowflake Kisses

Berry and Mia are given a second chance but not without some unexpected obstacles in Alane Middleton's next tantalizing novel.

Snowflake Kisses

Available for preorder.
Read on for a preview ...

Snowflake Kisses

Ten Years Earlier

"Ah, Berry, come in." Mr. Porter, an older gentleman who'd worked at Harper High in the English department for what seemed like a hundred years, held out a stack of papers. A sickening worry settled in Berry's stomach. He eyed the pages as if it were a coiled snake about to strike. There was only one reason Mr. Porter would be handing him back his assignment – his recent attempt at explaining the symbolism in The Scarlett Letter had fallen short.

"You wanted to see me, Mr. Porter?" Berry crossed the threshold, apprehension weighing down on him with every step he took.

Berry always thought Mr. Porter resembled an owl. His thick brows sprang out over the wireframe of his glasses, and his pale blue eyes were as sharp as ever. Mr. Porter had a way of making him feel as though every move he made was being scrutinized.

"Indeed. I'm glad you could stop by. I understand Coach Sherdan offered to help clear your grade requirement so you could continue to play the remainder of the football season."

Heat crawled up his neck and burned the tips of his ears. "Ah, I...that is, I wasn't going to take him up on his offer."

It was common practice at Harper that when certain athletic students were struggling in any of their classes, the teachers would "help them out" by giving them passing grades until the end of the sports season. Until this year, he hadn't had a problem with his grades. Whether it was the teacher or the class, he couldn't say, but Berry learned he hated English. The sooner he never had to write another essay, the better.

"I'm glad to hear it. I think we do a disservice to the students when we 'help them' in this way. Additionally, I believe this strongly reflects the type of person you will become. If you apply this same kind of dedication to your work, I think you will be surprised at how well you can do. With that settled, I wanted to review your recent essay."

Berry's eyes fell on the report he'd turned in last week. Red marks streaked the top sheet, and he knew it wouldn't be any better on the next page. Resigned, he snagged the papers from Mr. Porter's hand.

"I know it looks bad, but I promise this assignment was much better than your last. I think what you need is a tutor."

"A tutor?" Berry scrunched his nose. "I don't know about that."

"Berry, I'm going to be frank with you. If you don't show marked improvement in the next essay about the woman of Shakespeare, you will fail this semester and won't be able to graduate."

"I'll fail?"

"I'm afraid so. If you remember, I listed all this out on the syllabus at the beginning of the school year. Essays account for seventy-five percent of your grade. Even if you turned in all your other assignments, you still wouldn't have enough points to bring your grade up to passing."

Frustrated, Berry ran a hand through his blond hair, brushing it away from his forehead. He looked with disgust at the F scrolled in bold ink at the top. "I don't understand. I followed the directions and did the assignment the way you specified."

"True. But you didn't cite your work, and grammatically, there were too many errors to grade. What happened to the reference sheets that I handed out at the beginning of the semester?"

Berry shrugged. Panic churned in his stomach as he weighed his options. "I wouldn't even know how to find a tutor."

Mr. Porter smiled with victory. "That's all right. I have the perfect person. She was in my class last semester and is in college English this year. I think you will work well together. Mia had a head for the details, and she never misses an error. Just listen to what she says, and I'm sure you'll pull this around."

"A college girl."

"Oh, no. You misunderstood. She isn't in college. She's a senior at Harper. She is simply taking a few college courses with her schedule."

"Oh. Did you say her name is Mia?"

"Yes. I'm sure you've seen her around. Although I doubt you have any of the same friends. She isn't the type you usually associate with."

With a sigh, Berry stuffed his essay into his backpack. "When am I supposed to meet with her?"

"I've already made the arrangements. You will meet in the school library after school for an hour on Mondays, Wednesdays, and Fridays. Just remember, she is doing me this favor, so be nice."

Berry sent him an exasperated look. "Why wouldn't I be?"

"Because I've seen you in the hallways. I don't want you teasing her."

Great. Now, he was going to have to spend an hour three days a week with some mousy girl and try not to ruffle her feathers. This was just how he wanted to spend what was left of his senior year, Berry thought wryly. "Fine, whatever. I promise I'll be on my best behavior."

"Good. She's waiting for you in the library now. Why don't you head over there? I am going to give you a week to fix the essay and get it turned back into me. But only this once. If you listen to her advice, you won't need to turn a paper in more than once from here on out."

Berry groaned as he hoisted his backpack over his shoulder and turned to leave. He paused at the door and said, "Thanks, Mr. Porter."

The high school library also served as the public library, and anyone who wanted to check out a library book could do so after school hours and on Saturdays. The space, although not large, offered several tables for studying and a couple of small classrooms that people could use for work or whatever they might need.

Berry made his way through a few clusters of students who liked to hang out after school with friends. He nodded to a few he knew and smiled at a few girls he recognized from campus but couldn't remember their names.

When he came to the assigned study area, he found two tables occupied. At the one closest to him was a brunette, trim and striking. He might need to get her number if she was still around after his tutoring time was over. At the other table, his date for the next hour sat. Her strawberry blonde hair was twisted and knotted on top of her head, held by a yellow pencil. Her oversized shirt held the logo of some band he didn't recognize. On the table in front of her were stacks of books and papers in a jumbled mess, leading him to wonder where exactly she was expecting him to sit.

Berry stood next to the table, holding out his hand. When she didn't look up, he cleared his throat. "Hi, Mia. I'm Berry. Mr. Porter sent me to meet you."

She lifted her head, giving him the first real look at her, and he supposed she matched what he expected from someone already taking college classes. Clearly, she didn't spend time on much else.

Her eyes reflected annoyance, her brow furrowed in impatience. "I'm not Mia."

"Excuse me?"

"My name. It isn't Mia, and I don't have a class with Mr. Porter."

"Oh, sorry about that." Perplexed, Berry turned around and found himself staring into the most beautiful brown eyes he'd ever seen. They were dark, rich, and gleamed with humor, causing him to grin. "I suppose you're Mia?"

"You suppose correctly." She admitted. Her lips curled into a secretive smile that made his toes curl. How Mr. Porter thought he would be able to concentrate on a word she had to say was beyond him. Didn't the man have eyes?

He ambled over to the table where she sat, admiring every detail of her appearance. "I don't remember seeing you on campus."

"It's a big campus."

"Not really. Not that big, at least. I know I would have noticed you had I seen you."

She tilted her head, her eyes narrowing slightly. "Oh, why's that?"

He had the sickening feeling that she was leading him around by the nose, and he was about to land himself in a heap of trouble. However, he had never been one to back down from a challenge, and it seemed as if she was daring him to acknowledge that he found her attractive.

With his hand planted on the table, he leaned forward, rewarded immediately with the sweet scent of flowers and exotic spice. He took in her heady aroma and wanted nothing more than to breathe her in for the next hour. His mouth curled into his signature smile, one he knew from years of practice drove girls crazy. "Because I make sure to know every pretty face in the school."

He waited for her response, expecting her to giggle or bat her eyes at him as all the other girls did. In fact, as the crowd of girls did, standing by the library doors. Yet she didn't smile or laugh. She didn't blush or tease him back. Instead, she leaned back in her chair. Her dark eyes simmered as she glared at him. "I just bet you do."

"That was a compliment." He said, wondering if she had misunderstood him.

"Oh, I realize that was *your* idea of a compliment."

"What's that supposed to mean?"

Mia held up a piece of paper and read out loud a sentence he had written for his writing assignment. He had tried to explain the art of flirting for the expressive language essay. He'd gotten an F for his efforts and a call home for his attempt at humor. Heat crawled up his neck as he struggled to maintain eye contact. He didn't particularly care for his past mistakes to be rubbed in his face.

Berry pulled the chair out and sank into the seat across from her. He crossed his arms over his chest and gave her a sardonic smile. "Look beautiful. It's not my fault God gave you a face; men slay dragons, for any more than I can help to appreciate beautiful things."

"Yes, I'm aware of your lack of depth. I don't suppose you will ever be able to see beyond the superficial, which will lead you to a series of shallow and meaningless relationships until you finally settle for a loveless match. But hey, at least she'll be beautiful. After all, what else can a face like yours expect in this life but to be surrounded by an inordinate amount of brainless bimbos? But at least they will be beautiful."

"What's your number?"

"Excuse me?"

"Your number." Berry held up his phone, waving it in the air. "You know, so I can text you later."

"Have you lost your mind? I'm not giving you my number."

"Why not?"

"Because I don't like you."

"Sure you do." He laughed at the incredulous expression on her face. "There's no reason to lie. Besides, you are my tutor, remember? Don't you think we'll need to reach each other?"

His grin widened. Watching her bristle under his gaze gave him as much satisfaction as listening to her attempt to blister him. Lucky for himself, he'd heard everything she said before. Countless times, in fact. It was one of his mother's favorite lectures. He never saw what the problem was. So what if he liked pretty girls? As long as they liked him, where was the harm?

"What's happening, man?" A familiar voice spoke from behind. The intrusion was as unwelcome as it was irritating.

Berry turned to find Chance and Isaac from the football team crowding behind his chair. He pushed back, forcing them to move as he stood. "What are you two doing here? I didn't think either of you knew where the library was."

Chance shoved him. "Shut up, man. I could say the same for you."

"Come, now. You know I can always be found where the lovely ladies are." Berry turned to wink at Mia, who sat with an open look of irritation. "Now, if you don't mind. I'm in the middle of something." He said, gesturing to Mia.

Isaac gave him a knowing smile. "Don't let us interrupt, man."

"Too late," Berry grumbled as he watched his teammates leave. When he turned back to Mia, he was surprised to see her packing her things. "You aren't leaving, are you?"

"What do you think?" She snapped as her delicate fingers shoved the papers into her backpack.

"But we haven't even started yet."

"Oh, we have done more than start, Berry. From where I sit, we have finished. Now, if you'll excuse me, I'm going to see if I can catch Mr. Porter before he leaves."

Berry reached out, catching her arm. "Why? I mean, you haven't even given me a chance. Don't you think I at least deserve the opportunity to prove you wrong?"

He could see the indecision in her eyes and pushed forward. "Come on. I promise I'm not that bad. Besides, I was just teasing you before." He held up his hand. "I swear, no more jokes. I'll be totally serious. Please."

The moment he saw her relent, a knot in his stomach loosened. He couldn't explain the desperation that seized him a moment ago any more than he could explain why he couldn't take his eyes off of her.

"All right." Mia sighed, dropping her bag back into the chair beside her. "But all business from here on out."

"I promise."

THanks For reaDING!

We hoped you enjoyed *Frosted Christmas* by Alane Middleton.

If you enjoyed *Frosted Christmas* and would like to get updates on new releases and exclusive content sign up now to join Alane Middleton's mailing list. Be the first to hear about ARC reader opportunities and special promotions!

Sign up now!

ABOUT THE AUTHOR

Alane Middleton is an artist at heart and loves anything she can use to express herself. She has been married for 15 years and has five young children, one of whom was born with a severe congenital heart defect (HLHS) and another diagnosed with autism. Special needs have become a way of life for her and her family, and she views it as a blessing to be introduced to a world she never knew existed. The challenge of having two children with special needs that are very different from each other has given her a level of strength she didn't know she had and an increase of courage she hadn't realized she was missing. Because of her experiences with her children, Alane was able to write her first novel and, in doing so, found a whole new way to express herself. Alane found a love of books when she was sixteen. After reading her first romance novel, After the Night by Linda Howard, she didn't realize a book could take her on such a journey, and she discovered delight in exploring the worlds that authors create for us. Alane wants to provide such an outlet for others. Writing has become a passion she loves to share with others.

Follow her on:

ALSO BY

Alane Middleton

Dunton Legacy Series

Storm Rising

Tempest

Aftershock

Vortex

Firestorm

Home For The Holidays Series

Frosted Christmas

Snowflake Kisses (November 2024)